EVOLUTION

EVOLUTION

BOOK TWO OF
THE DEVOLUTION TRILOGY

JOHN CASEY

PHiR Publishing
San Antonio

PHiR Publishing
San Antonio, TX
phirpublishing.com

First edition: May 2021

ISBN: 978-1-7369081-2-9
Library of Congress Control Number: 2021905941

Printed in the United States of America

ALSO BY JOHN CASEY

DEVOLUTION
Book one of The Devolution Trilogy

REVELATION
Book three of The Devolution Trilogy

RAW THΦUGHTS
A Mindful Fusion of Poetic and Photographic Art
(with photographer Scott Hussey)

MERIDIAN
A Raw Thoughts Book
(with photographer Scott Hussey)

THE BARN
A Mystery Novella
(co-authored by Doug Campbell)

For my children, John and Cayla

"There is no illusion greater than fear."
— Lao Tzu

WHAT CAME BEFORE...

In DEVOLUTION, Michael Dolan was introduced as a stoic perfectionist and former special operations pilot working a staff job at the Pentagon who accepts an improbable CIA request to help prevent impending terrorist attacks in Europe. The Agency had reached a dead end and was in desperate need of an agent they could quickly embed within the terrorist organization without raising suspicion.

After being vetted and receiving a bare minimum of training Dolan found himself back in Paris, France where he'd experienced a terrible tragedy years before while attending the Sorbonne University on a military scholarship. Dolan's French girlfriend at the time, Claire Fontaine, died after falling from the balcony of a hotel room. Dolan never fully recovered from the tragic and questionable circumstances of her death. He was close friends with Sharif Lefebvre back then, son of Hakeem Lefebvre, an Algerian oil industry mogul who later became the leader of the al-Mulathamun Army (AMA). The AMA was a newer terrorist organization in Africa with historical ties to al-Qa'ida. The CIA believed Sharif might be involved with his father's shadowy plot to attack American interests in Europe using a weapon of mass destruction. The CIA's plan, codenamed Operation EXCISE, tasked

Dolan with rekindling the friendship in order to collect and report on Sharif while maintaining his cover as an employee of a multinational intelligence-sharing organization led by the French government.

Meanwhile, François Martin, a wine industry engineer and past colleague of Sharif established a base of operations for the terrorist cell and finalized plans to attack in both France and Germany. As the story evolved, Dolan became intimate with Anne Bernard, Sharif's ex-girlfriend and onetime best friend of Claire. As difficult truths about himself and what really happened to Claire began to surface, Dolan realized the CIA kept him in the dark about many aspects of the mission and found they were spying on him using his cell phone. Faced with mounting obstacles and with no one to trust except Anne, Dolan decided to go dark and try to take out the cell himself, one terrorist at a time.

Lauren Rhodes, leader of the CIA black unit SCALPEL, did everything she could to keep the mission on track while holding threats from leadership to close the unit down at bay. Ultimately, she left Washington for Europe to help Tony Stone, SCALPEL's field operative in Paris, in a desperate attempt to salvage the mission after Dolan went dark.

DEVOLUTION builds and winds its way through jaw-dropping plot twists and psychoanalytically charged, heart-stopping action until the final chapter when Dolan concludes his mission in dramatic fashion. But there are unanswered questions and business left unfinished. The story continues here, in EVOLUTION...

CHAPTER ONE

Issam wiped the perspiration from his brow and continued walking along Hasan Abu Ghanima Street. He looked straight ahead and tried to act normal, as if he had a perfectly good reason to be in this area at this hour. It wasn't hot, in fact it was quite cool for two in the morning. Maybe 20 degrees Celsius. But his backpack was heavy, and he was very nervous. He'd already done four practice runs but this was it, the real deal. He was worried about being caught or prevented from finishing his mission.

At seventeen years old Issam was honored to be trusted with doing something so important. His mother wouldn't understand and had no idea about it. His father, however, would have been proud. He never knew him—he left before Issam was born and never returned. Issam found out later he'd traveled to an al-Qa'ida training camp in Khost, Afghanistan to fight the holy war. He was a hero in Issam's eyes, and what he did today he did in his name.

He and his mother emigrated to Jordan from Syria when he was four. 'To find a better life,' she had told him. Now she worked for a Non-Governmental Organization that provided assistance to Syrian refugees seeking asylum there. She didn't make much money, but it was enough for a one-room apartment in Zarqa, just to the east of the city. Issam worked there too from time to time and had helped his al-Mulathamun Army brothers Saleh and Fadi get into Jordan. They'd brought what was needed with them, hidden in their personal items, and after about three months of laying low and planning, they were ready to act.

A little further on Issam stopped in front of a large, vacant lot, opened his backpack and took out a small crowbar, a pair of gloves and a flashlight. He looked up and down the street and listened for anyone approaching, then put on the gloves and bent down to pry the manhole cover loose. He slid it two-thirds of the way off the opening and climbed partway down, then struggled and ultimately succeeded in replacing the heavy iron disk. Only then did he turn on his flashlight. He swept the area with the beam, noting that everything was as he had last seen it. Issam descended the last few rungs of the ladder, put his backpack down and walked a few meters east into the tunnel. There were several pipes and wires of various circumference on the walls and floor that branched out further on to a myriad of businesses, homes and government offices. There was only one pipe he was concerned with, however. Scraping away some loose dirt, he uncovered the bag he'd left hidden after his last rehearsal. He pulled it out of its hole and swatted the burlap sack with his hand to remove the dust, coughing as it clouded the area around him.

He removed the contents of the bag and his backpack, laying them out on the ground in front of the three large pipes that traversed the south wall of the tunnel. Issam selected a hinged clamp apparatus, placed it around the middle pipe and fastened it loosely, making sure the chalk 'X' he'd scrawled last week was visible through the threaded hole. He used a wrench to tighten the clamp. Next, he screwed a specialized component into the threaded hole, one that was geared internally to an auger that would drill through the pipe. He picked up the large double-walled stainless-steel container he'd brought with him, removed the cap and mated it to a fitting on the boring component. The pressure on each of the seals was important; they shouldn't be too loose, and they shouldn't be too tight. He screwed the oblong container into the component until he was sure the seal was strong. It was still cold to the touch. *Good*, he thought. *All is going according to plan.*

Sweating profusely now, he used a wrench to turn a bolt on the side of the boring component, pressing the tip of the auger within up against the pipe. He put a custom bit in his cordless drill and inserted it into a hole on the side of the component and pressed the trigger for ten seconds, then he turned the bolt again, advancing the auger. The bolt became easy to turn after repeating the process thirty-two times—the auger was through. He then turned the bolt in the opposite direction until he could feel that the auger had completely withdrawn from the pipe.

Issam placed the burlap bag and his tools in his backpack and surveyed the immediate area to make sure he hadn't left anything behind. Satisfied, he turned the valve on the stainless-steel container so its contents could trickle into the water supply. It would continue to do so for about three days, he'd been told. By that time, his Syrian brothers would be back across the border, and everyone would be paying close attention to their televisions as news of a cataclysm unfolded that was horrific beyond anything the world had ever seen.

Issam wiped the pipe and the apparatus down with a rag. There shouldn't be any fingerprints on anything—he had been meticulous. It was one of the steps he'd practiced countless times and by now it was routine. Before he finished wiping, however, he realized he should perform a final check to make sure the contents of the container were flowing. He put the rag in his pocket and grabbed the valve once more and tried to twist it. Just as he was about to release, a tiny, high-pressure jet of water shot out of the fitting between the container and the auger component, squirting Issam in the face. He instinctively launched himself backwards, dropping the flashlight and hitting his head on the far wall. Disoriented, he frantically wiped the water off with his shirt and picked up the flashlight. The leak had stopped as soon as he let go, but the damage was done. He had to get out of there, get home and shower as quickly as possible. But by then it might be too late. Maybe it already was.

He collected his things and began to cry as he climbed the ladder, again struggling with the manhole cover. This wasn't supposed to happen—he'd taken every precaution, done everything as he was taught. They practiced the execution of it so many times over the past two weeks, but not once on a pipe that was actually pressurized. As he began the long walk home, he became resigned to the fact that if something bad happened to him, it was the will of Allah. And if he died, he would die in jihad, and this was preferable to any other death. He didn't know what was in the container or what it would do to him, exactly. Maybe nothing would happen since he did not drink it. Saleh and Fadi had told him that whoever drank the water would die a slow, incredibly painful and grotesque death. And there was no cure.

CHAPTER TWO

Michael Dolan smiled as he drove, crossing the Charles River north into Cambridge. It had been another good day. Good days had become his status quo of late, and he was grateful. That evening he taught a taekwondo class as he did every Wednesday at six p.m. and for the first time since he began teaching, he was bested by one of his students. One of the important tenets he preached was never underestimate your opponent, and he'd done just that. Dolan was completely comfortable during the match in part because the twenty-one-year-old was only a second-degree blackbelt, and he was fourth degree former national collegiate sparring champion. His unbeaten streak at the school ended amid great fanfare as the rest of the group erupted in congratulatory clapping and hooting for their classmate.

Dolan was surprised by how much he enjoyed teaching, and as it turned out he was exceptionally good at it. He'd been an instructor before, teaching other pilots how to fly the AC-130 Spectre gunship back when he was in the Air Force, but this was different. Being an instructor pilot is one-on-one, and he was challenging an entire room full of people to learn and excel. The dynamic was fundamentally different, and likewise more challenging. He was also teaching in his day job, as an assistant professor at the Boston University Pardee School of Global Studies. He had to go back to school and get his master's degree before the faculty would hire him, an endeavor that made sense as there wasn't much else he could do in his first year back as he slowly recovered from the injuries he received in Berlin.

Berlin.

There weren't too many days that went by when he wouldn't think about what happened there and in Paris. What became of Sharif. What the EXCISE team was doing now. At first, he wallowed somewhat in his own misery, bedridden and in pain. After six weeks he requested a transfer to Mass General in Boston so his parents wouldn't have to drive so far just to be with him. He was discharged three weeks after that and decided to stay. Once he was able to drive, he returned to D.C. to get his things, still in storage near his old apartment in Rosslyn, VA. He found a nice two-bedroom apartment in Cambridge, relatively close to BU and the commute wasn't bad. Sometimes he just rode his bicycle. He underwent physical therapy for his right forearm and left hand for a few months more as he began easing back into a normal workout routine. The rigor of getting his advanced degree helped keep his mind off the pain and many other things, including Anne.

As he parked his car and walked up the six steps to the door of his apartment he thought about her, wondering if he'd handled their relationship correctly in the aftermath of Berlin. He didn't have the opportunity to see her before being flown back to Washington and had called her from his hospital bed in Bethesda. That was two weeks after he'd last spoken with her, at her workplace in Paris. Rhodes had already been in touch with her to let her know about his condition and that he'd be leaving Europe immediately for continued treatment. She told her he had been on a routine but classified courier mission, simple really, to transfer documents from Berlin to the Five Eyes Plus France office in Paris. But he'd been ambushed and left for dead, and they still didn't know who was responsible. It irritated him that he couldn't let her know what really happened, but it was what it was.

After their phone call Anne flew to Washington to spend some time with him. Dolan was incredibly grateful at the time. Having her there was a great comfort. His parents came down the same week and were able to meet her. And of course, they were enthralled, and Dolan could tell they thought she was 'a keeper.' But things never did pan out. Rhodes had given him the option to go back to Paris after he healed—they would keep his position open for him. But he felt he couldn't. Despite the great catharsis he experienced half dead in the Berlin safehouse, there were still so many things at the time that he had to work out. To work on. And it wasn't that his catharsis and subsequent self-understanding were somehow spurious or drug-induced, they were *real.* The fact was, he needed time to analyze and adjust how he thought, how he interpreted and reacted to life events and to other people. He had to rebuild his paradigm of thought completely and practice within that new structure until it became habitual. Dolan determined that the thing he felt had been missing all those years was *empathy.* He had to practice understanding how other people felt. At first it made him uncomfortable, but the more he tried it, the easier it was. And after about a year, he was beginning to feel it. That was the moment he considered himself fixed. Or at least, most of the way there.

It took longer than he anticipated, and by the time he felt comfortable with himself and within this new mental framework, Anne had slipped away. He was heartbroken, and so was she. But he understood why she left him. He couldn't expect her to wait while he cared for no one but himself for so long. *It is more honest to say that I left her.* It was a difficult sacrifice. At least, he hoped it had been a sacrifice.

For a time he wondered if he'd been selfish, that pushing Anne away was really part of a self-defense mechanism. But eventually he put those thoughts aside. It truly was a sacrifice, and it was the right thing to do. If Dolan had put her first, he'd be returning to Anne as some facsimile of the broken and marginally sociopathic man he'd been for so long. In that case, there could be no hope of a productive and happy future. For either of them.

As Dolan prepared his dinner, he acknowledged that not everything was perfect. Far from it, actually. The revelation that Claire had been murdered still haunted him. It was something he allowed to happen on a regular basis—a necessary, procedural departure from his old, deconstructed mental paradigm. It was the one box he'd left intact and imprisoned in his mind. There had been no good way to deal with it. No closure. To the contrary, her death had gone from being something he'd felt responsible for to an unimaginable crime with no clear path towards vengeance or reparation. The result was a stalemate between his subconscious and his waking mind, a ceasefire that Dolan hoped someday would be broken by a bullet to the head of his onetime best friend, Sharif.

It took seven months to cut his ties with the CIA. Not that they had any further use for him after Berlin, but because of the incredible amount of paperwork, debriefing, and administrative issues that ensued as he recovered. A lot of it had to do with indemnification, something the team had not planned out very well in the lead up to Operation EXCISE. Dolan figured they never seriously considered that he'd be hurt or involved in anything other than observing and reporting. The CIA covered all his medical bills and provided him a generous compensation package for his injuries. In return, Dolan signed documents stating in no uncertain terms that the government was not to blame, in any part or capacity, for any physical or mental damage to himself or anyone else at any time. Or something like that. Only after those months of tedium was he read out of EXCISE, agreeing that the team didn't exist, that he had done nothing for the CIA, and had never met any of them. And all of that was fine with him.

CHAPTER THREE

Lauren Rhodes strode quickly down the hall, irritated she was called in to Langley without so much as a hint of what it was about. She was hoping she'd get there before the briefing started so she could talk to Dittrich about it. As it turned out, traffic didn't cooperate, and she was late. She'd have to find out during the meeting.

She keyed in her code, held her badge to the reader and opened the door to the Sensitive Compartmented Information Facility and went in. Everyone at the table looked up as she entered. Dittrich was there, and she recognized two analysts, one from the Algeria Desk, and another from one of the Middle East countries. Other than that, no one looked familiar. A lady with a laser pointer paused her briefing as Rhodes came in. She took one of two empty seats at the long wooden table.

A map of Jordan was projected on the screen with a red circle around the capital city, Amman. There were smaller circles scattered around the outskirts and a 'CDC' logo in the top right of the slide. The lady continued. "When notified of the first cases, we analyzed the limited data and at first glance it had all the typical characteristics of the Ebola virus. After testing blood samples from symptomatic patients at our embassy, however, it turned out to be Marburg Hemorrhagic Fever."

Rhodes glanced around as a few in the room gasped or muttered disbelief. Others, including her, remained quiet, waiting for this lady from the Center for Disease Control to explain what they were up against.

"Marburg Hemorrhagic Fever is caused by the Marburg Virus of the Filoviridae family, which includes Ebola. It is called MARV for short. The symptoms of these two are nearly identical. Given the outbreaks of Ebola in Africa in recent years, the CDC and World Health Organization have been quick to react whenever they pop up. Further, the incredible surge of attention, funding and effort dedicated worldwide to reigning in the Coronavirus pandemic of 2020 has put the world on edge—we are much better prepared now for something like this. While outbreaks of Ebola come and go, though, Marburg is far rarer. The last known case was in 2014, in Kampala, Uganda and there was only one casualty. The last significant outbreak was in 2004 in the Uige Province of Angola. There were 252 cases there, of which 227 died. That's a 90 percent mortality rate, which is about right for Marburg outbreaks in third world countries with less than adequate response capabilities or sufficient medical facilities.

"A little more background. In 1967, German scientists from Marburg and Frankfurt were exposed to tissues of infected grivet monkeys. These were the first reported cases. In 1990 there was a case in Russia attributed to laboratory contamination. Other than these, there has never been an outbreak outside Africa. Given the number of cases, their dispersion pattern, and the rapid initial rate with which the cases were reported in Jordan, it is our conclusion this could not have been caused by a carrier traveling from Africa or elsewhere, nor could it have originated in the Middle East. This appears to be intentional, a weaponization of Marburg." She clicked to the next slide displaying information about the virus.

The room erupted with side discussions at that point and the CDC representative waited. Finally, Dittrich cut in. "Alright everyone, please keep it down. We are not finished here. Linda, please go on."

She nodded to Dittrich. "I mentioned earlier that Marburg is similar to Ebola symptomatically, but let's be clear. Marburg is much, much worse. With the right response and care for those affected, Ebola has a mortality rate of about 50 percent. As I mentioned before, Marburg can be as high as 90 percent. It is rated by the World Health Organization as a Risk Group 4 Pathogen, and when weaponized, as a Category A Bioterrorism Agent by the CDC. The Department of Health and Human Services categorizes it as a 'Select Agent' under U.S. law, which basically means it has the potential to pose a severe threat to public health and safety. There is no inoculation or treatment, other than to keep the affected comfortable and hydrated. Just about a year ago an effective vaccination was developed for Ebola, and it has been distributed to areas of concern in the third world, but it has no utility whatsoever for Marburg.

"There is another, related virus that causes Marburg Virus disease, or MVD, called the Ravn virus, RAVV for short. However, we've ruled out that RAVV might be the culprit here. MARV was researched and weaponized by the Soviet Union during the Cold War, and it is rumored they conducted testing, but we don't have good information about how successful they were. What is happening in Amman appears to be the result of the first known use of weaponized Marburg Virus. We have a rapid response team in Amman now working closely with the local government and medical community to contain the outbreak. The World Health Organization is involved in an advisory capacity. We have contacted our counterparts in Russia for whatever information they can provide but have received nothing so far. We expect they will be cautious with how they collaborate with us, as they know that we know about their historical attempts at weaponization of the pathogen. They will not give us any information they think might create a perception that Russia had something to do with the outbreak.

"Luckily, Marburg is not an airborne virus and is spread primarily through bodily fluid transfer, which includes sexual intercourse. This is why we have seen numerous family members of initial, direct cases become infected but not too many others outside that circle." Linda took a breath and placed the slide clicker on the table. "This concludes my briefing. I'd be happy to take any questions you might have."

She answered five or six inquiries from the group. Afterward, Dittrich stood up and walked to the head of the table beside Linda, thanked her and walked with her to the door where an escort was waiting. Then he moved back in front of the group.

"OK team, now you know what we are dealing with. For those of you who were brought in at the last second and don't already know, the al-Mulathamun Army claimed responsibility for this attack via a video online about an hour and a half ago. I'm sure that since we assembled here it has hit the news and if it hasn't it will soon. What may not go public, at least not yet, is that we know the virus was likely introduced into the public water supply. By the time anyone thought to test the water, it was clean. But the density and pattern of cases closely matches the map of water distribution lines in the western side of the city, something discovered by one of our officers in Amman. If this is correct, the AMA had detailed knowledge about the water system and was careful about where they attacked. The greatest concentration of cases…" Dittrich picked up the laser pointer and moved back to the map slide with the red circles, "is over here, in this area. This is where our embassy is, along with the embassy of Kuwait. Some of the housing for our State Department personnel is located there, along with restaurants, clubs and shops frequented by our embassy personnel and other westerners."

He leaned forward and put both hands on the conference table, looking at each person in the room in quick succession. "Folks, the ambassador and forty-seven other U.S. citizens from our embassy are infected, and another twenty-six of their family members. All told, there are over nine hundred reported cases in and around Amman and the number grows with each hour. Most of them are likely to die, and it's a horrible death. The AMA probably chose Marburg because of its high fatality rate, but also because it is not airborne—this allows them to use it in a targeted manner. To target us. The United States. The AMA just declared war, and our job is to find them all and eradicate them.

"What our friend from the CDC did not elaborate on was that weaponizing the MARV virus via a water supply should not work very well, but it did. Normally, a water treatment plant would remove the vast majority of viruses in the filtration process alone, but the AMA introduced it into the distribution system, after it had already been treated. However, the plant that services Amman uses chlorine to reduce bacterial and virus counts. The chlorine should have greatly reduced the effectiveness of the attack, but it didn't. This points to a highly sophisticated attack, one that either used an engineered strain of MARV that is particularly resistant, or they figured out some other way to keep the virus viable, perhaps by adding something else to the water.

"All of this points to technology and methods that only a state government would be capable of. As Linda mentioned, the Soviet Union spent some time trying to weaponize Marburg, but to our knowledge, not by delivery in this manner. There are many unknowns right now and we must operate under the assumption that this is not a one-time event. The AMA has the capacity to strike again with weaponized Marburg Virus using the same or similar methods. We know the AMA and have done our best to mitigate their efforts, but it hasn't been enough. This is the first time they've claimed responsibility for an act of terror, but it's not the first they've committed, or endeavored to, against us and others. Remember Berlin and Paris. The difference now is, where we've been marginalized historically in our efforts to locate and eradicate them, we are now in a position to receive collaboration from governments whose countries have been affected, both directly and indirectly, by this unconscionably evil event.

"This SCIF will be used as an operations center going forward. We'll be working twenty-four seven for the foreseeable future. Everyone here is on the team, and we'll pull in other assets as necessary. I'll get a forensics team on the video immediately, and I want everything we have on the leader, Hakeem Lefebvre and on his son, Sharif. We'll meet every morning at eight to go over updates and progress.

"OK. That's it for now. Let's huddle again this afternoon, let's say four O'clock? By then I think we will have more to go on. Lauren, can you hang back?"

They waited for the room to clear. Then Dittrich sat down again, motioning Rhodes to do the same. "Sorry for the late notice. Obviously, with the AMA taking responsibility it makes sense to get SCALPEL involved. You don't currently have anyone in the Middle East, do you?"

"No, we never have. In fact, we don't even have anyone in Africa right now. As you know, we haven't yet found a replacement for Tony Stone in Paris. We read Mike Collier back in and put his guy Stan

Bolden on the team, so we have two in Berlin. We've looked at several candidates for the vacant position, but none have stood out. We were waiting on vetting of a new hire before deciding where to station them. And we have Welker."

"OK. If I think of anyone who might fit the profile, I'll let you know. Whoever it turns out to be we should strongly consider placing them in Algeria. In the meantime, what's the status on Rolf Haussmann in Chile?"

"Actually, we should have him on a plane as early as tomorrow. We had some issues with customs and immigration in Santiago, but it's cleared up now. By tomorrow evening he should be at our safehouse in Annapolis."

Dittrich looked pleased. "Good. We may be able to get something from him about his dark web communications and numbered account transactions. It would be helpful if we could better understand Lefebvre's financial footprints. Frankly, I can't believe Haussmann eluded us for this long."

Rhodes nodded in accord. "Yes, he was a slippery one. We'll have plenty of time to work with him, and I'll get someone on it the minute he's at the house. Listen, I'll do my best to work with the Amman team. We have a lot of good data on Lefebvre's network, but nothing that suggests they have a presence in Syria, or Jordan either. This could be because our geographical focus has been too narrow— we will widen that to include the Middle East. On that note, there's something I've been meaning to discuss with you. Before EXCISE was even an idea, Thomas built an elaborate electronic web that tracks electronic data across North Africa, one he refines daily, to catch any transaction or chatter that has anything to do with the AMA, Hakeem, and now, Sharif. We average around twenty hits per day, and ninety-nine-point nine percent of them are spurious or not actionable. But three weeks ago we intercepted a communication in French that is, and we think it came from Hakeem. In it the sender refers to the 'IMD.' We don't know who the message was sent to, though we are confident it was sent to someone, somewhere in Europe. To date, we have not seen a response. There's more to the message but essentially it instructs someone to 'find and eliminate the IMD,' and it mentions payment. We know Hakeem was extremely unhappy about the way things went down in Paris and Berlin. Remember, the Berlin attack was supposed to be his retaliation for our drone strike near Algiers that killed members of his family, and of course both the Berlin and the Paris attacks were thwarted. Sharif knew who was directly responsible for stopping those attacks. He escaped from France shortly after that and is now presumed to be working with his father in Algeria. Sir, I believe the 'I' in 'IMD' stands for infidèle, and that Hakeem Lefebvre has contracted a hit on Michael Dolan."

CHAPTER FOUR

This was one part of the job he didn't look forward to. Grading papers. He wished he could set them aside and continue working on his doctoral dissertation, but such is life. Of the forty or so stacked on the desk in front of him there might be two, perhaps three that would prove interesting. About twenty would be acceptable, ten that were marginally bad, and the rest would be trash. On average. Occasionally, he was able to inspire a student who turned in consistently bad material to go the extra mile, to go 'from garbage to gold.' It was rare, but part of what made it all worth it.

Resigned to making it a late night, he took a paper off the top of the pile and began reading as the evening news played in the background on a television hung on the wall. He hadn't paid much attention to the news these past couple of years. Much of it wasn't really news anymore. Everything had become so partisan, so political, that finding truth in any of it involved too much effort. Today's broadcasts were tailored to certain demographics and rife with opinion and 'analysis.' It wasn't even commentary. It was targeted entertainment fashioned to generate and sustain discontent, and to improve ratings among a certain scope of viewers.

Three hours later he checked his watch. Eight p.m. He was beginning to get hungry but only halfway through with his work. The news program continued to drone on in the background, but something had changed. The tone of voice of the reporter onscreen. There was no conjecture, no sarcasm. No overeager disdain. Instead he sounded genuinely concerned, with even a hint of fear as he spoke. Dolan looked to the TV as he grabbed the remote and turned up the volume. A red banner emblazoned the bottom of the screen with the words TERROR IN JORDAN. The reporter stood in the hallway of a busy hospital as people in white coats moved back and forth behind him. Everyone, even the reporter, was wearing a surgical facemask. Over one thousand cases of Marburg Virus in Amman, seventy-two had already died—mainly children and the elderly.

Holy shit. This story had been morphing over the past few days. Initially, it was said to be thirteen cases of Ebola and a possible outbreak. The numbers had climbed each day and apparently, they had gotten it all wrong. Dolan had never heard of Marburg Virus, but the news broadcast made it sound like an apocalyptic situation. The reporter was fumbling through some of the statistics and limited information he had written on a sheet of paper, nothing of real consequence or interest until noting that the al-Mulathamun Army, a relatively unknown offshoot of al-Qa'ida based in Algeria, had claimed responsibility in a video uploaded to the internet just a short time ago. He felt his heart skip a beat, a chill run down his spine as his photographic memory instantly thrust every ugly detail from Operation EXCISE to the fore of his mind. Images of twenty-year-old Karim Hamidou, the Algerian terrorist he shot, collapsed and dying in the tunnel back in Potsdam. Martin lying on his back in the panel truck covered in blood. The sound of Sharif's voice as he admitted to Dolan he had killed Claire.

Then he shut it down. He couldn't allow himself to let those things bother him. He'd moved on and accepted everything that happened, and life was good. There would always be these triggers, reminders of what had happened. Revenants of his dark side, from darker times. He turned off the television, deciding to check his inbox and then call it a night. As he scrolled though the seven or eight new emails, one caught his attention with a sick, yet exciting sense of déjà-vu. From Lauren Rhodes. He thought it strange he'd often feel two ways about the same thing—two emotions or reactions that were diametrically opposed. He would wonder if that was normal, and decided after many years of speculation that it was not. Just another reason to compartmentalize. In this case it made sense in some way. A lot of bad things happened in Berlin that were somehow overshadowed by a few, monumentally important personal victories. Her email must have something to do with what he'd just witnessed on the news broadcast, but what could they possibly want with him at this point? How could he possibly help? He was convinced he had nothing left to offer.

'Just shutting things down' is something he still allowed himself to do on occasion. It was still useful in certain situations. The difference between then and now is that he figured out where to draw the line—knowing when compartmentalizing something was beneficial and would be unlikely to cause problems down the road. The question he had to ask himself each time was, is there anything he can do *right now* to solve the problem, or to make things better? If the answer was no, then he did his best to accept it. To understand it and to acknowledge he had no influence over it. To let it evolve and perhaps, at some point, it might find its way into his sphere of control. Or not. If the answer was yes, he might choose to put whatever it was into a time capsule, a semitransparent box where he could devise the best way to deal with it without letting it affect him mentally. There weren't too many of those boxes now. He'd dealt with all of them two years ago, mountains of them all at once as he lay near death on the safehouse bed back in Berlin. All but one. Some were new now, but he was working on them, and they came and went where before they would accumulate to the point there were too many to manage.

Dolan opened the email from Lauren Rhodes. The subject line simply read "Important."

Michael,

I trust this email finds you well. As you may have heard, current events have led to a new interest in our old friends. There is a recent, related development of critical importance about which I must speak with you…"

The email went on to request a meeting tomorrow morning at seven, across the harbor on Deer Island, near the water processing plant. Dolan stared at his computer screen, reviewing the content. Not much to go on. If the AMA was involved with what was happening in Jordan, it meant they'd recovered from the blow dealt by Dolan and the EXCISE team two years ago. Expanded their reach. It meant that the CIA had not been able to effectively follow up afterwards, to find and capture or kill Sharif and Hakeem. There was nothing that led him to believe he'd be of any value to them.

Ultimately, Dolan had been successful but had pissed off the team in the process. The CIA had reasons to never want to see him again, let alone ask for his help. The only thing he could think of, the only thing that made sense, was they needed him to deal with Sharif again. Sharif had shown signs of weakness leading up to the end of the mission, cracks in his psyche were exposed. Maybe they wanted him to try to turn Sharif against his father and the AMA. *Sharif, who murdered his Claire.* The one semitransparent box he'd left untouched in Berlin began throbbing then, strobing malevolently. He'd made the decision to leave it alone in the event he'd have the opportunity to deal with it later, however slim those chances might be. It was a calculated risk at the time. Leaving this dangerous artifact of his old mental self intact could have been a bad decision. Without closure, this aphotic remnant could catalyze an insidious reversion to his old self, undoing much of the progress he'd made. But if this meeting was what he thought it was, it meant he may have made the right decision after all.

CHAPTER FIVE

A complex mélange of emotions stirred inside as Dolan drove along the waterfront toward Deer Island. He welcomed it. After two years he'd come to appreciate the great value of dealing with things he'd previously bottled up. Interpreting and learning from them. To become a better person. It was an ability that helped him deal with both important issues and superficialities. To be able to quickly and accurately separate one from the other. Superficial things like the traffic that was just beginning to get bad but eased as he approached his destination, an area of Boston on the water with more of an old-world feel. The houses and small shops here had history that the soulless concrete and aimless bustle of the big city lacked. There were so many areas of Boston like this. Having grown up nearby, it was one of the main reasons he loved the city so.

Dolan pulled into the small, mostly empty parking lot. There were no buildings here, save the water treatment plant structures that were just out of sight on the other side of the hill. The rest of the island was a park overlooking the bay, the Boston skyline in the distance. Normally a popular place for sightseers, bicyclists and joggers, the island was unusually quiet this overcast early September morning. He remained seated in his meticulously renovated, red 1966 Ford Bronco, watching out the left window for Rhodes' arrival.

There she is. She was driving a dark blue Chevy sedan rental and pulled up in the spot next to him, smiling curtly as she came a stop. Dolan grabbed his suit jacket from the passenger seat, got out and put it on as he walked around to the driver's side of her car. He waited as she retrieved a file from her briefcase and then opened the door for her.

"Michael, so good to see you." Rhodes shook his hand as Dolan shut the car door. "Let's go for a stroll. How's the hand and arm?" They started across the lot towards the street, looked both ways and crossed together.

"Nice to see you as well, Lauren. The arm is fine, the hand is still a little stiff. The good news is, now I can tell when bad weather is about to roll in." They both smiled and he decided to wait before saying anything else. He knew she understood what his questions would be and had already prepared how to answer them.

At the water's edge they stopped, standing on the large, flat granite rocks that lined the edge of the island. For a moment they both stared across the bay. Then she turned to him and broke the silence. "I'm sorry Michael. The way things went down in Paris and Berlin. For bringing you in with insufficient training. For not telling you everything. Keeping tabs on you. We didn't have a lot of time and had very few options. It was the best we could come up with but in the end, it may have been the wrong way to do it. And while it was easy to blame you for deciding to do your own thing, that would be a copout on my part. It wouldn't be a stretch to say we might have failed in preventing the attacks if you *hadn't* done what you did. The whole mission was very risky. You know, Dittrich forbade any of us from apologizing to you, for admitting any fault. We were in the middle of all the indemnification paperwork, and the Agency lawyers… Anyway, the whole thing made me sick, and I wanted you to know. I apologize."

She looked much the same as when they first met. In fact, he was almost certain she was wearing the same navy skirt suit she wore that day he first met her in the Pentagon courtyard. Only something about her had changed. He looked closer and understood what it was. A few fine lines around the eyes. Her smile had more of a serious quality now, and she had lost a few pounds. He surmised the events in Berlin had taken a toll on her as well. She was relatively new as the team lead back then; it had been baptism by fire for both of them. *And she lost Stone*. Dolan nodded. "There was enough blame to spread around, I think. Certainly, some of it was mine and you should know that I have no grievances. To be honest, the only real regret I have is that somehow, Stone might still be alive if I had done things differently."

Rhodes winced and just as quickly gathered herself. "This is the business. Unfortunately, some of us must give our lives to ensure our national security is not compromised. We sign up for it. Having served in the military, from your combat missions, you know this better than most. Stone knew it too. He knew what he was doing. If it helps, I don't believe you could have done anything, or done anything differently that would have changed that outcome."

Dolan nodded again. He understood. Seven servicemen he deployed with died in combat in Afghanistan. One of them was a good friend.

With the apology out of the way Rhodes changed her tone. "As you have probably heard, the AMA claimed responsibility for the biological attack in Jordan. Rather than retreat and lick his wounds, Hakeem Lefebvre circled the wagons and fortified his organization, then began branching out. As far as we can tell it's limited to the

Maghreb and Syria but suffice to say the AMA is much larger and more geographically dispersed than it was two years ago. The bioweapon is advanced. It's not something that should be possible for a terrorist group to engineer. We believe they had help from a state government." She watched Dolan to gauge his reaction.

He looked down at the large granite rock they were standing on and kicked a pebble into the bay. He watched it hit the water. Then an aircraft caught his eye, climbing away to the north from Boston Logan as another landed from the south.

"Lauren, let's get to the point. Why are you here? What is it you think you need from me?"

The breeze off the water was cold. She should have dressed differently. "It's complicated, Michael. I can't tell you everything here. What I can say is that your life may be in danger. We have reason to believe the AMA has contracted someone in Europe to assassinate you. The details are sketchy at best, but we think now that Hakeem Lefebvre has expanded and strengthened the AMA. We believe what happened in Amman was not the main attack, that it was a test run, a capability demonstration. That there are more attacks planned and what we've seen so far might be the tip of the iceberg. And he hasn't forgotten about you—he wants revenge for what happened in Berlin."

Dolan was incredulous. He thought Rhodes would be asking him to come back to EXCISE, to help them take down Sharif and Hakeem. Instead, she was a messenger with a serious warning. He turned to her squarely. "Holy shit Lauren, are you sure? How long have you had this information? Do you know the identity of the assassin?"

"No, we don't. We intercepted a coded communication about a month ago that originated in Algeria. It contained the initials MD. We couldn't determine where that message was sent. A few days ago there was a response originating from somewhere in southern Germany,

Offenbach we think. It was confirmation of receipt of payment. Again, the initials MD were mentioned but there was more. The communication mentioned a location, BU. Though we can't be certain, it's safe to assume that stands for Boston University, Michael. Whoever the AMA contracted knows where you work and may already be on their way here."

Now Dolan felt a chill as well, and not from the breeze off the water. Just as he'd found balance in life and some semblance of peace, disquieting vestiges of his past he thought he'd reconciled long ago came roaring back. He bottled it up quickly. "OK, wow. That's not much to go on but I assume there's more to it. What is the plan? I am assuming you are doing whatever you can to locate this guy and take him out before he gets here. What am I supposed to do?"

"Unfortunately, we have very few leads. We aren't even that sure about the origin of the second communication. And even if it was from Offenbach, it doesn't mean the assassin is from there, or even from Germany. Michael, this is about as much as I've been allowed to reveal. I've already told you more than I'm supposed to. Dittrich instructed me to come get you. Bring you to Harvey Point, brief you in fully and come up with a plan. We have facilities there, in North Carolina. I can't force you to go, but I'm urging you to consider this the safest, most logical path. We don't know what will happen with this, or how soon. Getting you away from the university, away from Boston altogether, could very well prevent harm to others." She paused to let Dolan absorb it all. "I hate to have to bring this up, but you should also assume they may try to attack your family, even before they come for you."

She knew how his mind worked. *The most logical path.* The chill down his spine set in and grew colder. As she mentioned his family, his parents, he began to feel sick. His weak attempt to compartmentalize the swirl of emotions was failing. It was easy to deal with when things were balanced and simple. This was heavy. Complex. He fortified his efforts, quickly constructing the barriers needed to keep his mind clear. To remain in control. The chill and nausea dissipated.

"I'll be honest, Lauren. I am conflicted about all of this. I have a good life now. My body is healed, for the most part. I've resolved many things in the past two years and I'm at peace. Being pulled back into this, in whatever way, would probably be a bad move for me personally. That said, there is a part of me that wants to finish what was started. And it seems like you're telling me I have no choice. If we're being honest with each other, Hakeem is not the only one who wants revenge. I need to know now what we are talking about, exactly. I have a life and a job that I've come to enjoy. I don't want to lose that." He looked at his watch. "In fact, I need to leave soon if I'm going to make it for my nine-a.m. class."

Rhodes stepped slowly off and away from the rocks, onto the grass. "Go teach your classes today. We are still working on the plan, and I think we have a way to make this work without negatively impacting your position at the university. Thomas and I are almost there and can have most of it done by today. But if you want to know more... and more about how to help shape the way forward, you'll have to come with me to Harvey Point tonight. Every hour we delay puts you and others in increasing danger. You should pack for two weeks. I've already booked you a flight."

CHAPTER SIX

The flight from Logan to Norfolk was quiet and uneventful. His seat was five rows behind hers, probably on purpose. He was sure she didn't want to deal with any more questions until they arrived. Dolan passed the time drafting emails. One to the university staff, one to his students, another to his parents, and one to his taekwondo school. There were details he'd have to fill in once he understood more. He was nervous of course—it's not a common thing to be the target of assassination and it helped him put his life in perspective, starkly. There was also a part of him that was excited. *Rightly so.* To find out what transpired after Berlin, where Hakeem and Sharif were, what their involvement was with the attack in Jordan, and what his role would be, if any, moving forward.

Then there was the part of him that was angry. Angry that Sharif kept coming back into his life, creating chaos. He'd been relatively happy up until the moment Sharif killed Claire. There were a few years of disconsolate soul-searching. Then he pulled himself together only to be thrust right back into the place where it all happened, with Sharif as the centerpiece. Those few months saw him devolve mentally and near the end, physically, as he received several severe injuries and almost died. *Here we go again?*

He was worried about how Rhodes and Freeman were going to cover for him at BU. He knew he'd always be welcome back at his dojang, but being a professor was altogether different. He had important responsibilities to hundreds of students and to his colleagues. Luckily, the semester had just started and if needed he could hand off the syllabus content he created over the summer for his three classes to whomever they appointed in the interim. Rhodes said it would only be two weeks. He would probably be involved in some advisory capacity. He could give them information and provide his opinions remotely, safe and sound here in the U.S. *Nothing like before.* Regardless of where he was, the matter of leaving Boston wasn't up for debate. If there really was a contract killer coming after him, the best thing he could do is what he was doing—getting out of town. The chances anyone else at the university, his taekwondo school, or his parents would be hurt would be reduced significantly.

They landed at Norfolk International, retrieved their bags and got a rental car. On the way there Rhodes didn't say much. There was some small talk about Dolan's work. She asked him if he'd kept in touch with Anne. She seemed surprised that he hadn't. It was a sore spot for Dolan, so the conversation petered out and the rest of the trip was more or less spent in silence.

Harvey Point Defense Testing Activity is situated on a peninsula along the Albemarle Sound in Perquimans County, North Carolina. Commissioned in 1942 by the Navy as an air station for blimps conducting anti-submarine surveillance over the Atlantic, its tenants and missions had evolved over time. The base now hosted explosives testing and paramilitary and counterterrorism training facilities for the FBI, the Bureau of Alcohol, Tobacco, Firearms and

Explosives, and the CIA. Dolan was aware of the base only because of television reporting about the mockup of Osama bin Laden's compound in Abbottabad, Pakistan. It was constructed there for use by Seal Team Six in preparation for the assault that killed him on May 2, 2011. Beyond this, very little is known about what goes on there.

It was dark by the time they pulled up to the massive front gate. Armed guards approached the car as Rhodes came to a stop near the blockhouse. Dolan noted the tire shredders across the entryway as Rhodes gave her badge and his driver's license to one of the guards who then went back into the blockhouse while the second guard watched them. A few moments later he returned, handed her badge back saying, "Welcome to Harvey Point."

Rhodes drove slowly through the gate and onto the base. "There is a lot that goes on here, and the Agency is the primary tenant. We do a considerable amount of hardcore clandestine training here. Camp Peary, near Williamsburg, Virginia is where we teach the basics. You have probably heard it referred to as 'The Farm.' You could say this is where we send CIA officers for graduate school."

"So I've gathered," Dolan replied. As they drove the streetlights cast eerie shadows across occasional nondescript buildings and numerous, towering cypress trees covered in Spanish moss. There were very few vehicles, no one out and about. The place had southern ghost town feel to it.

"Thomas is here, along with Howard Welker. Welker is quite a character, but don't let his penchant for jocularity fool you. He knows what he's doing, and he's been doing it a long time. He's a prior member of the team and stays read-in so we can call him up when needed."

"And what does he do, exactly?"

"Quite a bit, actually. What doesn't he do… It's better if you ask him yourself. Here we are." Rhodes turned off the main road onto a wide gravel driveway that led up to what looked like an incredibly large warehouse with no windows. High-power lamps positioned at intervals on the ground lit it up on all sides. It was perhaps five stories high and could house a football field. There were a few trees and a handful of smaller buildings nearby with paths winding here and there. Various man-made obstacles and vehicles scattered about. From what he could see of the field, it was a paintballer's dream playground. *Only they don't use paintballs…*

They pulled up to the building and parked next to three other vehicles near an unmarked door. "Leave your bags in the car. And your cell phone," said Rhodes.

They got out of the car and approached the door. Rhodes pressed a button on a small callbox to the left and looked up at a camera eight feet above. There was a short buzz as the door was unlocked and they went in. The lights came on automatically as they entered a claustrophobically small foyer with an empty receptionist desk and three doors, one each to the left and right and one straight ahead. Rhodes directed him to the left and followed him in. There was a small table, three chairs, and nothing else.

"Have a seat, Michael. We have a few administrative things to get through first. It's the same exercise as last time—you were read out of EXCISE after Berlin, and I need to read you back in before going any further."

Dolan took the seat facing the door as she pulled a file from her briefcase and sat opposite him. She opened the manila folder and handed him the sheet on top, then closed the file. It was another nondisclosure form. Except for the date, this could have been the exact same form he signed almost two and half years ago. He looked at her kiddingly, but serious at the same time. "I'll need to see your credentials first."

Rhodes regarded him blankly for a moment. "Yes, of course, sorry." She remembered being asked by Dolan to do this once before, in the courtyard at the center of the Pentagon. She reached back into her case and produced her wallet, holding it out for him to see.

Dolan smiled at her. *She looks tired.* "Thanks Lauren." His eyes went back to the form as she slid a pen across the table. Then he realized it was not the same form. It was identical except for one very pertinent detail. There was no mention of Operation EXCISE. In its place was Operation SCALPEL. He signed the form and pushed it with the pen back across the table. Rhodes glanced at his signature and placed the form underneath the thick stack of papers in the file.

"Before I read you in Michael, I will need a commitment from you. I am not talking about secrecy; that is what the nondisclosure is for. When you were read into EXCISE, we developed your role before ever approaching you. EXCISE was created just for you. It allowed us to have you on the team without the need to brief you in on the larger picture. Whether or not that was the best, or even the right thing to do, that's the way it went down and though there were things that could have been done in a better way it was considered to be a highly successful mission.

"You will be read into our organizational mission. It is much broader than what was entailed with going after the al Mulathamun Army, Lefebvre, and his son Sharif. As you are aware the AMA is central to our current efforts, but after some discussion with leadership we decided our best chance at success against them includes briefing you in completely. What is different this time is, we do not have a defined role for you. That means a few different things, and how events evolve going forward will dictate the extent of your involvement. It could take a month, or it could be longer. What I need from you is a commitment to be part of the team at least until we reach a certain level of success."

Dolan tilted his head in thought, keeping his eyes on hers. He wondered if it were possible that this was a sham—that Rhodes was making an overture at transparency just to get him on board. It all made sense; she had planned it well. The apology, the threat against his life that could extend to his parents and students. She gave him no option but to follow her here. This was, increasingly, a perfectly formulated rabbit hole he had no alternative but to dive into.

"You told me to pack for two weeks. This sounds like it is longer than that. Before I can commit to anything, I need rock-solid assurances that my position at BU will be unaffected, with an explanation about how you will pull that off. And if my parents are in any danger at all, I expect the Agency to do what is necessary to protect them. There are a lot of other questions I have, but I assume many of those will go unanswered without a commitment."

"That is a good point," Rhodes acknowledged. "Two weeks is the duration of your training and preparation. The mission would come afterwards. So yes, I asked you to pack for two weeks because that is how long you would be here at Harvey Point. As for your job, Thomas has been working on the plan and is ready to execute it, when and if you come on board. He can explain the details later, but essentially, we've created a semi-structured sabbatical opportunity for you. And yes, we know you are too new at BU to qualify, heck you haven't been there a year. We created the appearance of a once-in-a-lifetime, use it or lose it scenario. You were requested by name to participate due to your exemplary work with foreign governments at your Joint Staff job at the Pentagon, and because you've quickly gained a good reputation at BU that has been noticed by the right people. You'll be hosted by an organization called Atlantik Brücke, a German non-profit association that focuses on German American relationships. One of their missions is to provide support for study abroad opportunities for teachers. It will be uncomfortable for multiple reasons, mainly the suddenness of it but you will have to sell the story to your colleagues, friends and family. It is fully funded and includes a significant grant made directly to your department at the Pardee School of Global Studies. The sabbatical, or whatever you want to call it, is real—you would have to actually do the research. Since you are currently working on your Doctoral degree, you should shape the opportunity to support completion of your dissertation.

"Now, when I say it is 'semi-structured' I mean there will be occasional events you will have to attend, and Atlantik Brücke will be monitoring your progress. We have a contact for you there, a professor from Free University of Berlin, where you will be doing your research. His name is Lutz Möller. He is unaware of your cover of course—as far as he is concerned, this is nothing more than a collaborative research program.

"Though it's not finalized yet, for now I can say you will be paid a minimum of four hundred dollars a day, for every day you remain on the team. If your contributions are deemed substantive and the mission is successful, there is a five-thousand-dollar bonus at the end of it. We have an apartment set up for you in Berlin. Finally, we conducted another background investigation on you, which checked out, and you will have to take another polygraph. It will cover the period from your last poly in 2019 until now. We have it set up in the other room. I can tell you more once you pass it." She watched Dolan expectantly. "What do you say?" Rhodes picked up the pen and tapped it a few times on the table.

Dolan was thinking while he listened to her, comparing and measuring the possible outcomes. The polygraph didn't concern him, but some of the unknowns did. "What happens if I turn it down? Will you put a tail on me, so you can keep an eye out for this assassin? Will you involve local law enforcement? How will you ensure my parents are safe?"

These questions made her visibly uncomfortable. "We… there is a plan, but again I can't say anything else until you come on board. And I get it, some of this becomes moot if you do. We wouldn't be able to guarantee your safety or anyone else's for that matter. But of course, we would do everything we can to prevent the AMA from moving forward with the hit, and to capture those involved. I think you know by now that it would be more difficult for us to do any of it without your involvement."

Again with the tapping. *She is worried I won't commit.*

Dolan was surprised at the CIA's level of preparation in advance of this meeting. To ensure he would join the team. He was familiar with Atlantik Brücke and if set up well, it was believable and could work. Except for the fact that he wasn't eligible for a sabbatical. Not even close. The grant was unusual as well, but what university would blink if it were a large enough sum? "How much is the grant?"

"One hundred thousand euros."

Holy shit. "Wow Lauren, that seems like a lot. How in the world do you justify it? I mean, what am I being expected to do that might ever approach the value of such a grant? What is the logical reason behind such an amount?"

Rhodes was beginning to get exasperated. "OK fine Michael, I'm supposed to wait but frankly I need you on board, so here it is. The dean of the Pardee School, Kenneth Freihoff, used to work in the intelligence community. We approached him directly and made it a matter of national security, which it is. He's already on board and the 100K is what he brokered. Atlantik Brücke gets fifteen percent of that. Apparently, he's also a good businessman. The amount of the grant won't be public. He knows nothing about the details of the mission or about your prior involvement with the Agency, and he signed a nondisclosure agreement. The only other request he made was that the 'sabbatical' lasts no longer than three months. Anything longer and it would raise too many eyebrows. Added to that, he values you as an assistant professor and wants you back at work. This is something he understands, and we are lucky this was so easy to set up. You will only need to convince your friends and colleagues about your cover. Freihoff will take care of the rest."

They really had thought of everything. Dean Freihoff never spoke much about his time with the National Security Agency, but it was no secret he had been a spook. His seventeen years with the NSA culminated in a senior director position and it was mentioned in his biography on the school's website. Dolan was painted into a corner, and there was not much else he could think of to ask at this point. He wanted his parents to be safe. He did not want anyone else hurt, either. The stability and relative happiness he'd managed to build and sustain would be disrupted, but it wouldn't be anything he couldn't repair. Moreover, this could be an opportunity to accelerate the timeline of his doctoral degree. And maybe, to help bring Sharif and his father to justice. The positives seemed to outweigh any negatives, and in any case, he didn't really have a choice. Which made it easier.

"OK Lauren. I am willing to go along for the ride. But we cannot call this a sabbatical because no one is going to buy it, especially my colleagues at BU. As you said earlier, I am already working on my PhD. We can call it a joint German, or European and U.S. security research project. Something that has been identified as a requirement or a clear need. I already have a topic for my doctoral dissertation, but I'm not so far along that I can't amend it somewhat if needed. It would be nice to kill two birds with one stone. And this is something Atlantik Brücke would actually do. 'Brücke' means bridge—it is what they exist for, to enable activities and partnerships that strengthen our trans-Atlantic geopolitical ties. Before I agree to come back on board, though. I first need you to make a commitment to me."

Rhodes gave him a quizzical look. "What is it?"

"If I am going to sign up for this, I ask that you promise you will not surveil me unknowingly or keep me in the dark. About anything. I am a full partner, or I walk."

She leaned forward a bit, seriously. "Michael, as I said earlier, what we did before, we thought it necessary at the time. In hindsight, I would have done things differently and this is a completely different agreement. You have my word on both counts."

"OK. Let's see where this rabbit hole goes then."

CHAPTER SEVEN

"Hey there, Howard Welker. You must be Michael. Nice to meet you!"

Dolan stepped forward and shook his hand. "Nice to meet you as well. Good to see you again, Thomas." He shook Freeman's hand and the four of them took their chairs around a metal table in the middle of what looked like a very large and old aircraft hangar. Four stacks of intelligence files graced the table, with water bottles at each seat. The towering sliding doors at the east end were closed. There were several rooms or offices down the south wall and a staircase leading up to a second level walkway that ran the length of the building, with more doors. On the opposite wall there were thirty of what looked like oversized garage doors, side-by side from end to end. Dolan noted drains in the floor, interspersed every twenty-five feet or so. Other than that, it was one incredibly large, empty room with a gray painted concrete floor. Their voices echoed under the bright mercury vapor lamps hanging high above.

Welker wasn't what he expected. He stood about five feet seven inches tall, was mostly bald and somewhere north of fifty-five years old. It was hard to tell; he could have been sixty but was in good shape. He was wearing a purple sweatshirt and jeans. Rhodes was right—Dolan's first impression of him was that he was a little *too* happy. Too affable for this line of work. Jocular. *Maybe he is some kind of nerdy specialist.*

Rhodes began. "OK team, now that Michael and Howard are acquainted, it's time to get down to business. Michael signed the NDA, passed his polygraph and has been read into SCALPEL. I will go over the high-level details, then Howard will brief us on what we'll be doing for the next two weeks." She looked at Dolan. "After that, Thomas will brief you on all of the actions you will need to take to finish setting up your cover, and to keep it secure." Dolan nodded.

She continued. "Our mission is classified Top-Secret SCI, in support of a larger mission codenamed Operation CLEARCUT. Everything I'm about to brief to you, and quite a bit more is contained in the files in front of you. You are responsible for studying and memorizing them, and at no point do they leave this building. The AMA claimed responsibility for the Marburg Virus attack in Jordan, and we believe this to be true. As of today, there have been one thousand five hundred and twenty-nine confirmed positive cases, sixty-two of which are U.S. citizens. Of those, three hundred and ninety-eight have died so far, fourteen from the U.S. The AMA has increased their reach and influence over the past two years and has begun to gain the allegiance of certain al-Qa'ida organizations. This was not considered to be a possible outcome two years ago, as the AMA had a falling out with them and split off. Due to their ideological differences, what remains of ISIL, or ISIS, has not joined the AMA ranks. Nonetheless, there has been chatter that shows winning them over is one of the AMA's goals.

"Lefebvre and his son are believed to be in hiding somewhere in Algeria, however there is no evidence to suggest they couldn't be hiding elsewhere. They haven't been seen in the past two years, but we know they are still leading the AMA. Lefebvre has been smart about building the organization. AMA literature we've studied shows they are less radical, more of a mainstream Islamic fundamentalist group that welcomes all branches of the faith, but with one unifying goal—to destroy the West and most importantly, the United States. After the July 2019 attack in Berlin we shared key details with the government of Algeria with the aim of getting them on board as a partner against the AMA, and initial indications were positive. They branded the AMA as a terrorist organization and promised to root them out, locate Lefebvre and bring him to justice, but they did not agree to extradite him or Sharif if captured alive.

"Despite our best efforts to establish a bilateral arrangement in rooting out the AMA, the Algerian government is continuing to try to go it alone. Historical events that hampered collaborative efforts leading up to the planned Berlin and Paris attacks continue to be a barrier to partnership. What they managed to do was seize most of Lefebvre's oil empire, which is now state-controlled. There is still a large portion of it that is privately owned and controlled, however, because there is no legal proof that Lefebvre has any ties to ownership and because much of it is not located in Algeria. We believe he set up part of his empire many years ago in a way that would make it very difficult, if not impossible, for the Algerian government to seize his entire empire. There are fifty-seven installations in Algeria and elsewhere across North Africa where we think Lefebvre could be hiding. Of those, there are six where we have a higher degree of confidence, and we have prioritized those and are getting satellite coverage of each, but mostly visible spectrum and infrared stills using flyovers. There are too many of them at this point, and too much uncertainty to justify dedicating NRO satellites for real-time video surveillance. There is also a large amount of funding still being funneled to the AMA, and there is no opportunity presently for us to count on the Algerian government to work with us on that or other matters, so we are going it alone."

Rhodes paused to take a drink from her water bottle. "As each of us here is aware, Lefebvre has motives beyond conquering the West, and they are more personal. He is still bent on revenge for the death of his four brothers in the drone raid outside Algiers. He knows through his son Sharif that Michael here was partly responsible for preventing the attacks in Paris and Berlin, and he has hired an assassin to take him out. Though we don't know yet know his identity, we assume the assassin is a resident of Germany, perhaps living in or near Offenbach. Since we do not know who he is, we have no idea where he is at this time, or if he has already travelled to the United States. Our plan will be to keep him in Germany, or if he is in the U.S. now, to compel him to return there. We will send Michael to Berlin under cover with support from Howard and Berlin Station to draw the assassin out, capture him, and rendition him back to the United States for interrogation."

Partly responsible. One might argue he stopped the attacks single-handedly. "How are we going to draw him out, specifically?" asked Dolan. *I am the bait.*

"Howard will explain all of that in a moment. Now, pay attention because this is very important. Intelligence suggests Lefebvre and the AMA received technological assistance from a state government in planning the Amman attack. Evidence points to Russia, but it could also be a former Soviet satellite. We also believe they have the capacity to launch similar attacks at any time, most likely in North Africa but possibly elsewhere, including Europe or even the United States. Given recent events, it is not out of the question that Lefebvre would instruct his assassin to transport and use the virus on you,

Michael. And given the indiscriminate nature of a bioweapon, many Americans could die if their plan is to attack Boston University when they know you are there. If this is the case, the logistics would be complicated and would take time—probably much longer than the two weeks that have elapsed since the order was given. Bringing Michael here would have subverted that outcome.

"Finally, we may have a lead in Amman. One of the earliest Marburg cases is a young boy who lives in Zarqa, an eastern suburb that is well outside the attack radius. His mother works at an NGO in Amman proper, but the office is outside the radius as well. We think he may have been involved and are questioning him and his mother. He is in pretty bad shape but it's possible he could pull through. He has denied involvement thus far, but there are a lot of things he is telling us that don't add up. He and his mother are immigrants from Syria, and his father was a member of al-Qa'ida in Afghanistan.

"While we are here, DEVGRU, better known as Seal Team Six, will be in and out of the building and in the adjacent field, prepping for a final assault and extraction that will happen once we have Lefebvre's location. They are referred to as Task Force Blue within the Joint Special Operations Command community.

"The building we are in used to be a blimp hangar." Rhodes extended her arms, "Quite a few modifications have been made over the years. We have a team that can transform the interior into an entire city block or simulate a field with trees and a single building. Any kind of weather or time of day can be replicated for training and strike preparation purposes. It's called 'The Stage.' There are speakers throughout the facility to add whatever noise and sounds we need. There are specialized sprinklers overhead for rain. We can simulate fog and snow, up to fifteen-knot winds and even the correct positioning and brightness of the sun or moon," she pointed upwards. "This place is a lot more high-tech than it looks. The garage-looking doors along the side wall contain all the structural components, furniture, streetlights, and other props for setting it all up, and what they don't have here can be brought in. The buildings snap together like Legos. It's amazing, really. The team of forty-eight at our disposal does all the setup and teardown and they do it fast. It takes about a day to do something complex; a simpler scenario can be finished in a couple hours. We receive the blueprints from a specialized intelligence analysis group at Langley. The team will be here shortly to construct the first scenario. You can expect the fun to begin around ten p.m.

"You probably noted the hangar doors. Due to the fact this used to be a hangar, there is a taxiway from the airfield that leads straight to this building, very useful in case we need to fly something in to complete the mock-up. The DoD also does Top-Secret program weapons systems and aircraft experimental and developmental testing in here. For our purposes, we can simulate up to a three-story building inside the hangar, away from the prying eyes of whatever satellites may be passing overhead. DEVGRU will practice raids on each of the six sites in this building over the next three months, or however long it takes. But our goal is to strike within three. As our intelligence improves, that list of six will be adjusted and narrowed down.

"Do not attempt conversation with the Seals. If they initiate with you, fine but don't ask them any personal questions and don't use anything but first names. Whatever name they use will probably be an alias, in any case. We will remain clear of this area pretty much the entire time and will be doing our training and planning upstairs in those rooms," she pointed to the top of the staircase, "at the range, and a couple other places. Our sleeping quarters are downstairs, numbers seven through ten. The numbers are on the doors. We have an operations center set up on the second floor, in the Maple conference room. Michael, your training each day will be in the Hickory conference room, about five doors down from Maple. The rooms are soundproofed, but once DEVGRU gets going in here the noise and vibration can be significant. I recommend you wear earplugs to bed. The Seal Team has quarters elsewhere.

"As you have probably gathered by now, CLEARCUT is a broad operation. The President has authorized it and will give the execute order for the strike on Lefebvre. There are elements of the DoD besides DEVGRU that are involved, along with the NSA and other intelligence organizations. Everyone is doing their part. One thing that no one knows, however, is that SCALPEL is involved." She looked directly at Dolan. "Remember that even when working within a larger, joint team with a common goal, SCALPEL does not exist. For the purposes of this operation, all other stakeholders believe we are run-of-the-mill CIA case and counterintelligence officers assigned to gather, analyze and provide intelligence, and to assist in the overall success of the mission.

"It is essential we rendition Lefebvre and Sharif alive if possible as the AMA will quickly assign new leadership and continue to operate without them. We will need as much insight as we can get into their organization, and we will get it from them and whatever physical evidence is found during the raids that take place. If CLEARCUT is going into Algeria within three months, it means SCALPEL has one to two months to nab Michael's would-be shooter and extract everything we can. Lefebvre's location is the prize; the lab where they cultured the virus is the secondary target. Hopefully, the two are one in the same. We already have someone in custody who had ties to the AMA from Operation EXCISE, though it has been difficult thus far to get anything out of him. Our success in Berlin could be critical to the success of the larger operation. No one else, I mean no one, is aware of

SCALPEL's plan to capture this assassin. And at least for now, the Berlin mission is the extent of the scope of your involvement, Michael. Any questions?"

"I don't think so," responded Dolan. *'At least for now'—what does that mean? And who is this person in custody?*

"OK, I think that covers everything I wanted to brief."

Dolan had a quite a few questions. He knew many of them would probably be answered in the Top-Secret file on the table in front of him. "Lauren, I do have one concern. You said no one else is read into our mission in Berlin. I assume that means it is not being coordinated with the German government."

Rhodes inhaled. "No. Normally we would want to, and we did work with the BND on our last mission there. However, this is a situation where we are intentionally cornering a terrorist on their turf, perhaps even luring him back there from the U.S. In our analysis, they would never agree to our planned approach. And even if they did, given our intelligence shows the target plans to strike in the U.S., the German government would want the whole thing to go down in the United States and not in Berlin. The second complication is, we are certain that if the shooter is a German citizen, they would never let us extradite. And even if they did it's possible we'd be unable to interrogate him the way we want while extradition proceedings are ongoing. So no, they know nothing of it and hopefully, they never will."

"Understood," Dolan responded. This was why SCALPEL was involved in the first place. Once again, a situation where the host government was not able or willing to assist, so the U.S. is going to violate international law. And he would probably be going in, once again, without diplomatic credentials.

"Good. Howard, go ahead," Rhodes concluded.

Welker, who seemed generally disinterested as Rhodes spoke, was suddenly happy to take over. He folded his arms across his chest and smiled. "Michael, I am damn excited to be part of this and happy to meet you. I know what you did in Berlin, and though the Agency might not like how it went down, I was impressed with what you were able to accomplish there. I can't tell you how many missions Lauren here has pulled me into that were boring as shit. This one is the real deal, however. We are going to have some fun!"

Dolan couldn't help but smile as Rhodes shook her head, ever so slightly. Welker was putting on a bit of a show, and it seemed to be OK with both her and Freeman. This is just who he was...

He went on, more serious. "Over the next couple of weeks you and I are going to work on greatly improving your counterintelligence skills—abilities that will allow you to plan for, locate, and react appropriately to foreign assets who are surveilling or attempting to surveil, or influence, or manipulate, or harm you in any number of ways. And then we will learn how to use the information you gain from that knowledge against them and their organizations, without them ever knowing it was you. You are going to be tired. We are going to go at it for sixteen hours every day, with only two thirty-minute breaks to eat. Every day but one will be spent here at The Stage. We will also go to the range and do some other, equally manly stuff. All of this will be some of the most important training you have ever had because there will be situations in the future where your life will literally depend on how well you internalized it."

He stopped to think for a moment, as if he may have said something incorrect, then continued, "Yes, your Air Force and SPECOPS training was very important as well, and we took all of that into account of course when deciding how to tailor this course, but I'll bet you never had to worry about a professional assassin trying to kill you before. Using CI knowledge and methods we will lure the scumbag out of the shadows, identify him and capture him. Thomas and I will be coordinating with Berlin Station and other assets to create an electronic and human intelligence net around and within a perimeter near your apartment in Dahlem, a suburb on the southwest side of Berlin, where we can maintain constant oversight and control. You will wear an earpiece and have at least two friendlies monitoring you and your environment. There should not be a single moment when you are not in our sights or out of communication. It is likely the assassin will spend a period of days or even weeks doing his research and watching you before making his move. He'll want to know how you get to and from Atlantik Brücke, your local grocery store, etcetera and your preferred methods of travel. He will want to know about your neighbors and what their habitual activities are. He won't make his move until he has decided where and when it will take place, for which he will need to know your daily routines and have developed a solid risk mitigation plan and an exit strategy. We will grab him before he gets to that point.

"There are a lot of moving pieces, many unknowns. It is possible there may be more than one of them, or that the assassin has other resources helping but for now, indications point to a single target. You will need to leave our controlled perimeter at times to meet periodically at the Atlantik Brücke headquarters, for instance. We will try to keep these situations to a minimum and will widen or reshape the perimeter as we can to adapt to evolving situations. I will be there, directing the whole thing. Additionally, there are probably more spies in Berlin per square kilometer than any other city in Europe. With its Cold War history and the fifty-two or so embassies in town, there is always a lot of surveillance and counter surveillance going on. Our operation could stand out if it is not done perfectly. We do not want to have it blown up by a third party or the host country so we will be operating very, very carefully."

The main entry door opened, and The Stage suddenly filled with echoing voices and laughter as a stream of men and a few women began to filter in. The group looked just as Dolan envisioned, like a construction crew. Welker stopped speaking abruptly, watched them for a moment, then continued. "It's the setup crew. Anyway, we have a lot to go through and we will get started at six a.m. in the Hickory conference room. You still have a couple hours of boring administrivia to go through, but we can end my part of it here for now. Thomas will finish briefing you upstairs. The bottom line is," he smiled widely while rubbing his hands together in anticipation, "we are going to catch this motherfucker, and yes Michael, you are the bait."

CHAPTER EIGHT

There were foam earplugs in the room, but Dolan decided not to use them. At around three a.m. he woke to muffled cracks, booms and reverberations. He decided to go ahead and put them in. It wasn't that big a deal; he'd learned to sleep in environments much more uncomfortable than this. After another two and a half hours of sleep the alarm clock buzzed crudely. It jerked him up and was somehow far more irritating than the muted noise of DEVGRU's warplay. The alarm was a break from his routine of the past few years. With his cell phone in the car there was no opportunity for waking gradually to the slow, methodical build of Nine Inch Nails' *La Mer*. No reminder of his daily affirmation. Nothing can stop me now. He whispered it to himself instead, got up and took a shower. He could feel occasional vibrations through the floor as he walked barefoot around his room. Task Force Blue was still at it.

As he got dressed Dolan thought again about the extent of SCALPEL's preparation for him that went on prior to Rhodes' email just two days ago. It was amazing so much could be done so quickly. And all of it gambled on his acceptance of the role they prepared for him. They must have considered he might turn them down, as badly as things turned out at the end of EXCISE. He supposed they assumed he not only had a knack for the work, but that he enjoyed it. And that was true. As pleasant as his quiet, contemporary life had been recently, it lacked adrenaline. Teaching taekwondo was the extent of his weekly excitement, and much of that was demonstration and choreographed activities. He had only one student, the promising twenty-one-year-old second-degree blackbelt that bested him earlier in the week, who could even challenge him. It wasn't enough. *Not nearly.* He needed more.

Dolan opened the door, closed it and leaned against the railing that ran the length of the interior of the huge building. Where last night there had been nothing but a small card table and four chairs occupying the center of a vast open space, there was now a two-story building, several modestly sized trees in oversized planters, quite a few man-made rocks here and there, and three older vehicles. There were white lines and other markings on the floor—positioning points, safety zones and other directions and reminders for the Seal Team as they practiced their incursions. The floor markings were initially included as recommendations from the analysis team at Langley, based on sight lines, probable positions of enemy guards, and best places for the team to take cover as they approached the building. Those markings would change over time as they refined their plan.

DEVGRU was either on a break or had finished for the day. Dolan wondered why, in an enclosed structure such as this where they could mimic any time of day or night, that they wouldn't simply train during normal waking hours. He figured it was probably related to time zone acclimatization, to make sure their biorhythms were in sync. They were making every possible effort to train as they fought, as if they were already in North Africa. They will probably initiate the raid in Algeria at around three or four a.m., so last night's start time made sense.

He watched them with Rhodes and Freeman for about thirty minutes before heading to his room to read through his file. They had to wear night vision goggles to follow the action. To say it was impressive would be an understatement—it was unlike anything he had ever seen. Dolan worked in SPECOPS for years, but this was altogether different. Flying the AC-130 Spectre gunship was a mission that put him thousands of feet above his unsuspecting prey, which appeared as ghostly, dot-like figures on his targeting screen in the cockpit. His 105-millimeter M102 Howitzer would vaporize anything within several meters. This team of men were eerily quiet as they moved, communicating with hand gestures or inaudible whispers via their comm system. They met their quarry in close quarters, often face-to-face and with rapid and precise lethal force. Without fear or hesitation.

Before the show, the three of them went through what seemed like a mountain of paperwork, several emails and a few phone calls, all that was necessary to tie up loose ends. The university, his landlord, taekwondo class, Atlantik Brücke, his apartment in Dahlem, everything. They even thought to have a general power of attorney drawn up with his father as executor should it be needed while he was away. He would call his parents later and let them know about his last-minute 'sabbatical' and to expect a visit from a notary public. All that was left now was to get through two weeks of training with the interesting and peculiar Howard Welker.

◆

Dolan expected it would be similar in many ways with training he completed while in the Air Force. It turned out there were few parallels. Counterintelligence and counterespionage training was different than anything he had experienced before. CE is the branch of CI that actively penetrates and manipulates foreign clandestine operations. Though he'd gotten a taste of it before in Paris and Berlin, EXCISE had been planned as an intelligence gathering operation, for the most part. CI and CE are specific subsets of espionage that extract information from and manipulate another country's or organization's intelligence apparatus. In this case, they would be using CI methods to operate under the radar of the many foreign spies in Berlin, and particularly that of the Bundesamt für Verfassungsschutz. The BfV is the domestic counterpart to the BND and essentially, Germany's equivalent of the FBI. CI methods were necessary for SCALPEL to remain undetected as they executed their mission to capture Dolan's assassin. Whatever information is gained from the target will make it easier for them to employ CE methods to manipulate the AMA into making mistakes, increasing the probability for success of DEVGRU's raid and eventually, for the total eradication of the AMA. Dolan found out soon enough that his assassin was actually their second target.

Their first target was newly renditioned and in custody. Dolan wondered during the team's discussion last night who it was that Lauren had referred to, and it turned out to be a German named Rolf Haussmann, inventor of the Hemoxin gas Dolan had prevented from being used in attacks in Paris and on Berlin Station. *Yet another important thing they kept from me.* He expected there would be many more hidden details about his fateful participation in EXCISE that would come to light as Operation CLEARCUT gained momentum.

Haussmann had been moved from SCALPEL's safehouse in Annapolis, Virginia to Harvey Point days ago, and part of Dolan's training would be to observe Welker's interrogation of him. It would happen in the afternoon of that first day, but the morning would be used to lay the groundwork for everything going down in Berlin.

"Good morning sleepy head!" Welker was seated at the conference room table with a laptop, projecting on the far wall. "Did you get to watch DEVGRU at all last night?"

"Good morning. Yes, we watched for a little while. Impressive stuff."

"Yeah, they know what they're doing alright. It will be fun to watch that raid go down, if we're lucky enough to be part of the viewing party."

Dolan took a seat to the left of Welker. He looked again at the large screen on the wall. "Facebook?"

"Facebook and LinkedIn. That's all we need initially to either keep our assassin in Germany, or to head back there if he's already left for Boston. And it may help us further as the mission progresses. The first step was to notify all those close to you, personally and professionally, and you did that last night. It took me about three minutes online to find out you don't do much with social media. In fact, there is no record at all of you prior to your move to Boston. But that's OK, both your accounts are public and it's what the assassin will go to first to find out more about you. I noticed you also use an announcement service for your taekwondo class, we can tap into that as well. We will do some social media posting this morning. And it's not just for our target. Your cover needs to look, smell, and feel real in every possible way to family, to friends, to the German government. To everyone. So now you are going to let the rest of the world know about your once in a lifetime opportunity at Atlantik Brücke."

Dolan had been wondering how they would lure the assassin to Berlin. He felt stupid suddenly—this was so simple, and probably quite effective. It was something he should have anticipated. It was understandable that he wouldn't have thought of it, however. He'd only ever used those accounts to aid in establishing a new career in the civilian sector. Once he got his job as an assistant professor at BU, he hardly ever posted anything, almost never accessing the accounts. "So this is counterintelligence," he quipped. "I think I'm going to do just fine."

Welker turned away from the laptop toward him and flashed his wide, toothy grin. "Yep, this is counterintelligence. Some of the most effective methods we use are the simplest and the least risky, but their scope of usefulness is usually narrow. Of course, there is much more to it than this. Facebook works particularly well. I have a few accounts, for various things. Two are my personal accounts and if I need to, I use them for things like this."

"Why two? Doesn't that look suspicious?"

Welker chuckled. "Not really. I tend to post things that can piss off the super-sensitive, the politically correct, and anyone who considers themselves left wing. That amounts to about ninety percent of people. So I get put in Facebook jail a lot. They'll shut me down for thirty days at a time, so I switch to the alternate account and let all my friends know. I have fun with it. Anyway, it makes me look like a normal guy and I usually have pretty good cover if I ever go anywhere on a mission. I have my own business process management company, BPM for short. The work requires travel, and there's always a BPM conference or opportunity I can look into wherever I go that will give me a good reason for being there. I'm also an outdoorsman, and sometimes I will bring my road bike or my mountain bike with me, depending on where the mission is."

Dolan laughed. *This guy is a piece of work.* He liked him. But how could he be for real? Dolan knew enough by now to know if you were to be a successful spy you needed to blend in. To be invisible. And if you happened to be noticed, you should be so unremarkable that you are dismissed and quickly forgotten. Welker was not like that at all. "So what do we say about these two weeks I am here, where I am neither in Boston, nor in Berlin? Won't it seem strange to someone who is analyzing available data on my whereabouts when fourteen days are unaccounted for? And what is your cover, if I may ask?"

Welker cocked his head, then shook it. "No. We don't have to make anything up for this period of time. We simply make the posts vague enough that it could be you left already, or are leaving in a few days, or maybe next week. It would be logical to assume you needed two weeks off from work to prepare for such a long trip, and you wouldn't necessarily broadcast the details of that to the world, particularly if you don't have an active social media history. It could be as well that you traveled elsewhere during those two weeks to tie up loose ends, visit family or friends, whatever. If we try too hard to explain everything he might start digging and find out it isn't true. It would also look like a break from your normal posting behavior and raise suspicion. We don't want our target to think we are on to him. As for my cover, I'll be meeting with a few Berlin area startups to give them a briefing on what my company does and how it could make their processes more efficient. Germans love it when you tell them you can improve their delivery outcomes. If any of them are interested, I pass them on to my employees back here in the U.S. and let them take it from there. Yes, I'll be away from our team on occasion to knock those out, but it will have minimal effect."

That all made sense to him. "Got it." Dolan logged into his accounts and they crafted the posts together. It wouldn't require anything more than that, Welker told him, maybe one additional post a day or two after they arrive in Berlin. Dolan would then establish a routine, begin his research project and the team would be monitoring everyone and everything around him to identify the target. At the same time, Freeman would be sifting through terabytes of data each day, assisted by powerful Agency algorithms to gain additional information on the assassin to narrow their search. This included monitoring who views his social media accounts and sifting through online searches for Dolan's name in combination with certain key words. If they were able to pinpoint an IP address they think is the target's, then they had him.

There were two CI officers from Berlin Station doing what they could to identify the most likely locations in the Offenbach area where the assassin might live or work. It wasn't as easy as it sounded. At roughly fourteen percent, Offenbach had the highest concentration of Muslims in all of Germany. And they were banking their efforts on the assumption the assassin was Muslim—it was possible that wasn't the case. But the most likely scenario was he was of Algerian origin with ties to the AMA. A German citizen with a passport who runs a small business that caters to the Muslim community. Or at least, this is what the CIA analyst who wrote the report in Dolan's file thought. These factors narrowed their search considerably to relatively small geographic pockets.

After spending about three hours on the finer points of how to maximize the effectiveness of subterfuge using social media, email, and other digital communications, both Dolan and Welker were ready to move on to something more interesting. Rolf Haussmann was waiting for them in a room nearby, shackled and sensory deprived. Though he hadn't provided much in the way of useful information thus far, he hadn't met Welker yet. And Welker was very, very adept at extracting information.

CHAPTER NINE

Ivan Vasnetsov wiped beads of sweat from his forehead with his shirt sleeve and stood up from the metal stool at his workbench. The air conditioning did little to provide any comfort. He wondered how bad it would get if it were ever to malfunction. At least he could count on them fixing it quickly. Not for him of course, but for the lab. It was delicate work and years of preparation could be undone with something as simple as a change in temperature. As he pondered his predicament, the electric collar chafed his neck. What he wouldn't give for some lotion to ease the burning. At least he was no longer chained. He could walk about the lab now without knocking things over and use the restroom without calling the guard.

He looked to the corner of the lab where his stained mattress lay on the floor. That, a blanket and some clothes were all he possessed in this place. Then his eyes traveled to the door of the room where his Megachiroptera colony was sleeping quietly in the dark, upside down. He then lamented for the thousandth time that he was caught up in this horrible mess. That it was tragically ironic his fruit bats were the only real companions he had, and at the same time the root cause of his wretched situation. *Reduced to this.* It was supposed to have been a lucrative opportunity, a two-month effort to set up the lab and to train Hakeem's technicians how to do everything. His success in weaponizing the virus for his government many years ago had led Hakeem to seek him out for a secret and profitable collaboration. One that would require a few weeks of intense work, after which he would return to Vladivostok a million euros richer. At the age of 72, it would be the last work he would ever need to do.

At first, everything went according to plan. He was treated as a celebrity by Hakeem and his lieutenants. They gave him the best food and wines, women, and invited him out on occasion to celebrate reaching certain project milestones. But as time wore on, he came to realize Hakeem's technicians lacked much of the fundamental education and experience required for such work. He began to get behind.

Ivan communicated his concerns to Hakeem, but this was met with incredulity and derision. How could he question their abilities? "We are following a path laid out by God, it is his will that we succeed. Your role is to impart your knowledge—do it," he would say. But God had yet to find his way down into this underground lab. There would be no divine intervention in bringing Hakeem's lab technicians up to speed. In the end, it was taking too long and Hakeem grew frustrated. Two months turned into three. He began threatening Ivan and eventually made him a prisoner. The technicians no longer needed to understand how to extract the blood, grow the cultures, and to containerize, store and prepare the virus for weaponization. Ivan could do it all by himself, indefinitely. That was just over four years ago.

That a man of his stature, celebrated in certain scientific circles as a hero even, would fall to such a fate was inconceivable to him. A recipient of the Medal of the Order for Merit to the Fatherland, no less! The things he knew, the highly classified programs he had worked on—there were few contemporary Russian scientists his equal. He had no wife to mourn him; she passed years earlier, childless. And because he told no one where he was going or what he would be doing, Ivan suspected what family and friends he had left had given up by now. No doubt they assumed he had been disappeared, fallen victim to some government entity or dark society who wanted him gone for political or other devious reasons. It wasn't so far from the truth.

His pitiable reverie was broken by a noise in the hallway. The guard just outside propped the door open and Hakeem strode in, a big smile on his darkly tanned, gray-bearded face. Ivan gathered himself and faced Hakeem at attention, waiting for him to speak.

Continuing to smile, Hakeem spoke loudly, "Ivan! How is my favorite Russian scientist today?" His demeanor then changed, appearing concerned. "You are looking thin, Ivan. Are we not feeding you enough?"

"No sir... I mean, yes, forgive my English. Yes, the food is fine. I am just getting old, that is all." Ivan looked down. Hakeem was right, he was getting too thin. The veins on his hands and arms had never been so pronounced.

Hakeem laughed from his belly, bending backward with a hand on his barrel of a chest. He was much taller and bigger than Sharif. An imposing, swarthy man. "You are not much older than me, my friend. And look! I am getting fat. But it does not affect my work, mind you. I want to make sure you are healthy. Our job here is almost finished, but there are still some things left to do. Once it is all complete you can finally go home. You want to go home, don't you Ivan?"

Ivan did not think Hakeem would ever let him go home. If the work was to be finished soon, it meant he would be finished soon as well. He would die here, and no one would ever know what happened to him. "Yes sir, I do want to go home. It has been a long time, and I believe I have served you well."

"That you have, Ivan, that you have." Hakeem then dropped the theatrics, continuing seriously. "I need to know when this latest batch will be ready for delivery. I know you don't get much news down here, but you will be happy to know that the test was successful, beyond my wildest dreams. We will be ready soon to execute our primary mission, and I need to know when you will be finished."

Ivan shifted uneasily on his feet. Once he delivers the final batch, he will become unnecessary. He would be signing his own death warrant. "Sir, I still need to run some tests. I am worried this last batch may not be as potent as the previous three. I must determine the potency. If it is weak, I will have to run another cycle and add it in. This could take another two months, at least."

At that, Hakeem was angry. "This is not what I wanted to hear, Ivan. We do not have another month, never mind two and you know this." He paused to think for a moment. "I will tell Sharif to help you. I've had him working on other things, but he can do this, it is more important." He smiled again, sardonically this time. "It is probably a good idea in any case, to make sure you are not stalling for some reason. You are not stalling Ivan, are you?"

Ivan's eyes went wide with surprise. "No sir, of course not. I am a scientist. I do not play such games and my loyalty is to you." He hoped Hakeem believed him.

"Good, Ivan, good. You have three weeks to complete your work. Sharif will be down later, and you can bring him up to speed. In the meantime, I'll have someone bring you a coffee and some Mhalbi. It is rice pudding, delicious. You do like rice pudding, eh?"

"Yes sir, thank you very much."

Hakeem regarded Ivan for a moment more, grunted and strode out, the guard closing the door behind him. Ivan's mind was racing. Sharif was highly intelligent and understood quite a bit about the processes. It would be difficult to fool him. Complicating things more, Sharif seemed to be angry and brooding most of the time. He will be on edge and could lash out at him. Sharif was not happy here; he would rather be back in Paris living in his comfortable apartment leading his privileged life. Things were much different here than in Paris. Much different than in Vladivostok as well. To give himself enough time to plan an escape, Ivan would have to sabotage the current batch; it was the only way. Just enough to give him an extra couple of weeks without Sharif noticing what he was doing.

He scratched his neck again, just able to get a finger underneath the collar. It was impossible to take off—he had tried. And he tested it twice, each time swearing he would never do it again. On both occasions he made it past the bathroom, approximately ten meters down the hall before it went off. Twenty thousand volts of electricity coursing directly into his neck and head and throughout his body. He passed out quickly and was found unconscious in each case. If he could only locate the receiver, he might be able to disable it and escape. It was probably somewhere in his lab, but he had never been able to find it. The guard wasn't posted at night anymore, and the door wasn't locked so that he could use the restroom. But even if he managed to disable the collar he would still have to navigate out of the large building, and he had no idea what to do or where to go when he did. But it didn't matter, he had to try. Otherwise, he would probably be dead very soon.

♦

Issam coughed hoarsely, spraying a phlegmy mixture of clotted blood and sickness across his chin and chest. The nurse by the side of his bed quickly grabbed a white cloth and began wiping his face. He looked at her and wondered if she felt bad for him, or if she was afraid of him instead, worried she might catch his disease. It was difficult to tell as she was wearing a surgical mask and a clear faceguard. He wished he had a mirror, to see his face. The purple and brown lines traversing his gaunt arms and hands like spiderwebs, the oozing sores and his yellowed skin—he probably looked grotesque. A tear formed at the corner of his eye and ran down his cheek.

The two men were back in his room, also wearing facemasks. He was certain these two were not concerned for his welfare at all. Apathetic to his condition or considering it a karmic justice, he supposed. He'd talked with them several times already in the past few days, barely able to speak. Today, he was feeling better. *Praise Allah.* Each time they arrived his mother yelled at them to leave her son alone, and each time security escorted her out of the room. The two men waited a couple minutes until the nurse was done and then continued asking him questions. The American in the suit would say something in English, and then the other man, a Jordanian he thought, would translate the question into Arabic.

"Issam, tell us again how you think you were infected. You do not live or work near the area where the attack took place."

It was difficult to breathe, let alone speak and his throat hurt. But he continued. "As I told you before, I'm not sure how it happened. Maybe it was one of the immigrant families from my mother's work who gave it to me. I don't know." He thought it was good he was so sick; they probably could not tell how nervous he was right now. Then he realized, this is why he had the accident in the tunnel, why he was exposed. Allah had thought of everything.

The Jordanian told the man in the suit what he said, and he remained quiet for a minute. Then he bent down to reach into a bag or case, Issam couldn't see. When he stood up, he was holding the hinged clamp apparatus in one hand and the double-walled stainless-steel container in the other. He held them out for Issam to see clearly. Issam could feel his heartbeat thumping and suddenly the machine by his bed began beeping loudly in a rapid manner, which made him even more distressed. He was supposed to go back to the tunnel three days later and remove them but by then he was already in the hospital and in such bad shape he'd forgotten about it completely.

"Issam, I need you to tell us the truth. If you do, you could save the lives of many people. The men who gave these to you and told you to do this, they will do the same thing again, and many more people will die. But if you help us, you can stop all that. You can be the one to prevent thousands of innocent men, women and children from dying and suffering. You can make things easier on yourself as well. And you might be able to keep your mother out of jail. Issam, before you answer, you need to know, your fingerprints are on the metal container. We already know you were involved so it only delays the inevitable for you to deny it."

Issam's fragile, simple world then came crashing down around him all at once, much like one of those old buildings that engineers blow up intentionally, he thought—straight down with a huge cloud of dust. He saw it once on TV. How could his fingerprints be on the container? He had worn gloves the whole time. It was impossible. There were two canisters, one that was empty and one that stayed in the freezer. They never practiced with the one in the freezer of course, but had he ever touched it without gloves on? He tried to remember, back to when Saleh and Fadi had first shown it to him. He had held it then, he remembered now. Just for a moment, and then handed it back. And then he remembered being in the tunnel and wiping down the pipe and the apparatus, but he had stopped to check the valve. That's when the accident happened. He never wiped the canister.

He coughed again and more blood spattered. The nurse seemed agitated that the men were somehow making his condition worse, though she said nothing. He never considered his mother might be harmed by any of this. He believed what he had done was right, that it was the will of Allah, but how could Allah allow his mother to be hurt by righteous actions carried out by a true believer, and in his name? Issam realized at once he was a simple soldier and probably would never understand the answers to those types of questions. Whatever happened, he couldn't let his mother be hurt. She was all he had left. "Yes, it was me. I put the device on the pipe. In the name of Allah. I am his soldier. This is a war. You understand this and it was part of my responsibility. I was following orders and I would do it again." Issam realized as he said it that it wasn't true. He was very scared and should never have been involved in any of this from the beginning. This is why Allah would allow his mother to be hurt. *I did not do it for Allah,* he admitted to himself sadly. *It was for you, my father.*

CHAPTER TEN

Rolf Haussmann squirmed, trying in vain to get comfortable. His wrists and ankles were raw from being zip tied to the chair. The stench of his own filth had become less noticeable in the past few days. He was acclimated to it by now, as he was to the bag over his head, kept there despite the lack of windows or lights in the room. He was thirsty and tired, jerked awake periodically by low-frequency vibrations and rumbling most of the past twelve hours. After a time they subsided, and he was able to nod off for a bit. As luck would have it, he was now unable to sleep, despite the total silence.

All at once a thousand tiny points of light shone through the fabric over his face. Someone turned on the lights. A small shot of dopamine coursed through his brain as he contemplated the possibility of human contact. Even if it was more interrogation, it would be better than sensory deprivation.

He heard the door open and close and a chair slide across the linoleum floor. The bag was taken carefully off his head and he squinted, his eyes adjusting to light for the first time in hours. The man folded the bag and placed it on a table against the wall, then pressed a Styrofoam cup of cold water to his lips. He drank gratefully. When

Rolf was finished, his captor put the empty cup on the table and sat in a chair facing him, legs crossed. He appeared to be dressed for the gym, wearing matching gray sweatpants and a sweatshirt. He regarded Rolf silently. Rolf watched him and waited. After about thirty seconds, the man rose from his chair and took a pair of scissors from his back pocket, cutting the zip ties on Rolf's hands and feet. He placed the ties on the table and sat back down.

He finally spoke. "Hello Rolf. My name is Frank."

Then, nothing. He was waiting for Rolf to respond. "Hello."

"I am here to interrogate you. I think you understand that. By the way, I've heard your English is rather good, but if I say anything you don't understand please let me know, OK?"

Rolf felt uneasy. Frank was not acting like the others, he seemed to be nice. *Just part of the game.* "OK."

"Good. Now, I have a general idea of what has happened in each of your previous interrogations. I know that you have not provided any useful information to us, and it is my goal to change that. I believe I will be successful because I recognize that you have concerns and interests too, and I can use that as leverage. Bargaining chips. Am I being clear so far?"

Rolf's hopes jumped, just a little. Was it possible his demands might be met, at least partially? "Yes, it is clear."

"OK, thanks. First of all, I want you to know that I intend to be one hundred percent honest with you. I will never lie to you. Everything I say will be the truth." He smiled a bit then. "Now, we both know that early-on, there will be no way for you to verify if I'm being truthful, but I'm telling you this up front anyway because I think it will help us come to an understanding quicker. As part of my effort to be transparent, I want you to know this conversation is being recorded, and do you see that mirror there?" He pointed to the right, above the table.

Rolf already knew. But this man was right, it did seem helpful. *He knows what he is doing.* "Yes. It is a two-way mirror."

"Correct. There is a person back there who is watching us and listening in. You see, as long as I've been in the business, sometimes I miss something. Sometimes the camera misses something. It helps to have another set of eyes and ears to catch the little details, you know?"

"I understand," said Rolf.

"Alright. Additionally, my name is not really Frank. I can't tell you my real name, so I picked Frank. I'm sure you understand why, and it doesn't really matter in the grand scheme of things. But like I said, I will be one hundred percent honest with you the entire time. Let's get to it then. You've been through a lot so far—captured in Chile, put on a plane and flown to the United States, enhanced interrogation, sensory deprivation, all of it. It hasn't been fun, has it?"

Mister Frank did not appear to be amused or acting sarcastically, he actually looked empathetic. As if he had been through something like this himself at one point. "No, it has been quite difficult, in fact."

Frank continued. "I *could* say that the root cause of your difficulties has been your refusal to cooperate. But that's only a part of it, right? I must assume that our failure to get anything from you so far is related to an ineffective approach. You may have already thought to yourself 'so far, this is not like the other interrogations I've been through.' And it is not. This will be comparatively comfortable for you. But you do have a big problem; everyone in the world except me and my friends thinks you are dead. It means I can do pretty much whatever I want with you with no repercussions at all. I can promise you everything, and then give you nothing. Or worse. No one is looking for you. I can torture you. I can even kill you and no one will ever know or care. So if I were to offer you anything and expect information in return, my offer would need to be genuine and verifiable. The bottom line is, I need whatever I can get from you to help prevent future terrorist attacks, and I need it now. And to this point you have not provided any information because you want your freedom in return, and you want rock-solid proof that what we offer is real. Does that about sum it up?"

For the first time since his abduction, Rolf was beginning to feel hopeful. His efforts to stall, to make them desperate were succeeding. He needed to be careful not to screw this up—his life depended on it. He nodded, "Yes, that is correct."

"OK. You already know what we want—any and all of the online and dark web usernames, passwords, and sites that were used during all your interactions with Monsieur Blanc. We want you to show us the bank transaction details for whatever payments were made to you for your provision of Hemoxin gas to the AMA, and all other details and data you think could be helpful. In return, you will be treated as a member of my team. No more sensory deprivation, no more bonds. You'll have a comfortable bed, a television, books to read, good food. All the comforts of home for the next two weeks while you work with us. You will be guarded of course and will not be able to leave until after we are done, but in all other respects you will be unencumbered. You will also have the satisfaction of being able to atone to some degree for what you did.

"You know, several people died because of your actions, either directly or indirectly. Two in the fire you set in Hamburg, three in Potsdam, your co-conspirator Francois Martin in Berlin, and an American in Southern France. Two more were hurt, tourists who inhaled Hemoxin during the failed attack on the U.S. Embassy. Think about this Rolf; you are German so I know you will understand the gravity of it. Those two tourists, *they were Jewish!* Essentially, you were responsible for gassing two Jews at one of the most significant European Jewish memorial sites. *In Germany.*"

Mister Frank paused to let the facts sink in, then continued. "If the information you provide proves valuable, at the end of two weeks you will be set free, no strings attached. We will give you your wallet and Chilean identification card back to you and you will be released. But we will not take you back to Chile; you will have to figure that part out on your own. Do you understand all I have said so far?"

Rolf's sense of hope was building quickly. He did not know about the Jews in Berlin, and he felt bad about it, but it was as he told Monsieur Blanc; whatever they did with the gas would be no concern of his. If Rolf had never provided the Hemoxin, this terrorist group would have used something else. But it did sting a little, particularly the two Jews. "Yes, it is all clear. But how can I possibly verify all of this? Even if you give me a letter signed by the President of the United States, it could be a forgery. The only way I will know your offer is real is when I am released."

Mr. Frank unfolded his legs and leaned forward, serious and appearing completely genuine. "Rolf, I've given my word that I will never lie to you. This is important to me; it is part of my moral code. It is a difficult thing to do in my business, but I manage to do it and it works. Step by step, day by day, everything I've offered you will come to pass. By degrees, over the next week and a half and it will all end with your unconditional freedom. And I'll start with this." He reached into his back pocket and produced Rolf's wallet, extending it to him. Rolf took it and looked inside; everything appeared to be there, right down to the two hundred and twenty thousand Chilean Pesos. Mister Frank then got up from his chair and opened the door, motioning for

Rolf to leave. "Come on, let's get you a shower, some new clothes and a hot meal. Clifford is just outside; he'll be your escort while you are here. After you are cleaned up and fed, I'll introduce you to a couple other folks you will be working with."

Rolf was still in his chair, his mind searching for a better alternative, a reason to continue stalling. Was there any way he could ever get the validation he needed, a guarantee of his freedom up front? Probably not. He would play their game for now, give them a little bit and see what he got in return. If what Mister Frank said would happen for him continued to prove true, he would continue to cooperate.

Rolf stood up from his chair and wobbled a bit before stepping forward gingerly. Except for a few bathroom breaks he'd been seated in that position for perhaps twenty hours. It hurt to walk but as he took the next step it began to feel better. He approached Frank with his hand extended. "You have a deal."

They shook hands in the doorway. Frank nodded approvingly and smiled, looking almost ridiculous in his gray sweats. "Excellent, Rolf." Then another man approached from down the hall. "Ah, let me introduce you to your escort, Clifford. Clifford, this is Rolf, Rolf, Clifford. Oh, and his name's not really Clifford."

CHAPTER ELEVEN

"What was *that?*" quipped Dolan.

"That," returned Welker, "was an interrogation. And I think it is working."

They were back in the conference room, and Rolf's apparent capitulation was the topic of discussion.

"What makes you think so?"

"Well, aside from him saying we had a deal, my gut. I predict he will give us a few things and see how it goes. If we continue loosening his leash and making him more comfortable, he will continue to give us more."

Dolan was unconvinced. "But what if he doesn't? What if he's just telling us what we want to hear while he comes up with a plan to try to get a more formalized or legal agreement? And are you really going to let him go?"

"Listen. I know it wasn't what you expected, and we'll spend some time later this week on interrogation techniques. Rolf has already experienced some of the others, intended to inflict fear, humiliation, pain, anxiety, loneliness, etcetera. There are different ways to do it and which ones you decide to use depend on several factors. If your subject has already been exposed to certain techniques that didn't work, you may want to try something else. One factor is whether you have embarrassing or otherwise damaging information on the subject. Another is the person's state of mind, and whether they have specific weaknesses or not that you can exploit. How quickly you need the information is another, one that applies in this case. Now, we have a lot of damaging information on Rolf. But threatening to release that information doesn't necessarily help us, unless we are prepared to give the world evidence he is still alive. If we do that, we risk the German government looking for him and we don't want that.

"Traditionally, what we would want is for Rolf to break. To give up. But his concession to a deal precludes that from happening, at least for now. He feels as if he still has a certain amount of leverage, and he will continue to use it until he is free. If he doesn't keep his end of the bargain he goes back into solitary, back to the fear and pain. After a taste of comfort and a sliver of hope though, I am guessing he will do almost anything to prevent that from happening. And keep this in mind—the interrogation is not over until he does in fact break. Whether he knows it or not, he's being interrogated until that happens, or until we get enough out of him to release him. If he keeps his end, we let him go after we're done here.

"And it's true, Michael, I always try to be one hundred percent honest in an interrogation. That doesn't mean I have to tell them everything, it just means that what I do tell them is always true. It's that simple. There have been very few exceptions to that rule for me through the years. Clifford, or Thomas I should say, has the agreement on paper for him to sign. And it is legal, which doesn't matter of course because on paper, he is already dead."

Dolan smirked. "It seems to me that even with a death certificate, his detention would be considered illegal due to the fact he was renditioned."

"Michael, I'm no lawyer, and I'm fairly sure you aren't either. I'm just regurgitating what was said to me by the lawyer who drafted the agreement. Generally speaking, what is legal is not always honorable or ethical, and in this business, what is honorable or ethical is not always the right thing to do. There's a lot of gray here, so let's just roll with it, shall we?"

Letting this guy go did not sit well with Dolan. "Sure. I am just trying to understand the situation better. If you let him go, I assume you are not worried at all that he will try to expose you, to come after the Agency for his rendition and detainment because he'd be risking his cover, right? He wouldn't be able to do that without admitting he faked his own death. The new life he's put so much thought and effort into building would fall down around him, and he'd probably end up in jail. If not in Germany, then somewhere else."

Welker looked at Dolan pointedly and grinned. "Something like that."

◆

The days rolled by quickly. The training was intense, just as he was told it would be. Sixteen hours a day with thirty minutes each for lunch and dinner. The one major downside for Dolan was that there was no time for exercise. He wasn't allowed to leave the building, apart from going to the range. A few hundred sit-ups and pushups each morning was about all he had time for before starting each day with Welker. He missed his daily run. But even with the crazy schedule he was still getting six hours of sleep, which was enough for him.

The training was a very concentrated, very tailored version of what new recruits received at Camp Peary, with some additional topics folded in. It also included eleven grueling hours of testing. The tests gauged his aptitude for logic, mathematics, communication ability, spatial intelligence, interpersonal and behavioral skills and other areas.

A future CIA counterintelligence officer would spend four to five months at the Farm, and Dolan was getting just two weeks. However, in those fourteen days he would receive 203 hours of one-on-one instruction. And unlike the Farm, his training wasn't designed to accommodate the lowest common denominator. It was an executive-level course on steroids, essentially. Combined with his extensive SPECOPS and other military experience, training and education, and the limited instruction he received prior to participating in Operation EXCISE, he was getting 'everything he needed' to be certified as a CI officer. Welker informed him of this only after reviewing the results of all his testing. Apparently, he passed. They had left quite a bit out due to the compressed timeline, but he would have the opportunity when the mission was complete to get through a number of other formal and advanced training courses. For now, this would have to do.

Hiring him as a defacto CIA employee would grease the rails on everything from receiving a paycheck to provisioning medical benefits. Though his job as an assistant professor at BU afforded him a quality health plan, Dolan suspected it wouldn't cover him for accidents or injuries sustained while participating in questionably legal, clandestine activities in Europe. He would have the option to resign when the op was over, or he could stay on. If he decided to stick with it, he could retain his teaching job at Boston University. Welker told him that as long as Kenneth Freihoff remained as Dean of the Pardee School it was too easy to leave Dolan in place there. It was a good cover. Not perfect, but good. How often he would be called upon remained to be seen, and when he was it would be situational. He would be a sleeper asset, to be activated when needed. Dolan was intrigued by the whole thing but decided not to think about it too much until the current operation was complete.

On day seven he came out of his room and The Stage had changed. Instead of a single building there were now several, each two stories tall. The trees and vehicles were gone. It looked to be more of an urban setup. He made a mental note to get up in the middle of the night to come out and watch DEVGRU do their thing again.

He walked up the stairs to the conference room where Welker and Rhodes were having a serious discussion. They stopped abruptly when he opened the door.

He thought about excusing himself and waiting outside the room for them to finish but on a hunch, he chose to interrupt them. "Good morning," Dolan said carefully as he strode in.

"Good morning, Michael," Rhodes said warmly. "Come have a seat. We need to discuss something with you."

His intuition was correct—they were talking about him. Dolan sat down across from the two of them and Rhodes continued. "Michael, I made a promise to be completely transparent with you, and I wanted to make sure I do that to the best of my ability. Part of that endeavor means making sure you have the complete trust of everyone on the team; each of us must have your trust and vice-versa. Up until now you have been a contracted contributor—someone who is working for us, but not necessarily working *with* us. Once you complete this course there will be no question of that, however there is one thing we haven't told you yet."

Dolan's blood was instantly set to boil. His agreement to participate was based largely on their concession to include him as a full partner. What was this now? "Go on," he said, stoic as ever.

She glanced at Welker, cueing him to take over. "Michael, we've touched on these things, and I know you have a photographic memory, however, for the sake of this conversation I'm going to repeat myself. There are certain qualities and traits a CI officer needs to have and to nurture to be successful. I spent many years teaching at The Farm, and I can tell you that when a student had all these traits and worked hard to improve on them, they invariably did excellent work in the field. But some are more important than others. First, it is essential to be naturally curious. To want to find out the why and the how of things. This promotes and feeds our ability to obtain knowledge, which we use to do our jobs. A second important trait is the ability to recognize patterns. You have shown to be particularly adept at this; your results on that test were off the charts. Third, you must be interested in and to be able to understand people. I know that sounds broad and vague, but that's because people are complex creatures, and this ability is far more difficult to master than it seems. About ninety percent of people never become good at it, I mean really good at it. Even with long-term, professional training and experience it is difficult to master for most. If you want to boil it down to a single word, we are talking about empathy. Aside from sociopaths and hardcore narcissists, everyone has it, to one degree or another. But most cannot tap into it whenever and wherever they wish because their emotions get in the way. As soon as stress or fear is introduced into a situation, that ability becomes marginalized. This happens because it can be difficult, paradoxically, to control one's emotions while accessing the part of the brain that *understands* emotions at the same time. It requires great control. Losing that control cannot happen in our line of work. We need to be able to maintain our nerve, to be patient and to maintain a healthy dose of skepticism. And through it all we must be able to determine with a high degree of accuracy what is going on inside the heads of those around us. This requires empathy.

"Now, to the point at hand. Most people I know and work with are unaware of this, but I am a licensed psychologist. I don't hide it, but I also do not promote or advertise it. It is not something I need or use in my civilian job, though it does offer me many advantages there. I have several good reasons for keeping this fact about me in the dark that I won't get into but suffice it to say that I know what I'm talking about.

Welker stopped for a moment, watching Dolan to gauge his response. Seeing none, he continued. "The single biggest detractor in your file," with his forefinger he tapped a thick stack of papers on the table in front of him, "is that you may not sufficiently possess this ability and further, there is the question about whether you are able to work and play well with others. The results of your testing in these areas were essentially inconclusive. And we are all aware of what happened in Paris and Berlin when you ditched your team and went rogue. This is what Lauren and I wanted to make clear for you. You are only here because someone in leadership intervened and overrode the team's recommendation to keep you out of it. Some were concerned about your mental state and worried about the possibility you could have another breakdown, as you appeared to have during EXCISE. The compromise that was reached was to keep you monitored by someone with the ability to see it coming. Someone who could stall it, fix it. That someone would be me." Welker flashed his devilish grin while Rhodes remained serious.

Dolan was caught off guard. It never occurred to him his loyalty or mental state would be questioned. He could bring up the facts, the incomplete training, the illegal surveillance and watching of his movements. *They spied on me.* He had good reasons back then not to trust them. But he was also not in a good frame of mind at the time. He entered a downward spiral the moment he landed in Paris, and it didn't stop until he almost died in a bed at the safehouse in Berlin. Welker was right, at least partially. They had reasons to question him, but he and they both knew it went both ways. Rhodes had admitted guilt already and apologized. It could be that this collective guilt played a role in the initial attempt to keep him out of Operation CLEARCUT.

"So Dittrich made the decision then. Interesting." Dittrich was a risk-taker. It couldn't have been anyone else, though Dolan found it difficult to believe Rhodes may have voted against him. He was also surprised at the inconclusive results of his test. Had he not fixed these problems? Had he not found acceptance and dealt with all his long-compartmented issues head-on? Did he not now truly understand love? He was happy with his life and no longer bottled up his emotions. Or at least he made a continual, conscious effort to prevent it. But it was possible there were still cracks in his psyche that had yet to fully heal over. Or perhaps they had healed, and the scars were too prominent, bothersome. Ugly. Could it be that by being thrust once again into a situation that forced him to confront the tragedy of Claire's death, he was slowly reconstructing his old defense mechanisms? Subconsciously preparing those dark corners of his mind to once again lock up anything and everything that might hurt him? Then there was that lone, pulsating box hidden away in his mind. The one he had yet to reconcile. It was fair to say he hadn't dealt with everything yet.

Neither of them would confirm his suspicion about Dittrich. "Listen," Rhodes replied, "it doesn't matter who made the decision. What's important now is that you are part of the team, and we all genuinely believe you have what it takes to contribute great value to the

Agency. We are doing what we think is best to get you to that point. That includes providing you with the unique assistance Howard is capable of. And to be honest, he would have been part of this regardless of what we thought about your mental condition. It is only happenstance he is also a psychologist. You are probably aware that as case and CI officers, we all get psychologically evaluated from time to time. Some of the work we do makes it necessary and it's best to look at it as a benefit. We are not always the best evaluators of our own thought processes, and it helps to have an expert tell us when they are getting off-kilter."

With a nod, Dolan conceded. "I understand. No need to worry, I recognize the value of it, and I look forward to your insights, Howard."

Welker grinned again. "Super. You've got a good head on your shoulders, I think. There's just some junk in the attic we'll have to go through at some point. We all have it, and as I like to say, everyone is at least a little bit nuts. What's important is that *we are aware of it.*"

CHAPTER TWELVE

Sharif stood on the flat concrete rooftop and gazed out at the bleak landscape. Nothing but brown in every direction. A few trees here and there, a couple of abandoned ramshackle structures in the distance. One winding dirt road led from the building, disappearing at the horizon. The sun was low, appearing much larger than it should. He adjusted the visor of his crimson and white Francopharma baseball cap to get a better look. The now worn and dirtied cap was all he had left to remind him of his previous life. Despite the drab expanse of nothingness he tried to appreciate the beauty of the sunset, but it wasn't possible today. Not in this world.

Nothing could have prepared him for the condition of life he was forced to endure here. He wondered for the hundredth time how he could have made the decisions that led him to this fate. He was now just another of his father's lieutenants in a war he didn't fully understand or support. Yes, he hated the Americans for their invasions and occupation of the lands of his people and faith and for what they did to his family, but why did it mean he had to sacrifice everything? He'd been doing nothing but training since he came here—small arms, explosives, biochemical weapons design, communications, intelligence, and counterintelligence. But he'd been given no real role. He felt like a fifth wheel, and for what? So he could live out the remainder of his existence in this dump, ready to defend his father to the death when and if they were finally found? He wanted to blame his father for all of it. Badly. But to do so meant he would hate the one person he had left in his life. It also meant that the work he was doing in the name of Allah would be disingenuous, and that scared him. He wished Allah would speak to him somehow and reassure him of his path. Give him hope. This is something his father could not do. The only human being left in the world who cared about him. If he even did—it was difficult to tell at times.

A creaking sound pulled him from his thoughts, and he turned to see his father standing in the roof access doorway. "Sharif, I've told you before. We are not to come up here, except at night." He rolled his eyes up and pointed to the sky. "They are always looking for us. Come back inside."

"Fine. I'm coming."

He followed his father down the dark stairwell. At the landing Hakeem stopped and turned to face him. "Listen Sharif, I am worried about Ivan. I think he suspects we will kill him once this last batch is complete, and he is stalling. I need you to spend some time working with him and watch what he does. If you think he is dragging his feet, let me know. At the same time, be nice to him. If he does think his days are numbered, I want you to do what you can to change his mind. We cannot move the timeline for the next attack, too many things are already in motion, and we need the last batch without delay. OK?"

Sharif stood three steps up from his father, half listening. He did not look at Hakeem, instead he looked off the side, noting a brown stain on the wall above the railing. He wondered if it was blood, perhaps decades old or maybe just coffee someone spilled as they tripped going down the stairs...

"SHARIF!" Hakeem yelled, exasperated.

Sharif jumped and looked at his father dead in the eyes, defiantly. Almost immediately he thought better of confronting him and softened. "Yes father, I will do it."

"Alright then. Go to him now and get started." They continued down to the first floor where Hakeem exited the stairwell and Sharif continued to the basement.

The remote compound had been used in the past as a base of operations to prospect across this region of the country for oil and natural gas deposits. Hakeem had established seven of these facilities on subsidiary and family-owned lands across Algeria, Libya and Syria. Prospecting efforts were largely unsuccessful here, however, and the compound was abandoned quickly several years ago. There was still running water however, and they had electricity from three diesel generators in the basement, a primary unit with two backups. In addition, Hakeem had gone to great lengths to wire four of the seven facilities for internet connectivity, an expensive endeavor given how remote they were. For the three remotest sites he established mobile satellite internet services that could be packed up and moved anywhere at a moment's notice.

The lab in the basement had originally been set up to test rock and soil samples, and there were sleeping quarters for Hakeem's fiercely loyal skeleton crew, most of whom provided security and kept them provisioned. Supply runs were made once a month, and only at night. It was the perfect place to prepare for their attacks, and a good hideout. No one would think to look for them here.

Hakeem insisted that the two above-ground floors could not be used at all; they had to maintain the appearance that the property was abandoned. To make room for the operations center the basement had been enlarged long before they arrived, a process that required excavating a considerable amount of rock and earth. There was now more room in the basement than above, and Hakeem's entire crew spent all their time below ground.

They had a small information technology and communications team—two hardware experts, two coders, and Ahmad. Ahmad was Hakeem's longtime Chief Information Officer and his closest friend. They seemed to argue a lot now though, mostly about strategic messaging and planning. The two coders, Mukhtar and Taweel, were accomplished hackers and responsible for preventing anyone who might be looking from finding out where their communications were sent or originated from. They were remarkably busy most of the time. Their setup looked something like a scaled down Pentagon-style war room, with all the latest high-end technology. Hakeem called it 'The War Room.'

The door to The War Room was open as Sharif walked by. He stopped at the entrance to observe. Large screens on the wall showed various foreign news broadcasts. Deutsche Welle from Germany, France 24, Al Jazeera, and CNN. There were other screens as well scrolling lines of code and other seemingly important, unintelligible information. Amhad was speaking with Mukhtar and Taweel while the hardware guys just sat there, watching the televisions. Finally, Ahmad noticed him and they stopped talking, looking his way expectantly.

"Don't worry about me, guys. Just checking out the news."

They turned back and began speaking again and Sharif continued down the hall to the lab. As he entered, Ivan moved from his workbench, walking quickly toward him and stopped a short distance away at attention. He was wearing a facemask and surgical gloves.

"Ivan, there is no need to do that when I come in. Remain at ease."

Ivan relaxed his posture but remained standing there, arms by his side. "Yes sir. Thank you, sir."

"And call me Sharif, please. I am tired of all this militaristic behavior. Everyone here should try to loosen up a bit."

"Yes sir, I understand," he replied. "How can I help you?"

Sharif walked over to the workbench where Ivan had assembled several petri dishes, slides and a microscope. "Actually, I am here to help *you*. My father is concerned about our last batch, that it won't be ready in time." He took a prepared slide, inserted it beneath the microscope stage clips and peered through the ocular.

"Be careful, sir, those are live cultures. I mean, Sharif. You should be wearing protection."

Sharif looked back at Ivan, still standing near the door, and smiled. "Come on over here, Ivan. It's been a while since I've been involved, and I don't know where you are in the process. Lay it all out for me, OK?" Sharif took a seat at the table in the middle of the lab, motioning Ivan to sit.

Ivan sat opposite him, slowly removing the mask and gloves and placing them on the table. He regarded Sharif for a moment and began speaking. "We are perhaps two weeks away from being able to weaponize the final batch. But I am concerned about the strength, the virulence. It is weaker than the first three. I recommended to your father that we take more time. To grow more cultures so we can increase the quality of the batch. But he wants it on time. He doesn't understand the science."

Sharif removed the baseball cap, setting it on the table and watched Ivan's face as he spoke. He looked to be in pain. Not physical pain. It was severe mental stress. He felt bad for him. Ivan already knew there was no scenario where he would get out of here alive. "Well, that is why I am here, because I understand some of the science. Not as well as you, to be sure, but in general. What can we do to improve the virulence and still stay on schedule?"

"Mister Sharif, the only way to stay on schedule is to move forward with the batch that we have. I started a new batch and if any of it is ready at the end of the two weeks, we can combine the two, but I can't guarantee that it will increase the virulence without more time."

Sharif began tapping his fingers on the table, watching each finger strike the stainless steel with a dull thud. He continued tapping, trying to bring himself to think logically, to formulate a plan, to find a way through the problem. But he simply did not care enough about it. Just as Ivan saw no light at the end of his tunnel, there was no light at the end of Sharif's, either. Even if they were successful in this next attack, what next? Eventually, they would be found, and his life would go from bad to worse. Or he would be killed, along with his father and everyone else. That might be the best end result, another drone strike. In the middle of the night, when everyone was sleeping. A painless transition from a meaningless life of hardship to the gates of Jannah, the final abode of all righteous Islamic believers.

Then Sharif stopped tapping and frowned. He was not yet convinced his father's path was a righteous one. If it wasn't, it followed that *his path* was not righteous either. If he were killed, would Allah consider him a martyr? Would he end up in Jannah, or Jahannam instead? It bothered him greatly that there appeared to be no possible outcome where his future was anything but bleak and unbearable. He decided in that moment to have a conversation with Ivan that his father would never approve of.

"Ivan, you are an Orthodox Christian, yes? If you died tomorrow, do you think you would go to paradise, or to Gehenna?"

Ivan looked suddenly tense, regarding Sharif quizzically. "Sir, I do not understand. What is the meaning of this question? Do you think we will be attacked?"

"No, no. Well, maybe but not anytime soon, anyway. It's a theological question, a hypothetical one. In your religion, you have certain rules, a code you must live by, as do we as Muslims. Much of it is the same, to be honest. But if you were to die tomorrow, for whatever reason, do you think the summation of your life choices, your adherence to your code, would warrant you to go to heaven, or to hell?"

Ivan still looked perplexed, then resigned as he decided to answer the question. He thought for a moment and his visage changed yet again. Suddenly, he no longer appeared to be the frail, compliant shell of a man Sharif had come to know. He now looked resolute and almost confident. Knowledgeable. "Sharif, I have done things in my life that I regret. Some of those things I thought were the right things to do at the time, but I know now that they were not. And if we are being honest here, I regret having come here to work with your father. Nothing good will come of any of this, and people will die. People have already died, if what Hakeem told me is true, that the first attack was successful. At this point in my life I wish I could reverse some of those things, but I know much of that is in the past and there is nothing I can do. So if I were to die tomorrow, I am certain I would go straight to hell."

Sharif was watching Ivan intently as he spoke. It was the first time Ivan noticed that Sharif appeared genuinely interested in anything anyone said. Ivan went on. "But if I had time beyond tomorrow; if I were to leave this place and go back to my life in Russia, I would be able to change. To be a better man and to make better decisions. To do some kind of penance. My God is a forgiving one, and if He believed me to be complete and sincere in my efforts, when I eventually die, I believe He would reward me with a place in heaven."

Sharif was listening closely and knew Ivan was being sincere. He wondered what that might mean for him. *He* had made changes and decisions—to work with his father and the AMA, to make sacrifices and wage a holy war in Allah's name. This was the penance his father had prescribed, one that was supposed to guarantee him his seat in paradise. If that was all wrong; if his father was wrong and all of it was in fact the *opposite* of the will of Allah, then it was a terrible, damning and irreversible irony. *But maybe not?* What Ivan had said gave him the smallest sliver of hope in that regard. Maybe there was a possibility for reconciliation after all. To make things right, to have a future. *To be happy.* A plan began to form in his mind. One that might allow for his reconciliation. He would execute his part in the next attack, at least to the point where he could escape. Whether or not the attack itself was wrong was irrelevant he concluded, because he would be innocent; he was naive to Allah's true intentions. He would have to pray on it. Then he would begin anew. He would change.

CHAPTER THIRTEEN

As grueling and boring as the training was at times, it was also interesting and surprising. Dolan found he was exceedingly adept at deception, as if it were an innate ability. He was taught discreet photography, how to execute dead drops and brush passes, and various methods for defeating locks. He learned how to interrogate without the subject knowing they are being interrogated. How to beat a polygraph, how to surveil and counter surveil. He was introduced to all the latest gadgetry used for technical surveillance. He learned the latest techniques on how to mentally collate and analyze information quickly, something at which he'd always been exceptionally good. They also practiced how to evade and 'disappear' when being pursued.

Welker brought him to the range on base one morning where he was introduced to various weapons used by the Agency in the field. Some were traditional handguns, others looked nothing at all like weapons but were just as deadly. He was surprised, and Welker was pleased to find that Dolan had not only retained proficiency from his military days, but that he was uncannily accurate no matter which weapon he used. That afternoon they practiced defensive driving techniques on the taxiways near The Stage. Orange cones were set up in an elaborate course for the training, which lasted six hours. The final event consisted of a car chase in which Dolan was required to stay within the cones and evade two cars in pursuit. In each of the other vehicles men with paintball rifles were doing their best to prevent him from getting to the finish line unscathed. Dolan found this training event to be utterly enjoyable, a feeling like that of flying low-level through the mountains. Then he wondered if he'd ever have the opportunity to fly again...

The following day was set aside for hand-to-hand combat, right there in the middle of The Stage. The setup from the night before was still there, two one-story buildings and a couple of pickup trucks with large, potted trees here and there. Welker had drawn a large chalk circle on the floor between the two buildings.

Dolan was looking forward to impressing Welker, thinking he'd be doing the instruction. For this session, however, he brought Scott in. The DEVGRU lead had already been briefed that it was to be a training session, but also an effort to measure what Dolan already knew. Which was quite a bit considering his taekwondo prowess. But Dolan found that while he was able to get the better of Scott when he kept some distance between them, he was losing the battle whenever the Seal got close and inside his defenses. After a couple hours Welker decided to have them focus solely on wrestling and disarming techniques, chokeholds and the like. The Seal subdued Dolan easily on almost every try, but it became increasingly difficult for him as the day wore on. These were areas of self-defense that were more important, things Dolan had not practiced since he was in special operations. As the day wore on Dolan was winning every third fight or so. By ten p.m. they were finished, the three of them sitting on the floor drinking bottled water and sharing war stories. It was nice for Dolan to see there was a real human being behind a normally unreadable, tough-as-nails demeanor. He wondered if Scott was thinking something similar about him.

When all was said and done, Welker told him he was surprised, and satisfied with his knowledge and ability in hand-to-hand combat. And everything else, for that matter. Dolan had learned faster and performed better in two weeks than anyone he'd ever taught during his years teaching at Camp Peary. And students at The Farm had several months to internalize it all.

He didn't see much of Rhodes or Freeman during this time. They did poke their heads inside the door occasionally to inform Welker of important updates or ask questions. He passed them occasionally walking to and from his quarters and joined them with Welker at three one-hour, six a.m. meetings in the Maple conference room operations center. The meeting was held daily. But Welker felt that while it was imperative they stay on top of new developments, intel and planning, they didn't have time to attend them all. The Harvey Point team was in constant contact with the SCIF back at Langley via a 24-7 videoconference. Via a huge television screen hung on the SCIF wall, Langley could hear and see everything happening at Harvey Point, and the large screen on their conference room wall afforded them a reciprocal capability. In-between meetings both locations remained on mute but had the ability to 'buzz' the other to start a conversation. Scott represented DEVGRU each time. With a dense beard and prone to wearing Wrangler jeans and red flannel shirts, Dolan thought he looked more like a lumberjack than a Seal. He was able to speak with him a few times, and though they seemed to get along, Scott appeared hesitant to participate in any conversation outside of what was required by the mission. Dolan thought it strange, as they'd already broken the ice in hand-to-hand combat training.

During these meetings Dittrich led the discussions from Langley and various analysts and Agency officers from multiple locations took turns providing relevant intelligence updates and assessments. During the third meeting it was announced Amman Station had been successful in convincing the Syrian boy Issam Yassefe to provide them with information about his two AMA accomplices, who were now being pursued in Syria. Dolan found it interesting they said nothing about what they intended to do with the boy. He was a terrorist, after all. He killed many hundreds of people.

Amman Station was now working with a joint international team to analyze the virus delivery device to glean anything they could; where it was assembled, how the parts were manufactured, what country or countries the materials may have been from. They determined very quickly that the attack was more sophisticated than originally thought. Not only because of the quality of the design and manufacture of the device, but because the attack was so very carefully timed.

One point the CDC made was how well the virus survived, how long it remained viable within the water supply. Normally, after water from a public supply system is filtered, disinfectants are used to prevent growth of bacteria and to kill off viruses. Various disinfectants are used throughout the world but the most common and effective is chlorine. When used at the optimal concentration, chlorine will kill more than ninety-nine percent of all bacteria and viruses. However, there is a downside to using chlorine as the concentration will diminish quickly over time. As chlorine interacts and reacts with other substances, and as the Ph of the supply changes, chlorine becomes less effective. Among others, this is one operational reason why many communities will alternate the use of chlorine with monochloramine. While monochloramine remains effective within the system much longer, it can be up to 100,000 times less effective against viruses. The targeted Amman system had switched to monochloramine just one week earlier. The terrorists knew when that switch would happen.

Another important topic of discussion in these meetings involved information provided by Rolf Haussmann. It turned out that Welker's assessment of Rolf after the interrogation Dolan witnessed from behind the two-way mirror was spot-on. Over the course of his stay at Harvey Point he selectively released what he knew in a steady stream, a little more each day. Welker asked Rhodes to remain patient and not to threaten him for more or to give it up faster, but instead to dangle carrots in front of him. The big carrot was his unconditional freedom at the end. By the time they reached day thirteen, the team was confident Rolf had told them everything he knew about Martin and the AMA, including information about the financial transaction records and account numbers. He was also able to access his and Martin's dark web chat history. It was now all being analyzed at Langley and preparations were being made by Rhodes and Welker to release him.

The most important item on the daily agenda was the probable location of Hakeem and Sharif Lefebvre. There were seven spy satellites tasked to help find them, including four from the National Reconnaissance Office. The NRO's Orion was busy collecting telemetry, VHF radio, mobile phone, and mobile data link information across Algeria. Two Kennan KH-11 Evolved Enhanced CRYSTAL System satellites fed the Agency with a constant stream of highly detailed optical and infrared images of buildings, compounds and sites where the Lefebvres could be hiding out. The Quasar Satellite Data System relayed the imagery and other data from the low-flying KH-11s to ground stations in the U.S. The Agency also contracted three of Black Sky's ten reconnaissance birds. Black Sky was a private global intelligence company capable of delivering near-real time imagery and fusing it with social media, news and other data to improve the quality of analysis and insights.

All the data and imagery was being fed into the NRO's *Sentient* program. Sentient is an incredibly powerful artificial intelligence analysis tool that devours incredible volumes of all kinds of data, applying powerful machine learning to automate the intelligence tasking, collection, processing, exploitation and dissemination cycle. The intelligence community can then move forward with greatly improved situational awareness provided by Sentient scenario modeling to anticipate potential courses of actions of adversaries. The end goal was to be able to point their satellites toward what Sentient determined is the most probable location of Hakeem and Sharif.

Additionally, Sentient was crunching numbers to identify the timing and locations of the AMA's next likely targets. Dolan wondered how any large, organized and actively communicating terrorist organization could possibly remain hidden with such an elaborate and technologically advanced reconnaissance network brought to bear. It was only a matter of time before they were found. But the clock was ticking—they had to be found before they struck again. He also presumed that if there were ever a possibility 'Skynet' from *The Terminator* movies might ever come to exist, Sentient might just be it.

At the end of day thirteen Dolan went to bed, thoroughly exhausted. He looked forward to sleeping in for the first time in weeks. 'Sleeping in' for him usually meant getting up around eight a.m., but again, he usually needed no more than six hours. There were several streams of thought he'd been mulling these past two weeks and he usually worked on them for a few minutes each night as sleep arrived. He guessed it probably wasn't normal. It was probably more accurate to say that his way of thinking would be considered obsessive-compulsive when compared to a majority of people. From what he'd read and what he knew of others, trying to reconcile problems usually hindered the onset of sleep. But not for him. He had always assumed it was his ability to compartmentalize his feelings that allowed him to do this, and even though he'd taken great strides to break down those walls, to deal with issues as they came along, he found he was still able to perform his nightly mental collations and drift off in the process.

As he thought his mind turned to tomorrow's flight to Berlin. They'd spend one day in strategy briefings with officers from Berlin Station, test all their equipment and go over daily routines. Then they would begin. It was about to get real. He questioned Welker as to the true value of such an operation when they may not be able to get much at all out of the assassin, if they even caught him alive. The truth was, they suspected he was a member of an AMA cell based in southern Germany. If they were able to identify and capture the additional members of that cell, the resultant information would be a treasure trove. It was highly likely any intelligence turned up in the ensuing raids would narrow their search greatly for, if not pinpoint Hakeem and Sharif. They might also gain information on the date and place of the next attack.

Knowing this made him feel better, that the dangerous role he was playing was in fact especially important to the overall success of Operation CLEARCUT. Take down the AMA. Prevent future attacks and loss of life. Capture, or kill Sharif. He told Welker that if they were able to abduct him, he wanted to be part of the interrogation. Welker did not like the idea at all, for obvious reasons. But Dolan persisted, explaining logically and resolutely how their connection went deep, that Claire's murder was perhaps the one event in their shared history that only Dolan could leverage to break Sharif. And though he admitted it still affected him deeply, he knew better than almost anyone how to suppress those feelings while doing it. Welker capitulated, though he cautioned that Dolan would only be allowed to participate in a limited way—Welker would run the show.

One aspect of the op that didn't sit well with him was that he would have no opportunity to participate in the actual capture of Sharif. He wondered, given the opportunity to be part of it, if he would be compelled to kill him. Some part of him felt it was the right thing; his death would equate to justice in its truest form. An eye for an eye. The more he thought about it though, the more he decided it was less than that. Sharif killed Claire, and he killed Tony. In the Amman attack, he murdered many, many more. *It wouldn't be justice at all, not even close.* He needed to figure it out. As he laid there and almost without intention, Dolan envisioned the scenario, embedding himself with DEVGRU. Scott, the Seal Team lead was by his side. They both carried HK MP7 sub machine guns at the ready. Backs pressed against an outbuilding, waiting for a signal to storm the compound. Dolan peered carefully around the edge of the wall. It was dead silent and nearly pitch black— the resolution of the facility was grainy, even with their latest-generation night vision goggles.

"GO GO GO!" came the signal in his earpiece. Dolan turned the corner, quickly and deftly making his way across the dark courtyard followed at intervals by Scott and the rest of the team. With their backs now to the front of the hideout, Scott reached out and tested the doorknob. Unlocked. One by one they filed in and began casing the immediate area. There was commotion down the hall, and Scott warned the team. Dolan shut his eyes to avoid being blinded by NVG flareup and jumped as the flashbang grenade went off. He opened his eyes and followed Scott down the hallway where a dazed terrorist on his knees begged for mercy with his hands in the air. One of the team quickly zip tied his arms and legs together, gagged him and dragged him to a corner. They spread out across the first floor, announcing each room clear as Scott and Dolan made their way to the basement.

Scott held the door open for him and they moved silently across a large, strangely empty room. Dolan couldn't even see the walls, it was so large. A big, dark, empty space. He spotted a figure maybe twenty meters away, ahead and to the right. Terse updates from the team interrupted by reports from MK7s filled his ears as he moved silently toward the silhouette. Dolan glanced back but Scott was gone now; he was alone. He kept moving until the person began to come into view, his back to Dolan and head hung forward in defeat. Sharif. Standing in a corner, of all places. Unable to face him.

An uncontrollable rage mounted from within as Dolan struggled with what to do. Scott had gone back upstairs, no one was watching. He could tell the team Sharif attacked him or struggled. That he had no choice but to kill him. Before he could think about it more, he raised the barrel of his HK and squeezed off three rounds, two to the back and after Sharif fell to the floor, one in the head. Where he had stood, a grisly Rorschach pattern of spattered blood graced the walls. The shooting upstairs had stopped, his earpiece was silent. Dolan's hands were shaking. He set his weapon on the floor and flipped up his NVGs. Fumbling for the flashlight on his utility vest, he finally turned it on and shined it on Sharif's crumpled form, face down on the floor. But something wasn't right. A great sense of dread consumed him as he reached down, grabbed his shoulder and turned him over. It wasn't Sharif. It was Claire.

CHAPTER FOURTEEN

Dolan slept through most of the flight to Frankfurt. He also spent time ruminating on his dream from the night before. It struck him that what was supposed to have been a disciplined, waking effort to gain insight into how he might feel if confronted by Sharif had somehow morphed into an uncontrollable horror. He was bothered as well that he didn't understand what the ending meant, if it meant anything at all.

The other, persistent nightmare that plagued him for so long had ceased its recurrence with a cathartic finale. Near the end of his mission two years ago in Berlin it came to him one last time with a revelation that in that dream, Dolan was his own killer. That final iteration was enlightening in more ways than one and until now, it was the very last time he could remember having dreamt. If there was anything to glean from this new dream, it was probably that killing Sharif would be the wrong move. *But why Claire?* He thought momentarily about telling Welker of it but promptly put the idea aside. No need to worry him about his state of mind just as they began the mission.

He also pondered the reality of being an official clandestine operative. Before he left, they showed him his credentials badge, then took it back from him and locked it up. Their mission in Germany was deniable and if caught, they were to be disavowed. He was traveling on his personal passport. Mission deniability and potential disavowal aside, this was happening now, and it was real. He was a certified member of the team. *Things will be different this time.* He had expected to be more intrigued about it all, more excited. But as usual he found himself on an even keel. It was due in large part to his nature, he knew. There wasn't much in life that could shift him from a calm and methodical status quo. But he believed as well that he was quite comfortable with, and good at this type of work. Of course, he had little experience and still had much to learn but he was sure of it. This is what he was born to do.

Dolan made his connection to the newly opened Brandenburg airport in Berlin, getting there about ten a.m. After deplaning he went through immigration, retrieved his bags and cleared customs. He then got a rental that he would drop off the next day. At the desk, the attendant gave him the key fob, along with an envelope containing his apartment key and a cell phone left there by someone from the team at Berlin Station. Welker instructed him to get a van. They would use it tonight to pick up some larger diplomatic pouches from the military side of the older Tegel airport, located on the northwest side of the city. Welker flew in earlier and should already be deep into meetings at the embassy. Dolan was to drive to the apartment in Dahlem, unpack and wait.

The drive was uneventful. Along the way he was tempted to make a detour and retrace his fateful route through the Tiergarten. Maybe even to park and walk to the location where he confronted Martin as he attempted to launch Hemoxin gas into the U.S. Embassy courtyard. But he quickly dismissed it. Though unlikely, it was still possible his assassin already knew of his presence in Berlin. His CI network would need to be in place before he ventured out anywhere. Additionally, he had been instructed to steer clear of the embassy. There could be no behavior on his part that might link him to official U.S. business, appeared out of the ordinary, or that was not at least indirectly related to his work with Atlantik Brücke. Behavior that would cause anyone to question his cover.

Dahlem was the quintessential German village, made more so by the Oktoberfest festivities, which appeared to be in full swing this early Saturday afternoon. Germany was doing its best to make Oktoberfest bigger and better this year given its cancellation the year prior, a necessary precaution to slow the advance of the COVID-19 epidemic. Dahlem was close enough to Berlin city center to be easily accessible via the U-Bahn subway or by car, and just far enough away to maintain a small-town charm all its own. It was the perfect suburban Dorf and maintained a strong and tight-knit sense of community. Dolan slowed as he drove through the center square. Polka music played somewhere nearby. Lowering his window halfway to hear it better, he was met instantly with the smell of roasted chicken and a variety of others; difficult to decipher but he could guess—bratwurst, schnitzel, fried potatoes and Bavarian pretzels. Families, troops of friends and children milled about, every other adult or so toting one, in some cases two large beers. He smiled as he spotted a family of four sporting traditional Bavarian clothing. The mother and daughter wore sky blue Dirndl dresses complete with bodices, puffed sleeves and aprons. The father and son wore lederhosen and Black Forest Bollenhut hats. Banners and decorations hung alongside the street and above the intersections, adding to the atmosphere.

Eventually he came to 13 Fabeckstrasse, just south of the Dahlem-Dorf U-Bahn station. It was the left half of a stone and wood duplex, built in the 1960s and recently renovated. The right half was unoccupied and also leased by the U.S. government. Dolan parked the van in the driveway, took the housekey out of the envelope and unlocked the front door. He secured the van after moving his bags inside and walked around the entire building. It was one large, shared back yard with a chain-link fence along the sides and back of the property line. Though not large, it was private with mature trees screening the duplex from neighbors. English ivy grew thick over the four-foot fence. Afterwards, he did a walkthrough of the apartment. Nicely appointed with contemporary furniture and a wonderful kitchen.

Dolan moved his bags to the bedroom and unpacked most everything, then went back to the kitchen. Someone had already stocked the refrigerator. He made himself a Nutella sandwich and a cup of coffee, turned on the television and made himself comfortable on the couch in the living room. His German had never been that good, due mainly to the fact he'd never lived there and only studied the language while at the Sorbonne. Having a photographic memory made things easier, however. He understood most of what he heard and could get by verbally. Watching TV would help.

As he clicked through the channels, he noted many of the stations were still covering the outbreak in Amman. Though it was said to be mostly contained now, over three thousand people had died and an estimated four thousand were currently hospitalized with Marburg hemorrhagic fever. A great number of them would not make it. A handful of cases had popped up in Syria, three in Egypt, and another in Los Angeles. Most were likely visiting Amman and got on flights before their symptoms began to show.

The other major news item was the global economic meltdown that ensued shortly after events in Amman unfolded—all the major stock indices took major hits, similar to what happened in 2020 with

COVID-19. One of the positives of Marburg was that symptoms developed quickly. Those infected didn't have much time before they required hospitalization, which limited the spread geographically. News of the containment was pulling some money back into the markets today, but until the AMA was eradicated along with their ability to strike again, volatility would continue.

He had no idea how long he'd have to wait before Welker arrived. He was anxious to get on with it. Much of the planning and discussion about what would happen in the first few days was done back at The Stage, but there were things that were better left for after they arrived in Berlin, like familiarization with the communications gear and briefing the protocols for the various routes of travel. The Berlin team consisted of himself and Welker, the Station Chief Mike Collier, and a guy named Stan Bolden. Rhodes and Freeman had by now returned to their second-floor suite of offices in Clarendon, Virginia and were following all developments from Langley, Harvey Point, Berlin and elsewhere from The Pit, the name of their makeshift Sensitive Compartmented Intelligence Facility at SCALPEL headquarters in Clarendon, Virginia. Freeman and Rhodes would be taking shifts monitoring all electronic surveillance and communications from the Berlin team.

"Wake up!"

Dolan jolted out of his slumber to see Welker, Mike Collier and Stan Bolden standing over him. Welker had a big smile on his face.

"I'm up, I'm up." He stood and shook hands with each of them. After introductions, they all sat, three on the couch and Collier in an armchair facing them. "So, I see you let yourselves in."

Collier nodded. "You may have noticed the locked door in the hall. It's an adjoining door between the two halves of the duplex. We'll never come through your front door, for obvious reasons. In fact, I will meet with you here maybe one more time, and then I will avoid the place. My position is a little too high-profile. It could draw attention. Stan will be setting up shop next door, basically pretending to be a reclusive tenant. Because he is a resident diplomat and is known here in Berlin, whenever he comes or goes he'll be doing his best to remain invisible. The two of you should never be seen together. Never leave or arrive at the same time."

Welker was unfolding a large map on the coffee table. "We are here," he pointed to their location, which was surrounded by a large black circle. "I'm staying at the Hyperion on Prager Strasse, here. It's basically between Dahlem and the center of the city. I'll be coming and going as the mission dictates. And just as you and Stan will never be seen together, you and I won't either. As far as anyone knows, you are on your own here. We want to make sure it looks that way the entire time to the neighbors, to passers-by, and most importantly to anyone in the foreign intelligence community."

Welker then began tracing his index finger along several different colored lines on the map. There were probably twenty of them, some quite short and others going into town. "These are the only routes you will ever travel. As we discussed back in North Carolina, each of these routes have been cased and vetted. We know every alley, every vantage point, all the sightlines for these routes within the circle and we have verified our comm gear will be uninterrupted along the routes that go outside the circle. You can make minor deviations of course, in case you want to check out a particular store or restaurant, but you need to stay close and if you absolutely must deviate, tell us ahead of time so we can adapt our strategy."

It was difficult for Dolan to believe they could pull this off with such a small team. And unfortunately, it was his life that was being dangled out there. What really concerned him was the possibility the assassin was a radical Islamist trained as an assassin who was not a true professional. A true professional would take no risks that might lead to his own death or capture. He would go to great lengths to be careful, take precautions that went far beyond what was necessary to simply kill someone. He would want to remain invisible. Safe. Alive, to kill again. A professional assassin would be harder to spot. More difficult to capture. But when cornered, when faced with a choice of failure or the possibility of death, a jihadist would leave caution to the wind and come at him, guns blazing. If there were no team, if they didn't have the upper hand here it would be the opposite—Dolan would prefer the jihadist of course because he might gain the advantage against him one-on-one. But in this scenario, his chances of survival were better with a professional hitman.

Welker reached into his burlap satchel and pulled out a white vest. "You'll wear this at all times. Even in the house. It's the latest tech, noticeably light and thin. You'll have to dress appropriately so that it isn't noticeable. So, no T-shirts or V-necks. It's getting colder now, so that makes things easier." He handed it to him.

Dolan took it and felt the weight. Maybe four pounds. It was about a fourth as heavy as the Kevlar vest he wore in Afghanistan. "Is this going to stop a sniper round?"

Stan Bolden, quiet until now, responded. "Ultra-high molecular weight polyethylene plates are good enough to stop domestic armor piercing rounds and most NATO rounds, but not good enough for a high-power sniper rifle. What you are holding is next-gen moldable polyethylene. The plates can be bent to the contour of your body and the molecular density is nearly fifty percent higher than what is available on the open market. If you are unlucky enough to be hit by a sniper rifle you will feel like you just got hit by a truck and it might just stop the bullet, or it might not. But it will stop everything else."

It might not. "It won't do much for a head shot, will it?"

All three regarded him gravely, not wanting to make light of Dolan's facetious observation. Bolden responded. "Listen, it's a possibility. But regardless of what you see in the movies, assassins will almost always go for a body of mass shot to the chest or back first, especially from range. The last thing they want is to miss a head shot and fail in their attempt because now their target is scrambling for cover and everyone in the area is screaming and running around. He'll take the upper torso shot and if there is time, take the headshot once the target is on the ground. In any case, our objective is to identify and capture him long before that, before he's comfortable enough to execute. Remember, it is highly likely he will follow and watch you for days, maybe even weeks before he is ready."

Almost always. Highly likely.

CHAPTER FIFTEEN

They spent the rest of the afternoon and part of the early evening going through the routes and protocols, testing and familiarizing themselves with their earpieces and other communications and electronic equipment brought over from the other side of the duplex. Collier took about an hour after that to brief them on local risks, essentially a broad overview of the current and significant intelligence activities in and around Berlin. Their number one threat was the German intelligence community itself. This was their country, their capital city, and they always kept a close eye on U.S. activities. Tier Two was the Russian Foreign Intelligence Service, or SVR, and the Chinese Ministry of State Security. Tier Three was comprised of a host of countries—the French DGSE, Israel's Mossad, it was a long list. Collier made it plain that their job wasn't so much to worry about or try to figure out who might be watching them, but to remain so completely boring and ordinary that the only person who would be watched was Dolan, and that Dolan wouldn't be watched by anyone *except* the assassin. The team would be using all available resources to quickly pinpoint anyone who might be shadowing him, and then to surveil them until the team could confirm with high probability that it was the assassin, and then plan the abduction. If it was determined Dolan was being followed by the Germans or another foreign intelligence service, they were to halt the mission, regroup and assess.

Collier departed after the threat assessment and Welker made a pasta meal for them. They ate quickly. Welker instructed Dolan to remove two of the bench seats from the van, put them in the garage, and to drive to an address nearby at the edge of the Gruenewald where he and Stan would join him. Then they left. The three of them were going to Tegel airport tonight to pick up the diplomatic pouches. Dolan wanted to ask what they were but figured Welker would have told him already if he wanted him to know, so he didn't ask. It was probably just more surveillance equipment. The meeting location was a vacant lot, the kind used about one month a year to sell Christmas trees. Bolden took the driver's seat while he and Welker sat in the back of the van.

It was well past ten p.m. by the time they went through the gate on the military side of Tegel. Stan showed a badge of some sort to the guard who waved him through. They then drove slowly along the edge of the apron, following a maintenance vehicle with flashing lights. The vehicle stopped adjacent to a Gulfstream V parked on the tarmac. The cabin door stairs were extended. Next to the plane was an oversize golf cart-type flatbed loaded with a few large packages. A fuel truck was just leaving.

"You guys stay put, I'll be right back," said Bolden. He got out of the van and walked over to the German customs officer who was driving the maintenance vehicle. They talked briefly and Stan then walked to the plane, up the stairs and inside. About a minute later he deplaned and met the officer at the flatbed who checked Bolden's black passport and each of the packages, then wrote on something on his clipboard, tore off a sheet and handed it to Bolden. They hopped in the flatbed, rode over and positioned it behind the van.

"I'm going to help, one of them is heavy." said Welker. "Don't let him see your face."

Dolan looked straight ahead as they loaded the van. It took the three of them, grunting and cursing to slide the largest, cube-shaped package into the back. They put three other smaller boxes off to the side. By the time they finished the Gulfstream had started its engines and was already taxiing away. Stan followed the maintenance vehicle back to the gate and drove out of the airport. Everyone was quiet.

Dolan assumed they would be taking the boxes to the duplex, but soon realized they were not heading back to Dahlem. After about fifteen minutes of driving Bolden slowed the car to a stop at the side of the road in an urban area. The traffic was light at this time of night. A few people strolled the well-lit sidewalks. *What are we doing here?* he thought. His curiosity was getting the better of him and frankly, he was annoyed that he knew nothing of what was going on. Just as he opened his mouth to ask, Welker unbuckled his seatbelt and maneuvered into the back of the van, produced a boxcutter from his pocket and went to work on the largest package. Very quickly he cut off the top, revealing a square stainless-steel container within.

"Key," Welker commanded to Bolden.

"Here you go," said Bolden, and he tossed something over the bench seat to Welker.

Welker held up the key and looked at it momentarily, then inserted it into the top of the container, turning it. The lock clicked and he opened the refrigerator-looking door away from himself. Dolan unbuckled his seatbelt and turned around, up on his knees to better see what was inside. Welker looked with great satisfaction, first at Dolan and then at the inert body inside the large container. The man was sitting with legs bent and folded, his knees tucked up near his chin so he would fit inside. Welker grabbed a fistful of his hair and pulled the head back for Dolan to see. The deathly pallor of his face made it marginally easier to recognize him in the dim light. It was Rolf Haussmann.

"Holy shit," Dolan muttered in amazement. "Is he dead?"

"Not completely," responded Welker. He glanced up at Dolan. "Remember, everything I told Rolf during our interrogation was the truth."

He released two latches on the side of the steel container, and it sprung open under the pressure of Rolf's compacted form. Using the boxcutter he opened one of the smaller packages and removed a large syringe, which he plunged into Rolf's thigh.

Welker glanced around to make sure no one was watching them. "Help me get him outside."

Dolan moved to the cramped space in back, past Welker and opened the two rear doors. He grabbed Rolf's feet and pulled while Welker got up under his arms and they lifted him out, seating him on the cobblestone street against the rear tire. Welker steadied Rolf as he began to groan, opening his eyes halfway, dazed and unaware.

"Get back inside, I got this," said Welker.

Dolan stepped up on the bumper and back into the van, closed the doors behind him and took his seat while scanning for onlookers. There were a few pedestrians on the far side of the street, but they didn't seem to notice. *So far so good.*

"Stan, what exactly is going on? What is the plan here? If you are going to bring me along on this, whatever this is, I should know."

"Just sit tight, Michael. This is Welker's play and we're doing it the way he drew it up. I'll let him explain when he gets back."

When he gets back? From where? Dolan was getting pissed. Once again, he was not being kept in the loop and this was no ordinary situation. Despite his consternation he quickly decided the best thing to do was wait as Bolden instructed. He was a certified CI officer now, a partner this time around, but he recognized as well that did not mean he was an *equal* partner. He was the rookie.

Welker and Rolf then appeared from the back of the van on the left side, walking together across the street. Welker was supporting him as he was clearly having trouble moving. He could see Welker speaking to Rolf and offering a bottle of water, which he didn't seem to want. They made it to the sidewalk and moved slowly down the street, turning a corner at the intersection and out of sight.

About five minutes later Welker appeared at the corner and was walking casually but brusquely back to the van. Stan started the engine and left the curb as soon as he got into the front passenger seat.

After they were sure no one was following, Welker turned to face Dolan. "My guess is, you'd like to know what's going on."

"That would be an understatement," Dolan replied.

Welker returned an understanding smile. "The plan for how we would handle Haussmann when we were done with him was drawn up quite a while ago. At the time you weren't yet an Agency officer. Officially, anyway. Abducting and detaining him, certain parts of the interrogation, and transporting Haussmann here the way we did could all be interpreted as, how do you say, highly illegal, from an international law point of view. So, the first opportunity to brief you up on this would have been two days ago. The alternative was to wait until now."

Dolan wasn't buying it. "To me, it makes more sense to brief me in ahead of time, include me in the plan. Even if there wasn't enough time to do that, I was pretty much useless tonight, just additional risk. Why even bring me along?"

"You needed to be here. For one, there were possible outcomes where we would have needed more help from you than just getting him out of the van. Two, the best possible way to introduce someone to an unusually dynamic and stressful work environment is to shock them right away. No matter how much training is provided, a significant emotional event is the best possible way to fully capture the attention of a new field officer, to get them completely focused. And it's better that it happens early-on. I wanted to open your eyes. Moving forward in this operation, there is now much less that will catch you by surprise or knock you off your centerline." Welker stopped to let it sink in, then chuckled. "But most of all, you're a rookie and I wanted to bust your cherry."

Dolan chuckled at that, more than familiar enough with these types of antics from his Air Force days, though the real reasons Welker laid out made good sense to him. "OK, I understand, thanks. Now tell me what just happened."

"Everything I promised to Haussmann has come to pass. Sure, there are things I didn't promise him that were part of our plan, things he was unaware of, like being brought back to Germany. He's probably just now figuring out where he is. But we were never going to allow him the opportunity to go back to Chile, to his cush little life. Not after what he did to the U.S.A. And oh by the way, not after what he did here in Germany.

"What you didn't see was me taking him into the Polizeistation just around the corner. I explained to the desk officer that this man was stumbling on the sidewalk, didn't know where he was and seemed to be in some sort of trouble. All true. Then I gave the officer his German passport, which Stone found when he investigated his house back in

2019, after he disappeared. So I did exactly what I said I would do, I released him unconditionally. He walked in there of his own free will, sort of, and I didn't deliver him into custody—I only mentioned that he needed help. The officer will plug his name into a computer, scratch his head for a few minutes and then call his supervisor over. They'll bring Haussmann into a back office while they try to figure it out and decide to hold him until they can make sense of it. Then there will be a big investigation aided significantly by anonymous tips from the Agency." He made a motion of washing his hands, then turned back around. "Haussmann will spend the rest of his life in prison."

CHAPTER SIXTEEN

"It's time, Sharif, that I tell you what your part in all of this will be. You are ready." Hakeem Lefebvre put his arm around his son. "With your leadership it appears our Russian friend will be able to deliver the last batch on time, and then we will strike at the heart of our foes. Praise Allah." They were in the communications room. Ahmad, Mukhtar and Taweel were all tapping away on computer keyboards.

Sharif almost pulled away, instinctively. He wasn't used to amicable physical contact from his father. It felt disingenuous. But he didn't shrink from it. Instead, he returned the gesture with a halfhearted hug. It bothered him greatly that Ahmad, and probably Mukhtar and Taweel as well knew more about their plan than he did. After 'Destroy the West,' 'Operational security' was his father's favorite mantra. After two years, he will finally be told what his designated role is.

"You, my son, will be leading the team in Europe. I've thought about this a long time and to be honest, I was worried about you. You had become too comfortable in your westernized lifestyle. It was difficult for you to let it go. You yearned for the past instead of looking to the future. But I think this weakness has faded in you. Your work here, especially with Ivan, has been fantastic. You have good rapport with him and with most of our people here. More importantly, you are my son. It should be you who leads the charge."

Sharif was at once both excited and worried. Excited at the prospect of returning to Europe, back to civilization, and worried that whatever the plan was, he could be killed or captured. And afraid as well that if he wasn't killed during the attack, he might be later if he decided to escape and not return to his father, to stay in Europe. But he could lead the charge from the shadows, as he did in Paris. From a safe place. And then, to remain in the shadows, where no one could find him...

"Sharif!" Hakeem shook his son, his arm still up around his shoulders. "Are you hearing me? I want you to lead. To be Allah's right hand!"

"Yes father, I am just shocked and humbled. I am happy to do this and will not fail." Then he pulled away and looked at Hakeem, almost sideways. "And I am relieved that you are not giving this honor to Ahmad. I was beginning to wonder." It was a weakly delivered attempt at humor. He felt insincere and phony. Unfortunately, these were feelings that were not new to him.

Ahmad stopped tapping and looked over, a feigned scowl on his face. Hakeem laughed boisterously. "No, no, Ahmad was never in consideration. I think he is getting a little too old for that kind of action, and anyway I need him here. If our network goes down, we lose our voice. If we lose our voice, we lose control. And without control the organization becomes fractured and ineffective. This is what happened to al-Qa'ida, you know? After everything our brother bin Laden did for our people, when he went into hiding he did so quickly, with no plan for a secure, robust and redundant communications network. It was very ad-hoc, with no way to maintain the momentum he gained on 9/11 and it was all downhill from there. I have taken measures, gone to great lengths. Even if our place here is destroyed, there are two others with equivalent capabilities that can replace it. Ahmed and I are the only ones who know the locations of all three. *Operational security.*"

Even with the information he'd been privy to thus far, Sharif couldn't guess where the other two hideouts were located. "I understand. But please, tell me the plan. Who will be on my team? How will we get there, the targets, everything. I am dying to know."

Hakeem nodded and sat down at the utility table nearby, motioning Sharif to join him. "All in good time, my son. Some of the details will be revealed to you just before you leave, such as the attack locations. Others will be revealed after you arrive in Europe, including the method by which you will execute the attacks. Your colleagues are already there, preparing. As the leader you will be responsible for ensuring their security, providing resources, communicating with me and Ahmad, and for execution of the plan. They will listen to you and obey your orders; this is the direction I have given them. Most importantly, you will personally transport the virus and protect it at all costs.

"We have spoken at length about what went wrong in Paris and Berlin, so I won't go through all of it again. However, I want you to know I don't blame you for all of it. I blame myself, if anything. The bottom line is, it was a bad plan. I gave you a responsibility you were not ready for, one you were not trained for. As a result you adapted, you let François Martin take control of operations. But he was too eager, and not cautious enough. He took unnecessary risks and made things more complicated than they needed to be. This is how the Americans caught on to us. It wasn't your fault, not completely. But you have been trained now, as well as any of my followers. And you are smarter than all of them. You will have to lead with an iron fist this time, and I have no doubt that you will succeed."

It had been easy for Sharif to lay the blame at Martin's feet after escaping from Marseille to Algeria. His father had been livid; he went on and on about the complexity of using an unproven chemical gas. The novel delivery method. It had been Sharif's plan from the start, though. Every step, each detail. François hadn't done anything Sharif hadn't directed him to do. But Martin was dead, the truth didn't matter anymore, and he needed his father on his side. He had no one else.

"Thank you, father." It was probably the nicest thing he'd ever said to him, as far as he could remember. He felt warm inside and suddenly, a sense of purpose crept back into his mind. As if things just might be OK. With his father, with his future. He would weigh how he felt later, though. This could all change. He should leave all his options on the table.

Sharif then caught himself wondering about his father's motivations. He didn't speak like a fundamentalist, and he ran his AMA network as if it were a business. Perhaps that's all it was to him. The money was rolling in for sure, but his father had never needed it until lately. The Americans and Europeans had frozen much of, but not all his assets. And he had never been a particularly religious man either and only communicated with the Imams occasionally. When it suited him, or when he knew they expected it of him. It was essentially a quid pro quo relationship.

"OK, good. Taweel will go along, and you'll travel by boat of course, as there is no safer way to transport the virus. Tomorrow we will begin briefing you on the initial details. You will leave in three days."

Sharif asked a few more questions, they discussed some of the higher-level aspects of the plan and Sharif left to check on Ivan and the lab. When he got there Ivan began cautioning again about the strength of the current viral cultures, but Sharif wasn't listening. His interest in the status of the latest batch was overridden by a sudden urge. He held up his hand, motioning Ivan to be quiet and walked to the room where they kept the megabats.

"Sir, you should wear a mask, at least. It is dangerous, and you could contaminate the lab..."

"It's OK Ivan, I'm not going to touch them."

He opened the door and went inside. It was dark and eerie; a lone red spectrum bulb on the ceiling cast a sick bordello vibe within with just enough light to see. Five large, floor-to-ceiling chicken wire cages against the far wall held their thirty-two remaining carriers, the source of their wrath. 'Gifts from Allah,' Hakeem was fond of saying. He walked over slowly to within inches of the middle cage so he could see them clearly. There were sixty at the beginning, all brought in from remote caves in Uganda. They were dying regularly of late, about one every couple of weeks. Without being able to fly, to forage and live in their natural habitat, they seemed to be giving up. Over the past two years three females had given birth but in each case the baby bat died within a few days. Strange creatures, he mused. At about three pounds and with wingspans of up to five feet, they were huge as bats go.

Most people have never seen such animals. In the wild, they would be terrified if they did. The bats didn't appear so large or threatening here, though. Hanging from the ceiling in their chicken wire cages, wings wrapped tightly around themselves. One of them suddenly opened its eyes and looked directly at him. Startled, Sharif snapped back, then recomposed himself. After watching a little longer, he realized how vulnerable they appeared. But appearances could be deceiving. That they contained so much death within and remained unaffected by it themselves was a difficult thing to fathom. Why were they imprisoned here? Because they fulfilled a need. They could kill. *I am like them. I am here because...because I killed Claire. And I am needed to kill again.* And just as they were, he was trapped and withering away. Vulnerable, yet still capable of magnificently menacing things.

Sharif was still not convinced Hakeem's intentions were righteous, that following this path was truly the will of Allah. It could lead to freedom, however, whether he went through with the attacks or not. And as much as he wanted to shirk his responsibilities and somehow escape to a better life as soon as he reached Europe, as much as he longed for even a shadow of hope or redemption, he was also still very intrigued by the option to command great fear, to spread his wings wide and deliver a terrible pox on all those who had ravaged his family and forced him to cower in this dark, forsaken place.

CHAPTER SEVENTEEN

Welker spent Sunday at the Hyperion Hotel prepping a briefing for his BPM meetings, the first of which was Wednesday. Two others were conveniently scheduled three weeks and two months later. Bolden settled in next door and was putting the finishing touches on his electronic surveillance setup in the back bedroom. Six thirty-two-inch monitors hung on the wall above a large folding table with three laptop computers. One monitor was designated for videoconference capability with SCALPEL headquarters in Clarendon. Monitor two displayed a map of Berlin and showed the locations of team members and any targets being tracked. The first laptop was tapped into Intelink, the CIA's Top-Secret intranet, and a second served as the hub for all their video and real-time communications. The third was an unclassified system. Haussmann's refrigerator cube now sat in the corner of the room.

The hub laptop contained immensely powerful, proprietary software, the purpose of which was to hack into and exploit electronic surveillance resources of public and private utilities and companies. For this mission, they were targeting the traffic, S-Bahn train, U-Bahn subway and bus camera systems along each of the routes discussed the previous day. Within a five-kilometer circle of the duplex, they also had access to the systems of several shops and businesses. The suite of programs, codenamed Alpha Bright, allowed for facial, body, and gait recognition, as well as target tagging and automatic tracking. It used GPS data from their phones to error-check itself and to show positions on the map on screen two. Dolan was blown away that gait recognition technology was now so advanced that a person could now be identified, with a relatively high degree of accuracy, by the way they walked.

Four of their six screens could be assigned independently to display video of a tagged person, automatically switching between video feeds as that person moved along. As Dolan made his way along any of the routes, a green diamond would be overlaid on his torso, following him wherever he went. If Bolden or Welker were tagged, their overlays would be a green circle and a green square, respectively. A red circle would be assigned to anyone thought to be following Dolan, and if they believed it to be the assassin, it could be changed to red crosshairs. The technology behind Alpha Bright was so sensitive it could not be left anywhere unattended, not even in the twelve-thousand euro biometric safe bolted to the foundation of the duplex and hidden behind a false wall in the bedroom closet. The Intelink computer could be stored in the safe, but Alpha Bright was always to remain within sight and in possession of either Bolden or Welker, or checked back in to Berlin Station.

Bolden's primary job was to man the surveillance setup at 13 Fabeckstrasse. Welker's was to shadow Dolan wherever he went, protect him if necessary and collect on whoever might be surveilling him. Their assumption was the assassin would tail Dolan for several days before making his move, which should allow the team enough time to devise a plan to capture him unnoticed. Once identified, they would track him to wherever he was staying, most likely a nearby hotel, and abduct him there. He would be drugged and renditioned to the U.S. in the same stainless-steel cube they used to bring Haussmann back to Germany. If an opportunity with less risk presented itself, they would flex the plan but for now, that was it.

Dolan returned the rental van and took a taxi to a nearby Berliner Verkehrsbetriebe, or BVG station to buy a Monatskarte. The one-month pass was good on all forms of public transportation in the greater Berlin area. Then he made his way back to Dahlem via the S-Bahn and U-Bahn, walking the last half kilometer from Dahlem-Dorf Station through the Free University Berlin campus to the duplex. Walking through the campus could be problematic, as there were a few gaps in their Alpha Bright camera coverage. Bolden used Dolan's trip back to test both the tracking software and his earpiece connectivity. The earpiece was deep in Dolan's ear canal and invisible, linked to his cell phone. It required special tweezers to insert or extract. Communications were working as well as they could have hoped, though they soon realized camera coverage inside the train and subway cars was spotty. Either the cars weren't all equipped, or the cameras were in various states of functionality. Which made it more important that Welker was always nearby. There was risk involved in Dolan's trip downtown today without Welker to shadow him, but they assumed the assassin had not yet arrived in town. If they were wrong, Bolden figured they might have an opportunity to identify him early-on, but there didn't appear to be anyone following Dolan. Not yet, anyway.

Back at the duplex Bolden briefed Dolan on the initial test results and sent him back out, this time directing him from place to place within the five-kilometer radius. Dolan found the exercise enjoyable. He grabbed a bite to eat and stopped at an Apotheke, the German equivalent of Walgreens, to purchase some acetaminophen and a first aid kit. Then he meandered as Bolden directed, pretending to sightsee. It wouldn't be abnormal for someone new in town to get their bearings and check out the town, especially with all the festivities going on. When all was said and done, the tracking system was working like a charm, automatically switching as Dolan walked the town, from the U-Bahn security system to the intersection traffic cameras, grocery store surveillance to ATM cameras. All Bolden had to do at this point was watch the screens.

When they were finished Dolan returned and he and Bolden went through the data. They were able to canvass about a quarter of the routes in and immediately around Dahlem, a good test sample. Some of the video was less useful—lower resolution and older camera systems were prevalent. And others were not wide-angle, so a moving subject passed through the field of view very quickly. It was important that they map the gaps in-between the coverage. Knowing where they were allowed Bolden to keep Dolan apprised real-time if he was moving into an unmonitored area, a critical consideration when being followed.

Welker arrived at about seven p.m. with takeout food—Doner Kebabs and French fries from a street vendor. The Turkish meal had become a favorite in Germany over the years and could be found almost anywhere.

"So, how did it go boys?" asked Welker as he set the bags of food on the kitchen table.

"Alpha Bright is working great," replied Bolden. "There are gaps here and there, but we are mapping them. They will show up on screen two as grey squares. I am most concerned about the University since that is where Michael will be spending most of his time. I thought about installing a few cameras of my own, but the risk would probably outweigh the reward. The solution is for you," he pointed to Welker, "to have eyes on him, and in closer proximity than normal when he's traversing the area."

Welker grinned. "Super. What about Clarendon, are they in the loop?"

"I was in a video conference with Thomas for the last couple hours of testing, and he was able to see everything I was seeing. So that connectivity's working fine. They are keeping everything live and on-screen in The Pit."

Welker sat down and unwrapped his kebab, taking a big bite. "These are the best. I don't know why it is, but the best food in Germany isn't even German. Anyway," he paused to wipe the corner of his mouth with a napkin, "we need to plan out every move. Dolan has a meeting tomorrow morning at Atlantik Brücke, then another at Freie Universität in the afternoon, one O'clock I think, right? That one is with the professor Lutz Möller. Now, we have a mission here and it's our number one priority, but that begins to fall apart if the cover doesn't hold up. Michael, have you decided what you will be briefing this Möller guy on, the topic or topics of your research?"

It was something Dolan had put a lot of thought into. Welker was right, this part of the mission was important and only he could do it. It made sense to do it in a way that was beneficial to both his academic career and to Boston University. "I have a couple of ideas but the one I will lead with is U.S.-European collaboration on pandemic prevention and containment."

Both Welker and Bolden stopped chewing abruptly and regarded him as if he were kidding. Welker wiped his mouth again. "Seriously?"

"Yes. Why not? It is a topic that had everyone's attention with COVID-19, has everyone's attention right now with what's going on in Amman, and it will remain a hot topic for the foreseeable future. In the realm of international cooperation, it may be one of the top three current areas of concern, if not number one. And it ties in directly to our mission. You two may not know this, but my cover in Paris was uniquely suited to intelligence gathering on the AMA and it was the resources available to me as part of that cover that provided the one key piece of information that led me to their base of operations right near here in Potsdam. You never know, I could learn something that might help us."

Bolden and Welker looked at each other, then back at Dolan. Welker took another bite of his Doner and swallowed. "OK, I get it, but we don't want anyone putting two and two together. Not sure it will benefit us at all but like you say, who knows. Interesting…"

"Even if it doesn't it still needs to benefit Boston University and Atlantik Brücke. Otherwise, it looks like a sham. In any case, I've done my research on Möller and though it's not necessarily up his alley, I think he will find it intriguing. He's a former Luftwaffe fighter pilot and worked as a liaison for the Bundeswehr to German Parliament. He's a worldly figure and thinks big-picture. He will understand the value of it."

Bolden nodded in agreement. "Makes sense to me."

"Well, that was not a topic that was up for debate, but it sounds like it's settled," responded Welker. "What's important is you've done your homework and are ready for these meetings tomorrow. And based on your equipment test results, I'd say we are ready as well." He pointed to Dolan. "I am going to be shadowing you at a distance, but always within sight. If I'm doing it right, you will never see me. Don't ever look for me or even wonder where I might be. We should maintain radio silence the entire time unless there is a problem. You should never use the earpiece to talk to us unless you are in a situation where you cannot or should not use your phone. It looks weird when you are speaking to no one in particular, especially if it's obvious you aren't wearing a Bluetooth headset or earphones. You can, however, let us listen in on conversations. Just turn on the talk feature on the phone app and leave it on. Make sure to turn off the transmission when the conversation is no longer useful, as the battery will drain, and we need it to last. You will always be able to receive a transmission from us, and you have a short window afterwards to respond. In other words, the earpiece microphone automatically activates. It will deactivate three seconds later if you say nothing. If you respond within that time it will remain on until nothing is said at your end for an additional three seconds. But you will always have to initiate communication by using the app.

"When we do talk to you, don't be startled by it, there should be no visible reaction on your part. And there may be times when others, like Thomas or Lauren, are dialed into your earpiece. Keep doing whatever you are doing, even if you are speaking to someone else at the time. Just keep talking but listen as well. Again, we will only speak to you if it is important. There will be absolutely zero idle chatter.

"And whenever I am following you, I will be carrying a weapon. Of course, I will only use it as a last resort and only to prevent you from being killed. Note that I use the word 'killed.' I may intervene in a situation to prevent you from being harmed, but only if it looks like you can't handle it yourself. If I must use my sidearm our whole operation is at high risk of exposure. We could quickly find ourselves packing up and leaving and I don't want that to happen until we have the bastard comatose and folded up in my steel box."

CHAPTER EIGHTEEN

Freeman rubbed his eyes and finished what was left of his coffee. It was cold. He'd spent the last sixteen hours culling through mountains of telemetry, IP addresses, emails, video, photographs, VHF radio, mobile phone, and mobile data link information from the NRO's Sentient artificial intelligence program. It was a wider review than Sentient would normally kick out in its daily report, but they'd had very few useful results and he wanted to see if the AI had missed something. He reset the scope of what Sentient was instructed to look for and increased the geographic area to various parts of the Middle East and Europe, and certain additional countries in Africa. They were operating under the assumption that Lefebvre was probably hiding out in one of his own buildings and until now SCALPEL had focused primarily on properties currently owned by his sprawling conglomerate of petroleum companies. Now Sentient was looking at the entire history of ownership, as well as locations of companies he had done significant business with over the years.

Another assumption they made was that Dolan's assassin lived in Southern Germany. They thought this because intercepted communications about the contract on Dolan's life were sent and received from that area. Freeman was now casting the net wider. It could have been the messages were sent and received from there but relayed to and from another place. Another country perhaps. He was allowing for it because of the delay in responses on the topic from Germany back to Algeria. That part of Germany had a high concentration of Muslims, but the correlation did not mean the killer was part of the AMA or even Islamic.

"How's it going?"

Freeman jumped in his seat, then chuckled in embarrassment as Rhodes walked into The Pit.

"Sorry, didn't mean to startle you," she said.

"No worries. It's going. You know, for all the hype about Sentient, it's still only as useful as the information that is input to the system. I've widened the scope of what it is looking for in the hopes our original assumptions were either incorrect or slightly off. Right now, it's crunching a lot of data and I hope to see some better results soon."

Rhodes pulled a chair away from the conference room table and slid it over beside Freeman, taking a seat in front of the multiple monitors and keyboards. "That sounds like a good idea. What's the latest from Team Berlin?"

"Everything is up and running, Alpha Bright seems to be working fine. I have connectivity with Stan at the duplex in Dahlem. We are a go for this morning."

"Fantastic." Rhodes looked at the monitors, noting the empty room on the Harvey Point feed. On the screen directly above it, the Langley feed showed a busy room. Ten or twelve people making phone calls or typing away on Intelink. Dittrich was there, hunkered over someone, his hand on their shoulder as they talked about something important.

"You know, we really need to find out more about what kind of AMA presence there is in Germany. We must nail down who the likely cell members are, or at least where they might be located. If we get lucky and nab this assassin, it could be weeks before he tells us anything if he tells us anything at all. We've got to give Team Berlin something to go on before we get to that point. So they can pivot immediately after nabbing him to wherever that new information takes us."

"Agreed," replied Freeman. "That's part of the new dataset I programmed Sentient with. We didn't have it included before, because we were primarily concerned with locating Lefebvre and his son. Now it is looking for anyone who may be part of the AMA in Germany, which could in turn help with our search for Lefebvre. The only downside is the incredible amount of bandwidth that eats up, it is really slowing down the system."

"To get a little we must give a little. Have you thought about sending some of the imagery to Berlin? My guess is, though Michael won't have much downtime because of the research he has to do for his cover, Howard and Stan will. Why not let them spend it helping us nail down Lefebvre's hideout? The more eyes on it, the better. Plus, both of those guys are good at it. And Howard is really, really good."

"Yeah, that's a great idea. I think the best way is to send them satellite imagery Sentient flags each day, after I look at it. I can include my notes. Then they can review and send us their thoughts. Thanks Lauren."

"No problem. We're all in this together, and there is too much work not to spread it around. At the least, them not finding anything after you've already analyzed an image will help in removing the location from consideration."

"Agreed." Freeman grabbed his coffee cup and studied it, debating whether to refill it a fourth time. "Hey, have you heard anything on Haussmann yet?"

Rhodes smirked. "Yes, in fact. As we thought, he is telling a wild story about abduction and torture, and 'the CIA' is a big part of it. Of course, he has no idea who we really are or where he was held, but the German government is following up. And the more details he gives them about what we were asking him for, the more he implicates himself. He's in a catch-22. We are denying everything, you know how good Dittrich is with these things. He pushed them hard, demanding extradition and asking permission to interrogate Haussmann. From what I hear, he was convincing. They don't have any idea what really happened to him but should soon be able to corroborate the information we gave them about his manufactured identity and hopping a freighter to Chile. What they are sure about at this point is that he is the primary suspect for the fire at Vitale in Hamburg. His goose is cooked."

"Well that is good to hear. Glad he'll be getting what he deserves."

"He deserves more than what the German judicial system will give him, but it's out of our hands now. Listen, why don't you go home and get some sleep. It's my shift, and I'd like to settle in before we go live in Dahlem."

"OK, sure. Thanks Lauren. Call me if you need me."

"Will do."

Freeman got up, took his cup and walked tiredly out of The Pit. Rhodes got herself a bottled water from the minifridge in the corner of the room and waited for the videoconference and Alpha Bright screens to light up. It was nearing eight a.m. in Germany, two a.m. on the east coast. After a while one of the screens flickered and a digital map of the Berlin area appeared. Then the videoconference screen popped up with Bolden's face filling most of it, Welker and Dolan visible over either shoulder.

"Hello Lauren!" Bolden said enthusiastically.

"Hi Stan, nice work getting all this set up so quickly. Thomas tells me we are a go? Any issues?"

"Thanks. No, not really. We have some gaps in the video, and in some cases the quality or angle isn't good but it's acceptable. What about at your end? Did we get the analysts we were promised?"

"Unfortunately, no. I mean, everyone who can be assigned has already been assigned to the main team at Langley. We won't get anyone specifically for SCALPEL. With everything going on in Jordan and Syria, there is no available bandwidth. For now, we are going to have to review any intel specific to Germany ourselves. Which makes it even more important we watch AB carefully in real-time." She'd taken to shortening Alpha Bright to 'AB.' It hadn't caught on yet. "You and I, and Thomas when he's on shift, will need to remain alert and try not to miss anything. Michael, how are you doing? Are you ready?"

Dolan nodded and smiled. "Yes, as ready as can be. The vest is a little constrictive, but I'll manage."

"OK great. Stan, we're recording everything here as well, we can decide after each session how to split it up. But don't get too comfortable there, because starting tomorrow Thomas will be sending imagery with his notes for you and Howard to review. We want to put an extra set of eyes on everything we get from Sentient to locate Lefebvre."

"Darn," said Welker. "This is going to put a kink in my Oktoberfest plans…"

"Funny, Howard. Are you ready? Michael's meeting is in about an hour, right?"

"Yes, we're about to send him out. Fingers crossed," replied Bolden.

What followed was nothing more or less than uneventful. Dolan performed an audio check with the team, left the duplex and made his way north, through the Free University campus to the Dahlem-Dorf U-Bahn station. Then he boarded the U3 train and headed into Berlin. He switched to the U6 at the Hallesches Tor station and got off at Friedrichstrasse. Though he spotted no one suspicious along the way, he was still on edge. Then the ten-minute walk from Friedrichstrasse to Atlantik Brücke headquarters. Radio silence the entire time. On any other day he would have taken time to admire the sites along the way. He did his best to appear as if he were, but circumstances prevented his genuine appreciation for anything other than personal safety. He made it to his destination without ever noticing Welker, a good thing. The entire trip took sixty-five minutes.

He opened the front door and went in, noted the young lady at the reception desk and began to walk that way. Hans Koch, the Managing Director of Atlantik Brücke, came through a door next to the desk and intercepted him before he got there. At just over six feet with elegantly coiffed but thinning blond hair, bespectacled and wearing a fine-cut charcoal suit, Koch appeared the stereotypical European elder statesman. After introductions he gave Dolan a tour of the building, then they went to his office. The meeting lasted only thirty minutes, during which time Dolan outlined his plan for researching transatlantic partnerships in pandemic prevention and containment in support of his doctoral dissertation at Boston University. Koch showed genuine appreciation for the project and promised to email him a list of local professors and medical industry representatives in the Berlin area he could confer with during his research. With that he informed Dolan of the proximity of his next meeting, asked him to say hello to Professor Möller and walked him back to the foyer.

It was quick and about what he expected. Dolan's was just one of innumerable ongoing projects for the organization and he may have no need to see Koch again until he was ready to present his completed work. He smiled at the receptionist as he stepped through the door. As he did, he registered movement in his peripheral vision to the left. Someone standing up from one of the chairs against the far wall, slightly behind him. As he walked to the front door, he moved his head just enough to track their trajectory. The person was walking in his direction. Dolan turned to see who it was and stopped abruptly, utterly shocked and not knowing what to say. There she stood, smiling at him. Head cocked in that impossibly charming way as only she could, her auburn hair catching the light just so.

"*Listen you,*" she said coyly. It was Anne.

CHAPTER NINETEEN

Dolan immediately recognized the precarious nature of the situation. His first priority was not to blow his cover. Second was to keep the encounter as short as possible—he could not take the chance she might be identified as important to him by his assassin, if he was watching. And he had to try to do it all in a way that wouldn't hurt Anne or make her suspicious.

"Anne! What in the world are you doing here?" He stood facing her, glancing out the windows. Some pedestrians walked by outside, but no one appeared to be watching. He experienced a strange, sinking sensation as he succumbed to his feelings for her. It was a risk, but there was nothing else he could do. He strode purposefully forward and enveloped her in his arms, burying his face in the crook of her neck. As he held her tightly it came. As if flood gates were opened and he was caught in it, a turbulent river of emotion. He held on and realized then that even as he had become so completely self-aware over the past two years with what he thought was a profound understanding of love, of the very *meaning of existence*, he had at some point gone back to compartmentalizing things that might hurt him. He had boxed her up and put her away, lying dormant in the dark recesses of his mind. And it was all coming out right now.

"Hey, Michael," she whispered as the receptionist pretended not to notice them. "I am happy to see you too. Are you OK?" She released him and playfully poked him in the chest. "And whatever are you wearing under there?"

He forgot about the body armor. He was wearing a suit, nothing about his outfit looked strange with the loose-fitting jacket but she could certainly feel it during their embrace. Shit. Composing himself, he thought on his feet. "I'm fine Anne, I just can't believe you are here, and right out of the blue!" He touched his side. "It's a brace. I cracked a couple ribs last week, taekwondo. It should be fine in a month or so. But what are you doing here?" he repeated.

She took his hand and led him back to where she had been waiting and they both sat. She kept his hand in hers. "You poor thing. I hope it's not too bad! I'm in Berlin for an EU public relations conference, you know, for my job in Paris. It's just three days, I'm actually missing some of it now." She studied his face expectantly. *She's trying to read me...*

"Wow, what a coincidence. But what are you doing here?"

"Well, I saw on LinkedIn that you had earned this wonderful research opportunity at Atlantik Brücke, and so before I left, I called to see if you had arrived yet. They said you hadn't but that you had a meeting scheduled for today. So here I am, at the same moment as you. I think coincidence is the wrong term, Michael. That you and I are in Berlin right here, right now, it's possible this isn't coincidence, don't you think? Do you believe at all in fate?"

She watched him expectantly for a moment, then released his hand and folded her arms. *A defensive posture. My reaction is not what she'd hoped for,* he thought. He forgot he was connected to Anne on

LinkedIn. The possibility she would try to visit him never entered his mind. *Because I partitioned her away...* He put his hand on her arm and spoke from the heart. "Anne, regardless of why you are here, I am glad beyond measure that you are. Give me a minute to use the restroom, and I'll be right back."

"Sure." She uncrossed her arms, leaned back in her chair and smiled. Dolan smiled back, got up and asked the receptionist where the bathroom was. Back through the door and down the hall he found it, going inside quickly. He checked the two stalls to make sure he was alone and activated his earpiece. His heart was racing.

"Howard, this is Michael. Do you have eyes on me in the foyer? I have a problem."

Welker immediately responded. "I've been watching the front door. Clarify."

Dolan quickly explained the situation.

"This is the same Anne from Paris?" asked Welker.

"Yes."

"How long is she in Berlin?"

"For three days. I think that means through Wednesday, probably leaving on Thursday."

There was a pause, then Rhodes jumped in. "Go back to her, get her phone number. Take a few minutes to settle things, then explain you have another meeting to get to. Tell her to go back to her conference and you'll call her later. We can discuss how to handle her when you're back at the duplex. And Michael, leave the earpiece on."

It was what Dolan would have done anyway. "Copy. Heading back now."

Dolan used his phone to set the earpiece microphone to remain on, went back to her and did as Rhodes recommended. She wanted to talk longer, to catch up. Get a feel for where things were between them. Though she did her best to hide it he could tell she didn't fully understand his reaction; there was something off. He felt terrible about it and let her know that he wished beyond anything else that he could spend time with her, just cancel or reschedule his next appointment, but he couldn't. Inside, the sinking feeling he experienced earlier became more pronounced now with the realization he was unlikely to see her again before she left Berlin. To do so could put a target on her.

He got her number and hotel address and made a point of saying goodbye inside the building, checking out the windows again before giving her another hug and a kiss on the cheek. Then they walked out the door together. Just outside Dolan paused to see which way she would go. She walked slowly, head down just a bit. She wants me to notice that, he thought. He felt horrible as he turned off his earpiece microphone using his phone and departed in the opposite direction.

◆

He liked Professor Möller immediately. He was fifty-two years old and highly energetic with a lean, distance runner's frame. His physical appearance belied his age, with the exception that he was mostly bald. His English was impeccable, as was his French. The liaison position in Parliament was his final Bundeswehr assignment before retiring as a colonel. He took the position at the university immediately afterwards.

Like Koch, Möller was enthusiastic about the proposed topic of Dolan's research, though he lamented it was an area of study in which he had little expertise. Notwithstanding, his robust experience in politico-military and international cooperation could prove beneficial. Möller would be able to provide many of the contacts he needed to get started, but it was up to Dolan to do all the legwork. This included things like getting up to speed on and weaving in the relevant medical science like pandemic modeling, and historical data related to response and containment effectiveness. Möller had a colleague at the World Health Organization and another with their parent organization, the United Nations Economic and Social Council. He would introduce Dolan to both.

They spent some time building a rough timeline for the project and discussing how he might present it when complete. Dolan would need to funnel his research and conclusions periodically through a formal quality control process, ideally with representatives from the CDC, the European Centre for Disease Prevention and Control, and the WHO. There would be a period of validation and revision just prior to his presentation, after which his findings would be published and proposed for consideration with the appropriate national governments. Because he was required to provide a finished product before leaving Germany, defense of his dissertation would be a separate affair that would happen later.

The scope and gravity Möller was attributing to the project caught Dolan by surprise. He took his work very seriously and was expecting nothing less than a comprehensive, thoroughly researched and hard-hitting proposal with conclusions and recommendations that were innovative, unique, and that had real potential to change and improve how the world controlled contagion. Though he was fully invested and intended to deliver what Möller wanted, he worried about the bandwidth required—whether SCALPEL's mission would even allow for it. Without a crystal ball he had no way to know if it were plausible. He would have to move forward as if it were.

Möller showed Dolan his office, a modest and private room with an old wooden desk, a landline telephone and a nice view of one of the campus courtyards. It would be his daily workspace for the next three months. After three hours they wrapped it up and agreed to meet each Friday at two O'clock to review progress. Since Möller's office was one floor up from his, he could easily drop in if there was a need whenever the door was open. When they were through, he invited Dolan for dinner with his wife at his home that weekend, which he accepted graciously.

As Dolan walked the short distance back to the duplex he thought about Anne and what his options were. He would have to talk it through with the team. There were a few, but none were optimal. Recognizing this made him feel terrible all over again. He unknowingly compartmentalized her long ago and perhaps with her, his ability to love. He was out of practice. Seeing her again released it all, and he was more than a little irritated he couldn't use this opportunity to fix things. To embrace *fate*. As he saw it, his current situation would likely lead to her being hurt a second time. How could he be honest with her about how he felt without affecting his mission? He couldn't. His mind then went immediately to his troubling dream at Harvey Point. He was worried it might turn into another repetitive, evolving nightmare but it hadn't. Not yet anyway. He was confused about it still and couldn't divine its true meaning, if there was one. It might have had some twisted, predictive value had it been Anne and not Claire at the end. Or maybe Claire was just a placeholder in the dream for her. Maybe Claire was symbolic of his love for Anne. Though the previous nightmare had been foretelling and ultimately, cathartic, he wasn't sure this one was of the same variety. He did sense that it was significant, perhaps in some other way. Whatever it was, it was important somehow to his subconscious and he was not yet able to work it through an analytic process, towards reconciliation.

CHAPTER TWENTY

At the duplex, the team went through the day's events. Rhodes was there in the videoconference, looking haggard but alert. There was nothing immediately notable in everything recorded by Alpha Bright, and Welker didn't notice anything out of the ordinary while tailing Dolan. It appeared he wasn't surveilled by anyone on day one. So they jumped right into the topic of what to do about Anne. Rhodes kicked it off.

"Guys, here's my take on this. Yes, this took us all by surprise and it is a problem, but I don't see it as a *big* problem. Anne was tangentially involved with what happened in Paris and Berlin two years ago, and I even had the chance to meet her. Since she already knew me from when I was trying to track Michael down, I debriefed her after the attack in Berlin. As far as she knew at the time, I was a State Department official, and Michael had been involved in a bad car accident. We rammed her Peugeot into a tree before we brought it back to her to give the story some credibility. And then we cut her a check to get it fixed.

"However, I don't think she ever bought the story. She asked questions that demonstrated just how smart she is, and I believe she suspected Dolan was involved in something clandestine. I did what I could to put that to rest, and Michael, you explained it well from your end. The fact you two broke it off in the aftermath made things much easier.

"I think we have three different paths we could take. In the first scenario, Michael, you tell her you can't see her, that you have no time. It's impossible. We can come up with a way to make that believable. This is the safest bet, and she is out the picture immediately. Zero risk. In our second option, Michael meets with her for dinner, they have a nice time, and she goes back to Paris the next day, out of the picture. It gives you a chance to lay the groundwork for clear separation, so that she will not continue to call you or try to see you again for the duration of the mission. You can do this in a way that preserves the friendship. You refrain from intimate behavior, anything that might make our target think they could use her to get to you. We are still right at the beginning of this, and the assassin may not even be in Berlin, so the risk is low. Even if we were later in the game, he would likely wait until she was out of the picture before doing anything."

Welker stepped in. "Not to seem indifferent about Anne's safety, but this may be the best way to identify our target early on, in the event he is already here. When Michael is in transit, the target is moving as well. I am moving. It is more difficult to ID a target when moving between destinations. It is much easier at a destination because not only is he stationary, but he is also watching Michael. This makes him stand out. It gives me the best opportunity and the time I need to find him, and for us to verify his identity in a static, controlled situation."

Rhodes continued. "Thanks Howard, good points. In the third option Michael tells her he will meet for dinner, but then he doesn't show. And when she calls to find out why, he doesn't answer. Based on my assessment of her personality, I think she would not pursue it, and go home. Michael, I know you are probably not comfortable with that approach but there are several good reasons for doing it that way. Because you and she have history, and because of her past suspicions about the true nature of your work, she may wonder if you are involved in something else, something similar. Then we end up with a situation where she could delay in Berlin and persist. Try to force you to see her, worried about your safety and putting herself in harm's way. This would greatly complicate the mission."

"She wouldn't do that," Dolan interjected. "She may have had those suspicions, but it's highly unlikely she would react irrationally. Remember, we hadn't spoken in a year and half before today. That's a pretty good buffer." Both Welker and Bolden said nothing, looking back and forth between Rhodes and Dolan.

"OK," Rhodes replied. "It sounds like you are opting for either scenario two or three."

"Definitely not three," Dolan responded. "And I get why you like that option—it sends a strong message that I'm not interested in her anymore. It puts an end to it. But that is not how I feel. I would never do that to anyone, never mind someone I care about." He paused to think. "Obviously, I am biased here, and emotions are involved. I believe option one is best. We shouldn't involve Anne in any way that is a risk to her."

"Stan, what do you think?" asked Rhodes.

"Option one, without a doubt," he said with no hesitation. "Remove her from the equation. Don't gum up the works. We can create any number of similar controlled situations that yield the same result without involving a civilian."

Welker smiled. "True, we can choreograph anything we want. But you should know at this stage of your career, Stan, that nothing is as believable or works as well as the real thing. Right now, we'd either need Michael to be eating by himself somewhere, or square pegging someone who's not already involved into our round hole. Neither I nor you can do it. Certainly not Collier. Because Anne is unwitting, she is perfectly believable. Choreographing a scenario like that with anyone else wouldn't appear as natural." He turned to Dolan. "Where is she staying?"

"At the Ritz Carlton, near Potsdamer Platz."

"That's perfect. Take her to the Sony Center nearby. There's a good German restaurant there, forgot the name of it. But it is big and has an outside seating area, a beer garden that is open to the interior of the center. You'll be easily visible, both to me and our target. He won't feel confined or vulnerable. It's perfect for him and therefore, for me."

They all considered Welker's proposal. Dolan still didn't like it. Then Rhodes spoke. "OK team, I don't think there's a perfect answer. Not one that jumps right out at me. I still like option three but if I had to choose the one with the best risk-reward ratio, my gut says go with Howard's idea. I'll leave it up to you guys to figure out the logistics. Thomas is going to relieve me soon and I need sleep. If he finds anything on the Alpha Bright footage we missed in real time, you'll be the first to know. Oh, and he's going to send you the first batch of imagery for review. Michael, you're exempt as you have your own work to do. Stan and Howard, you'll be getting some every day so please don't get behind. You know how important it is."

Dolan remembered the Sony Center. He'd been there once, one summer long ago when he, Sharif, Claire and Anne, the 'Fab Four,' visited Berlin together. They only went to the center to watch a movie, but he remembered it. Anne would too.

"Sure thing Lauren. We absolutely *love* doing your analyst work for you," quipped Welker.

Bolden closed his eyes and shook his head. Rhodes feigned a stern look and said something about keeping it professional. He liked his team. They knew what they were doing and were good at it. They listened to and trusted each other. But involving Anne in this way seemed unethical. He was worried about her safety. He hoped they were right, that the assassin probably wasn't even here yet. That even if he were, he would essentially ignore her, wait for her to be out of the picture. *If anything ever happened to her...*

CHAPTER TWENTY-ONE

Sharif decided to check in on Ivan. It was clear to him now Ivan was slow-rolling production of the final batch of the virus. At first, he didn't even mind. He liked Ivan and felt bad he would probably be killed once he'd outlived his usefulness. But now that Sharif was to lead the main attack, he needed to make sure things went as planned. There could be nothing that stood in the way of him returning to Europe.

He considered shirking his duties altogether. It would be so easy to walk away from it all, to escape as soon as they got there. However, after much thought he decided he would go through with it. He concluded that though this may not be the path Allah had laid out for him, it was perhaps a first step *toward* that path.

His father had always considered him weak and was never afraid to tell him so. After so many years of being defiant and emotional about it, he came to realize his father was right. But no more. He would execute his part in the plan with precision and purpose. He would not fail. Only after it was complete would he consider his options. Returning to a third-world, fugitive existence in Africa or melting into the European background. Or there could very well be a third option; Allah may just illuminate a *new* path for him once he is done with the attack.

As he walked along the dimly lit underground hallway, he noted the explosive charges near the ceiling, placed at intervals over the main weight-bearing parts of the structure. His father had a plan for everything. Just as the attack in Europe began, Hakeem and his entourage would abandon the compound and head to one of the other two, *wherever they are*. There were motion detectors covering the first-floor doors and windows. As soon as anyone entered the building there would be a one-minute delay, and then the building would come down on top of them. One last 'screw you' to whoever came after them.

The guard was sitting on the floor in the hall next to the door, his back against the wall.

"You're not sleeping, are you?" Sharif said in a loud voice.

He jumped up quickly, instinctively putting his hand on his holstered handgun. "No sir! Everything is fine."

Sharif regarded the young man carefully. He had spoken to him before but didn't really know him. A local recruit. "It may seem like there is nothing going on, and you will be bored quite often, but there will come a time when you have to use that weapon," he pointed to the man's hip, "and when it happens you need to be ready."

He looked a little scared. Sharif wasn't sure if it was because of what he just told him, or if he was worried Sharif would punish him.

"Yes sir!" he replied, at attention.

Sharif opened the door and there was Ivan, dragging a step ladder to the corner. "What are you doing Ivan?"

He leaned the ladder against the wall and turned around. "Sir, one of the fluorescent lights was flickering. It was bothering me, so I fixed it." He looked nervous and began scratching at the edges of the electrocution collar around his neck.

"Ivan, I know you are slow-rolling production. I need you to finish the current batch, and I need you to do it now. I know *why* you've been stalling, and I assure you that your worry is unfounded. My father's promise will be kept, I will make sure of it. Once you are done here you will be released and sent home. And you will receive your full payment." He kept lying. Anything to get what he needed. "In fact, I will make sure you get a bonus to make up for your hardships. You've been here much longer than anticipated, and the only reason we've kept you a prisoner is because we were worried you would leave before finishing. But we are almost there, and this is something you should be looking forward to. I need you to finish, *now*."

Ivan stood still, staring at Sharif. Finally, he spoke. "Do I have your word?"

Sharif almost laughed but contained it. His word? He felt conflicted for a moment but shrugged it off. He and Ivan had a connection, but on this chessboard, Ivan was a pawn, and he was the king. Or perhaps it was better to say he was a rook, or a bishop. But Ivan was a pawn. "Yes, you have my word. My father listens to me on these things. It is in our best interest that we hold up our end of the bargain."

"But how is it in your best interest? I don't see how," Ivan questioned.

Sharif was getting irritated. But he had to maintain, at the least, an illusion of camaraderie. "Listen Ivan, this is obvious. If the AMA gains a reputation for not upholding our end of the bargain, no one will work with us. Our alliances will crumble, and our influence will wane. This is the opposite of what we are trying to do. Once you are finished, you will return home. OK?"

Ivan was not convinced. He kept scratching his neck absentmindedly. "OK," he conceded. "I will do my best."

"No!" Sharif yelled at him now, exasperated. "I don't want you to do your best. I want you to do it and to do it fast, OK? The only way we keep our end of the deal is if you keep yours. Do you understand?"

Ivan stopped scratching, looking defeated. He had no choice. "Yes sir, I will do it."

"Good." Sharif turned, got halfway out the door and stopped, then went back into the lab. He walked right up to Ivan. In a hushed tone he said "Ivan, I know what you were looking for. It doesn't work the way you think. It is not a proximity sensor; it is a transmitter. Once your collar gets out of range of the signal, that's when it shocks you. Disabling the transmitter is not going to help you escape. Instead, you would be electrocuted immediately. You must remove the collar."

Ivan looked stunned. "Why are you telling me this?" he whispered.

Sharif looked away and sighed. "Because what I told you before wasn't true. You won't be released. My father intends to kill you when you are done. But I like you Ivan, and I don't want you to be killed. I will be leaving once the last batch is finished. If you do your job well and do it quickly, I will give you the key to your collar before I go. It will be up to you to escape." Then he turned and walked out of the room.

Ivan stood there alone, confused that Sharif would suddenly be so kind. Perhaps it was due to their previous discussion of God. About the afterlife. About the consequences we must face for the choices we make. It was a bonding moment. Sharif wouldn't have offered him the key unless he felt strongly about setting him free, strong enough to undermine his own father. Maybe he was having second thoughts about the attacks. Or maybe Sharif suspected he knew he would never be released and was just playing a trick to get him to finish on time.

There was no way to know for sure, but it didn't matter. He had no other choice. He had to believe him. Because in doing so there was a chance, however small, that he might live through this after all.

CHAPTER TWENTY-TWO

The next two days went by without any sign of the assassin. Dolan walked the short distance to his office at the University and began his research, which at this stage consisted of phone call after phone call, email after email. Making his pitch to key pandemic and modeling experts, requesting volumes of data and numerous reports. He was relieved to find he was less linguistically challenged than anticipated—his German was getting better but was still lacking, however most highly educated Europeans spoke at least decent English, and many of them knew French. Möller popped into his office a couple of times to see how things were going.

At the end of each day he walked back. The routine he was establishing included periodic side trips into town for groceries and incidentals. Stops at the bakery nearby and the local café to enjoy a coffee. And all the while Welker was somewhere nearby, invisible to him yet within line of sight. Wherever he went Alpha Bright kept him in view most of the time, recording his movements and those of everyone around him. At one point Welker noted a Slavic-looking man sitting on a bench in the courtyard adjacent to Dolan's building at the university, drinking a coffee and not necessarily out of place. He could have been a professor, or just passing through. He moved on after a time.

Dolan had called Anne on Monday night and planned their dinner. It was a short call, as the team was listening in. He would meet her at the Lindenbräu restaurant in the Sony Center at seven p.m. on Wednesday. Though it was midweek, it would most likely be packed due to all the tourists in town for Oktoberfest. The assassin wouldn't try anything there, too many people and no good place to hide. No unmonitored route of escape. He told Rhodes he wasn't going to let everyone listen in on his conversation with Anne. Though they'd be watching he intended to use the situation to try to repair some of the fissures in their relationship. At least to the point where she wasn't upset or angry or worried about him. She understood and conceded. In any event, to leave the microphone on the entire time could fully drain the earpiece battery, and he needed it to remain functional for the trip back to Dahlem. Welker was OK with it, offering that Michael would be more relaxed with it off, a good thing.

On Tuesday evening Collier visited the team to discuss some of the finer points of the operation. He was there for about an hour and brought up something everyone had been thinking about, the possibility that for whatever reason the assassination could have been called off. Or that the contract might not yet be finalized. There was no reason to suspect either, but the team acknowledged that the evidence used as the basis for launching this mission had never been fully verified or corroborated. As such, the plan was to transition to Offenbach, after a time, without positive contact in Berlin. What they hadn't yet determined was what 'after a time' meant. A month? Two months? Three? It depended greatly on the type and value of any new intelligence gained on the suspected cell in that area. There were still too many variables in play. And when they went, would Dolan go with them? His cover kept him in Dahlem, at least until he could say his work with Atlantik Brücke was finished. Welker's cover was flexible—aside from a few meetings he could come and go from Berlin pretty much as he pleased. If after a month and with no evidence of their target, could they up and leave Dolan on his own? Probably not. They needed a contingency plan, one that would require resources they didn't currently have. As an alternative, Dolan suggested that he could focus on the Frankfurt area during his search for medical research companies and pandemic experts, something that could justify an extended detour from Berlin.

After Collier left, Welker asked him for a word and they left Bolden alone, through the adjoining doorway into Dolan's side of the duplex. Welker shut the door and they sat down in the living room.

"How are you holding up? So far so good?" he asked.

"I'm fine. Is this going to be one of my psychological checkpoints? To make sure I'm not going to wig out if things don't go as planned tomorrow night?"

He expected Welker to smile but he didn't. "Yes, that's exactly it. I wouldn't be as concerned if it were someone other than Anne. Using her this way is a bit of a monkey wrench but for the moment it's the best way to turn the nut. You two are emotionally invested in each other, for better or for worse. It can get in the way. And I want to be sure you realize that although the risk to her is low, there is still risk. That risk is mitigated greatly by the fact she'll be gone the next morning. If she weren't leaving, option B would have been off the table."

Interesting choice of words, 'for better or for worse.' He was probing at the depth of their relationship. To this point in his life, Anne was the only woman in the entire world he'd considered marrying. "I understand," replied Dolan. "I was against the idea at first. I still am to some degree but the more I thought about it, the more sense it made. I felt the risk was too high but as the plan came together, I became less concerned. I would be lying if I said I wasn't looking forward to seeing her. So, there's that."

Now he smiled. That unsolicited admission showed Dolan was opening up. "Good. Is there anything else, anything that's bothering you? Any concerns?"

Dolan hesitated. He wasn't sure if it was anything that would concern Welker, but he opted to tell him. "It may mean nothing. Our last night at Harvey Point I had a dream. In the dream I was part of a strike team to capture Sharif and his father. I ended up alone in the basement with Sharif and decided to shoot him rather than take him prisoner. But when I turned the body over and saw the face, it wasn't Sharif. Instead, it was Claire. I didn't know what to make of it at the time, and I still don't. I think if the opportunity arose on this mission, I would be strongly tempted to kill him, even if I were able to take him alive. I thought the significance could be that if I killed Sharif, maybe I'd be killing off a part of myself that is good." He sighed and shrugged his shoulders. "Perhaps the dream means I should distance myself from thinking about Sharif at all. He murdered Claire, and there's the possibility I'll never get over that. If I carry that around, it could have a negative effect on the mission, or myself. I don't think it really matters, though. Sharif is in Africa."

Welker had picked up a pen off the coffee table as Dolan spoke and was twirling it with his fingers, watching him intently. After a short moment of silence, he put it down and responded. "It's not an uncommon thing, to ask a psychologist about the meaning of a dream. It happens a lot. Truth be told, most of the time there is no real meaning. As humans we like to think there are metaphysical attributes to dreams, particularly those that cause us to be emotional after waking. We suspect there is some transcendental mystery associated with it, and if we were just somehow able to understand it, we'd be on some kind of path to enlightenment. The fact is, it's all just science. Biochemistry."

He shifted in his seat to get comfortable, as if he'd given this speech a hundred times before. "Our brain uses dreams to handle intense emotions, especially those that are negative. With an abundance of stress, one can enter a unique state during sleep called *epicenter tripping.* The brain will stimulate serotonin nerve receptors and at the same time, turn off the dorsal prefrontal cortex. This condition is called *emotional disinhibition* and results in emotions flooding the consciousness. It happens primarily during REM sleep, when we are dreaming. So, these strong emotions that are experienced during the day, or over multiple days, build up and can heavily influence what we dream about and how we feel and react *within the dream.* This can lead one to reenact events that led to the emotions in the first place. Or it can result in fantastical versions of those past events to play out in our heads, with symbolic elements in place of the actual trauma.

"What you might be worried about, I imagine, concerns the potential symbolism of Claire's death in your dream combined with the symbolism of you being the one who pulled the trigger. Does it concern me? Maybe. The fact you are still thinking about the dream days later, and because it is important enough for you to bring it up to me means, yes, it is significant somehow. But it may not be significant in the way you think it is."

Dolan watched him, waiting for more. *Wanting* more. He wanted Welker to tell him it was nothing, that the stress of these missions, of this type of work can manifest itself in ways like this, but that it was nothing to be concerned about. It was to be expected. That this was simply the way the subconscious dealt with it. Welker's explanation began but didn't finish that way. *He didn't finish*. Dolan knew there was something to it. It meant something. His previously recurring nightmare from years ago was indisputable evidence of that. He kept watching Welker, but that was it. He was done. It was just…*significant*.

CHAPTER TWENTY-THREE

Dolan arrived early so he could pick the table, one in the beer garden that was clearly visible from the huge, open interior of the Sony Center. Welker was in place somewhere out there, ready to go. They did a communications check and Alpha Bright was working well—there were numerous surveillance cameras within the common area with good resolution. The center housed Germany's Sony headquarters and was opened in 2000 on the historical site of the infamous Nazi *Volksgerichtshof,* or 'People's Court', established by Hitler in 1933 with jurisdiction over political offenses and operating outside constitutional law. Many German citizens were sentenced to death in what amounted to show trials by a kangaroo court for ambiguous violations such as 'treason against the Third Reich.'

The center was a sight to behold, grand yet minimalist, technology-focused but inviting with a multitude of stores, restaurants and spaces to shop, gather and dine under a soaring aluminum roof. It was one good example of how post-war Germany was not afraid of change; to the contrary, it exemplified how much they embraced it. Wherever in Berlin the war had reduced an urban area to rubble, it was common to find compelling, modern architecture, risen up between and above the undamaged, older buildings. It was eclectically beautiful, and impressive. There was no other city in the world quite like Berlin.

He texted her their table location. Within a few minutes Anne approached with a bright smile and outstretched arms. Dolan let himself get lost in the moment, briefly forgetting the gravity of the situation. *And the fact I am lying to her. Using her.* She sat down and they held each other's eyes for a moment.

"I'm sorry Anne."

She kept smiling but said nothing. As if she were thinking *'I'll need more context than that, Michael.'*

Dolan continued. "For abandoning you. For shutting you out. At the time I felt it was necessary, for me to heal. Not my physical injuries, but my head. My mind. As hard as I tried, I couldn't separate you from Sharif and Claire and everything that happened before. After the car accident in Berlin, things came rushing back. The pain of it. I was worried I would go down that same, terrible road I took after Claire's death and that scared me. To know that Sharif was somehow involved with what happened in Berlin, was part of this terrorist group with his father all along, it crushed me. I didn't see it. *I'm sorry.*"

She was watching him carefully. Empathetically, but carefully. "I forgive you Michael. But there is one thing that has been bothering me the past two years, and I can't come to terms with it." A waiter came to the table then; she ordered a beer and Dolan asked for sparkling water. "I can't help but think that you were somehow involved with that attack near the U.S. Embassy. You were there, in Berlin when it happened. You made a point of rebuilding your friendship with Sharif and spent so much time with him. It was understandable at the time but when I add everything up…and then I couldn't even see you until you were back in the States. In what world does that happen? The lady from your Embassy, I think I remember her name was Lauren, she was very nice but her explanation as to why I couldn't visit you before you left made no sense to me. Back then I thought perhaps it was because you were at fault in the car accident, and they needed to get you out of Germany quickly, that maybe someone else was hurt, I don't know. The next thing I know Sharif is all over the news, and this other guy Martin, and everything about the failed attack in Berlin. And then, when I finally came to visit you in D.C. you wouldn't talk to me about any of it. I need to understand."

She took a sip of her beer, then set it down and interlaced her fingers, setting her hands on the table. "So yes Michael, I forgive you. No matter what, I forgive you. But if you want to do it the right way, the apology I mean, you should give me some clarity on all this. So I can get some closure."

He expected this and was prepared. He, Welker and Bolden spent the better part of two hours brainstorming how to answer questions like these. "*Thank you, Anne.* You're right. I owe you that, at the very least. First, let me make it clear that I was not involved. Not directly, anyway. There is a lot that I was never told because I didn't have the clearance or a need to know. Remember, my job at the Five Eyes office in Paris was to coordinate exchanges of information between our countries. I was never involved in the why or the how, and I never knew what the intelligence would be used for. I was essentially an errand boy. And in any case, I had just gotten started.

"As for Sharif, my association with him was nothing more than what it appeared to be. We were old friends that had an opportunity to get back together, to grow that friendship and that is what we did. I never saw it coming, Anne. The coincidence is almost too much to believe, but that's all it was. I had no idea what Sharif was involved with; he gave me no indication. There was nothing out of the ordinary. It makes me think the attack couldn't have been a significant part of his life. I would have noticed, there would have been some evidence of it. He wasn't even in Berlin when the attack went down, he was in Marseille visiting his mother at the time. I even talked to him on the phone while he was there.

"That Sharif was involved shocked me just as much as it did you. Probably more. As for what I was doing in Berlin, it's as I said before. I was asked to be a courier for classified information that I was delivering to Paris from the German government. I found out afterwards it might have had something to do with the attack, information that might have even helped prevent it. And the car accident was just that, an accident. I think that this Rhodes lady or the U.S. government may have decided to get me out of the country the way they did because of the value of the intelligence I was delivering, that anyone tied to the whole affair needed to be protected. I didn't know what I was carrying, I was just ordered to get it there. I don't know. The other thing to consider was that I was badly hurt, my skull was fractured. It was unlikely the doctor would have let you visit, since you are not immediate family. Anyway, afterwards I was given a gag order. I was told by my government to say nothing at all until I was properly debriefed and signed a bunch of paperwork. That process took months, and I couldn't say anything to you about it until that whole process was completed. That's it, the whole story. Now you know as much as I do."

He reached across the table and took her hands in his, watching her reaction. She was normally easy to read, but not now.

She leaned toward him and whispered. "Let me see your arm."

He feigned confusion. "What do you mean?"

"Your right arm. You hurt your arm in the accident. It was wrapped in a bandage when I visited. I want to see it."

They covered this in their preparation as well, but she might not buy it. He pulled up his jacket sleeve, unbuttoned his cuff and rolled it up above the elbow, showing her the scar from the bullet exit wound on the inside of his forearm. She grabbed his wrist and turned his arm over, seeing the smaller scar on the opposite side.

"This is a bullet wound, Michael." She said it flatly, daring him to argue.

She released his arm, and he was granted a short reprieve as their waiter arrived to take their order. They both chose the Weiner schnitzel. He left and Dolan looked down at his scars, turning his arm over as if to analyze them and decide if what she said made sense. "I can see that. I don't have any experience with bullet wounds, but I can see why you think it looks that way. Anne, I don't remember how this occurred, honestly. It all happened so quickly, and I was found unconscious. I do remember the German doctor was curious about it as well, something had pierced my arm, a rod or sharp object of some sort. But there was no investigation into that, no need for it. The only thing that mattered at that point was to try to keep me alive. I was in critical condition."

She sat there, saying nothing as she evaluated his response. Clearly it wasn't enough for her. She still had her doubts. But that was OK, if they could put this discussion behind them.

He was about to change the subject, but she did it for him. "Père Aubertin passed away earlier this year. I thought you would want to know."

The suddenness of the change in topics caught him off guard. He was instantly and completely crestfallen. This kind, gentle and wise man had helped him. Not so much with his French, but with his mind. With the ability to manage life in a healthy manner. Normally. If it weren't for Aubertin, Dolan might have ended up in a much different place. The self-awareness he experienced while at the brink of death, that event may have never happened. He wondered now why, at about the same time he stopped talking to Anne, he'd also stopped emailing Aubertin. A pang of guilt hit him in the gut.

He reached out and took her hand again. "What happened?"

Her expression changed and she regarded him differently now, kindly. She was amazing that way, able to switch her attention instantly and genuinely to whatever was most important. "It was a heart attack. He was at Sacré Cœur when it happened. His funeral was there. It was beautiful—there were so many people."

"I'm glad he was well remembered. But when did you become familiar with him? And why?" She only knew of him from when Dolan was there in Paris, when Aubertin was his French tutor. He had told her about some of their deeper conversations, that they'd become friends.

"I sought him out. After you stopped speaking with me. It made sense really. He's a priest, and he knew you. I was looking for answers. Though he couldn't explain things to me in a way that gave me closure, he did help me. Just as he helped you. We became friends. I cried for days when he died."

Their food arrived and they ate. Dolan's earpiece remained silent. Just as suddenly as he had cut her off, Anne was right back in his life in a significant, emotional way. He hadn't dated at all since Anne left him. Suddenly he realized how strange that was. Two years. They talked about various things and eventually it came back to whether they should stay in touch with each other. They both wanted, *needed* to know. Whether there was a future. This meeting here in Berlin, this night, it couldn't be anything other than fate. What were the odds? And they were perfect for each other. Or maybe not perfect, but as perfect as life would ever offer. They had each other's phone numbers. Their email addresses were unchanged from before. Dolan would be in Berlin for nearly three months, and not far away. They both agreed to feel things out and try to get together again soon. In the meantime, they'd stay in touch.

Dolan played along with the promise to communicate but knew he might need to keep it in check. Until his mission was complete, to maintain any semblance of a relationship could put her in danger. He'd have to discuss it with the team and agree on the best approach. As he paid the check and they prepared to leave, he realized it would be unnatural not to walk her back to the Ritz Carlton. It wasn't far but escorting her to the hotel wasn't part of the plan. The team was expecting them to leave separately.

As they walked toward the restaurant exit, he stopped her. "Anne, can you wait here a minute? I'm going to use the restroom."

"Sure, I'll be right here."

Dolan wove his way through the throng of people to the men's room. There were too many people inside; he wouldn't be able to have a conversation. He decided to text Welker.

"I am going to walk her to the hotel. You OK with that?"

Three seconds went by, then a series of responses in quick succession.

"OK but be quick. Do not go inside room"

"I can't follow once you leave lobby, no cover"

"AB may not work"

"No target yet."

No target. That was a relief; there was no danger. Dolan put the phone back in his coat pocket and found his way back to her, seated on a bench just inside the entrance. She stood up as he approached.

"Mind if I walk you home?"

She took his hand in hers. "No, not at all. Let's go."

They walked casually, taking everything in. It was dark and the throng was beginning to thin out. Quaint wooden huts and stands set up outside the center were closing for the night, the last few still open offered beer and traditional Oktoberfest walkaround snacks. One merchant was selling Glühwein, a heated spice wine that would be found everywhere closer to Christmas.

They said little as they went, opting to enjoy each other's presence. Though their time together in Paris was short, and not necessarily physical or even romantic, it had been passionate and real. Their chemistry was undeniably strong. They each knew what was possible and they both wanted more. Two years ago, he couldn't jeopardize the EXCISE mission by becoming too close. Here they were again, at the edge of the same situation.

CHAPTER TWENTY-FOUR

They walked through the front doors of the Ritz and into the lavish main lobby. Dolan tugged her hand and they both stopped. He didn't want to appear presumptuous. "Should I walk you up to your room?"

Anne pulled him around and grabbed his other hand in hers. "It would be the chivalrous thing to do, don't you think?" Then she gave him a quick kiss on the lips and turned around, leading him to the elevators.

Without moving his head, Dolan scanned the lobby to see if he could spot Welker. No luck. *That guy is pretty good*, he thought. They took the elevator up to the third floor, exited and made their way down the hall. She unlocked the door and went just inside, then turned around. He leaned in and kissed her. A deep, meaningful kiss. She let go of the door and melted into his arms.

Their embrace was interrupted as a violent kick to the middle of Dolan's back slammed both of them against the partially closed door, into the room and onto the floor. The door smacked the inside wall and bounced back, caught by the left hand of the man who struck him. He stepped just inside the room and leveled a pistol with his right hand at Dolan, still holding the door. The barrel of the pistol looked oddly long with the attached silencer.

What happened next took less than a half second. Anne was dazed, on her hands and knees. Dolan's first instinct was to sweep at the man's legs with his right foot, knock him down before he could get the shot off. But he wasn't fast enough. As he began the maneuver the man squeezed off two rounds, the first impacting Dolan's back at the body armor plate just below his left scapula. The vest did what it was supposed to do but the force of the bullet slammed him back to the floor. He pulled the trigger again. At the same instant Dolan heard two additional, muffled shots as his arm was forced upwards, his weapon dropping to the floor. The bullet struck the ceiling and a few white crumbles of plaster fell to the carpet.

Welker, thank God, Dolan thought.

He was gasping in pain but managed to twist around. But it wasn't Welker. It was the Slavic man Welker had noted from before, the one drinking coffee outside his office building at the university. As Dolan reached for the dropped weapon the assassin fell forward on top of him. Dolan quickly pushed him off and from a seated position he took aim at the second man. Anne was still there on her hands and knees behind Dolan, incredulous and frightened.

"Anne, go sit on the couch," Dolan told her.

The black-haired Slav put his hands in the air, still holding the pistol. He was probably close to sixty years old and well-tanned, his visage that of a weathered warrior. A fine, whitish scar line led from his left ear to his Adam's apple. The door closed behind him.

"Anne, GO SIT ON THE COUCH!" he repeated, louder.

She heard him. "OK," she said meekly. She got up, stumbled to the couch and sat down. She put her hands in her lap.

"Drop the weapon!" ordered Dolan. The man calmly bent down and placed his pistol on the floor in front of Dolan and stood back up.

"Who are you?"

The man was way too calm. As if it was just another day at the office. "You have probably five minutes before this all gets out of hand," he replied. "Before we lose control of the situation. I suggest you listen and follow my directions." His English was good, but the Russian accent was unmistakable.

"Who are you, SVR?" asked Dolan.

"GRU, actually," he said. "But it doesn't matter, I am on your side. I just saved your life by the way, and I want to help, so please listen to me. Time is of the essence."

GRU. Why would Russian military intelligence be involved in any of this? Dolan looked over at Anne. "Are you OK?"

She nodded, still bewildered and clearly traumatized.

Dolan lowered the pistol but kept it ready. He wondered how long it would be before Welker called him on the earpiece. "OK, I'm listening. Talk."

"First, I must get the shower curtain. Otherwise the cleanup will take longer." He pointed to the dead assassin. Blood was beginning pool on the floor.

"Get it. Dolan motioned with the gun while bending down to pick up the Russian's weapon. He tucked it inside the beltline at his back, watching the Russian walk nimbly to the bathroom. He heard him rip the shower curtain down, then he was quickly back in the room laying it out on the floor beside the assassin with two towels spread out on top. *Smart...soak up the blood before it runs off onto the floor...* Then the Russian rolled him onto the shower curtain, checked his pockets and flipped the curtain edges up over the body. He placed a third towel over the stain on the carpet.

Anne was recovering from her initial shock. Tears were streaming down her face. "Michael, what is going on?" she cried.

"Anne, I need you to be calm for three minutes. I'll explain everything afterwards. We'll be fine." He wasn't sure, but his gut was telling him the Russian was being truthful with him.

"You can call me Yuri." He pointed to the dead man on the floor. "This man is Lugano Varayev. He's a Chechen assassin and a terrorist. One of our most wanted. We've been trying to catch him for almost twenty years. He killed many Russians. Diplomats, women, even children."

"Keep talking." Dolan felt Yuri was probably right, that they didn't have much time.

"But it is only good fortune I am able to take him out tonight; I did not come here for Varayev. I didn't even know he was here until I saw him following you. I came for you, Michael Dolan."

Dolan raised the barrel again. "What do you mean, for me?"

"It's OK, it's not like that. As I said I'm on your side. You see Mister Dolan, you and I have a common problem. We can help each other."

Dolan was getting irritated. "Get to the point. How do you think we can help each other?"

"The AMA. Four years ago, they took someone who is important to my country. Someone who knows things that we do not want anyone else to know about. Sensitive things. There was a CIA officer, his name was Collier. He's the station chief here now, correct? He was involved with your country's botched drone attack in Algeria. About two years ago I heard a recording of a phone call between him and another person, a woman. In that conversation it became clear to me the United States government may be close to identifying the whereabouts of Hakeem Lefebvre. If we knew where Lefebvre was, it followed we might be able to locate our missing compatriot. In that conversation they also named you, Michael. I came to Berlin quickly to see what information I could gather but I was too late, though I did find out you were successful in preventing the attack on your embassy. Nice job with that."

Dolan was shocked with how much the Russians knew about SCALPEL. Their cover was blown all this time and they never knew it. This revelation had serious ramifications and Dolan understood little about how far the damage probably went. But for Yuri to reveal all this was a serious breach in and of itself—he just gave away powerful and important intelligence. He could only have done so if he were instructed. That would only happen if there was something they needed very, very badly. This missing 'compatriot' had secrets the Russian government did not want revealed. Dolan glanced back at Anne. She had stopped sobbing and was now still, having recognized the precarious nature of the situation. Dolan turned back to Yuri.

He went on. "It was good fortune for both of us tonight that I was here. And again, I wasn't here for any reason other than to contact you. When you made it known you'd be in Berlin on Facebook, I knew something was up and came to town. I watched you for a couple days and saw you were running an operation. I made myself visible to your shadow the other day so that hopefully, when I approached you, it wouldn't be as much of a shock. But events unfolded a little faster, and a little differently than I anticipated."

"Get to the point. What do you want, and what are you offering."

Yuri smiled wryly. "You mean, in addition to saving your lives? He would have killed her too, you know." He crossed his arms. "First,

I will clean this up for you. The Russian embassy is three minutes from here, just down the road from your own. We have specialists there who can make this disappear very quickly, like it never happened. I will need both of you to leave the room for two hours. Next, I will give you everything we have on Varayev. This is an extraordinary thing, but the only reason this guy might be after you is because he was contracted to do it. And I'm willing to bet it's because you foiled the AMA's plans two years ago and they know it was you. I also think the reason one of your own guys is surveilling you is because you were trying to lure Varayev out and he is your spotter. It worked, but you weren't ready for it. In any event, information on Varayev might help you finally locate Lefebvre. In return, I ask that you tell me, as soon as you know, where Lefebvre is or where he would most likely be. Also, I need my weapon back. And I should take Varayev's as well. We can test it to see if it has been used for assassinations in Russia that remain unsolved." He held out both hands.

Suddenly Dolan's earpiece went active. "What's the holdup, are you on your way down?" asked Welker.

Yuri already knew about Welker and quite a bit about their operation. For the sake of expediency, Dolan decided to just answer him. "Everything's fine, I'll be down in two minutes." Then the earpiece went silent.

Anne looked at him quizzically while Yuri nodded in recognition, his hands still extended. Dolan gave Yuri's handgun back to him. "I'm going to hold on to Varayev's. And I can't promise you anything else. But we may have no other choice now that he's dead; we can't interrogate him. But you're right, it's a good thing you were here to intervene. You have my sincere thanks. I'll do what I can, I promise." Dolan then straddled Varayev's body and pulled back the plastic, took a picture of the dead man's face with his cell, then covered him again.

Yuri nodded. "Good. Take a photo of this as well—it's an email address." He reached into his jacket, fiddled for a second with his phone and held it out. Dolan complied. "I will have the information delivered to you tomorrow. It will be at a time and place of my choosing. When you have Lefebvre's coordinates, email them to me."

"Like I said, I will do what I can, no promises," Dolan responded.

Yuri acted as if it were a done deal. "I will only ever communicate with you, Michael. When I do, I may use someone else to deliver my message. But only to you. If anyone else tries to contact me I will know, and it will damage our working relationship. Just do as I ask, and we both get what we need. More lives will be saved."

Yuri then smiled at him, almost patronizingly. He'd probably been in the game now for thirty to forty years and Dolan felt like he could see right through him. Even with all their expensive toys, neither Welker nor anyone else on the team noticed Varayev—but Yuri did. And he wasn't even looking for him... It made Dolan wonder seriously if they were in over their heads.

Yuri set his pistol on the small table next to the couch and clapped his hands, as if to usher them along. "Now, you two take off so I can take care of this." He began to make a phone call and stopped, suddenly looking at Anne. "Dear, do you have any toothpaste?"

Anne looked at him, confused. "What?" she said.

"Toothpaste. Do you have any toothpaste?"

She shook her head in confusion. "Yes, I do, but why?"

"What kind is it; I mean is it white?"

"Yes, it's white. It's in the bathroom, on the vanity."

Yuri smiled at her. "Thank you, I will borrow a little, if that's OK." He looked up and pointed to the hole in the ceiling. "It's perfect for filling bullet holes. Once it dries, no one will ever notice."

Anne nodded dazedly as Dolan helped her up. As he did the pain in his back became unbearable in an instant and he almost fell over. *Lying to Anne about having cracked ribs has proven to be karmic*, he thought. He steadied himself and walked her around the dead Chechen to the door.

"Where is your purse?"

She looked at Dolan questioningly, then pointed to the nightstand. Dolan quickly went over and grabbed it. He used his jacket to unscrew the silencer, putting both inside and then ushered her out of the room. She gripped his arm tightly with both hands, leaning into him. He would have to take her with him, back to the duplex tonight. She needed to be debriefed and to sign a nondisclosure agreement. Dolan wondered how binding that would be since she wasn't an American citizen. After that he had no doubt they'd be up all night with Langley determining what to do about their compromised agents and mission. For a moment he felt somewhat consoled that he could now tell Anne at least part of the truth, but it was offset by the fact he'd nearly gotten her killed. The one person in the world he loved the most. If he was going to survive this mission, and if they were to succeed as a team, he needed to be much more aware. Prepared. Careful. They all did.

CHAPTER TWENTY-FIVE

Anne could catch attention in her distressed state; he needed to get her to Dahlem quickly, with as little drama as possible. And Dolan had blood on the front of his jacket. As they descended in the elevator, he took it off, folded and draped it over his unencumbered arm. The second he entered the lobby with Anne his earpiece erupted. Welker first, then Rhodes. Bolden piped in as well. He waited until they were done speaking over each other, then issued a quick demand while scanning the area for anyone who might be watching them.

"I have a situation. We are safe. Anne is returning with me, no other option. We will discuss it at the duplex. Dolan out." He hoped that would be the end of it until they got back, but no such luck.

"Negative," stated Welker flatly. "Leave her on a chair in the lobby, then move somewhere where you can talk. Bringing her to Dahlem is not possible."

Dolan kept walking with Anne toward the front doors. "There is no time, and we don't have a choice. She's coming," he said tersely. "Trust me. This is my last communication until we get back. Dolan out."

Bahnhof Potsdamer Platz was directly across the street. They walked out into the night and down into the large underground station. Before long they were seated and headed out. Anne still hadn't said anything. Dolan turned in his seat and looked back. He was surprised to see Welker seven or eight seats behind them, in the same car. *He wants to stay close. Makes sense.* They made eye contact; Welker acted as if he were any other stranger on the train, broke his gaze and looked down, probably at his phone, texting with the rest of the team. Dolan turned back and put his arm around Anne, pulling her in. She finally spoke.

"Michael, what was that? Are we going to the police? Why did this happen to us?"

With his palm he gently moved her head so he could look directly into her eyes. "Anne, I am so sorry about this. Thank God you were not hurt. I promise I will explain all of it as best I can when we get back to my apartment. I've already alerted the authorities and they will be there to discuss it with me and you. Everything will be alright."

That did little to satisfy her. But she said nothing more, resigned to waiting until they arrived. Thankfully, the team maintained radio silence the rest of the trip. Forty minutes later, Dolan inserted his key into the front door, and they went inside. He half expected Welker and Bolden to be waiting for them, with stern looks on their faces. Like parents after their teenager slinks in several hours after curfew. But they weren't. Instead he heard Bolden in the earpiece.

"Leave here on the couch. Tell her you're going to the bathroom, then come over here."

Dolan did as instructed, taking Anne's purse with him. After telling her he'd be right back he went down the hall and through the adjoining door. Bolden was there, standing with his arms folded across his chest looking worried. Welker was just coming in through the back door.

"What the fuck happened and why the fuck did you bring her here?" admonished Welker.

Dolan remained calm and stated matter-of-factly, "The assassin is dead in Anne's hotel room. I have reason to believe he's a Chechen named Lugano Varayev. My cover is blown, so is Collier's and I'm pretty sure yours is too," he pointed at Welker. "Let's go sit down. I have a lot to tell you."

The color drained from their faces simultaneously as they went to the back room and took seats in front of the surveillance screens. His earpiece was still active and Rhodes was still looped in, but she hadn't heard what he said. Bolden switched on the microphone on the table. Using a tissue from a box on the table, Dolan took the pistol and silencer out of Anne's purse and laid them down.

"Lauren, can you hear us?" asked Bolden, eyes growing wide as he watched Dolan produce the handgun.

"Yes. Now bring me up to speed. Michael."

Dolan looked up at Rhodes' image on the VTC screen. "I'll fill you all in, but we need to do this the right way. My assassin is dead in her hotel room, and she witnessed the killing. She was there for the whole thing. We were nearly killed ourselves. She's in shock and I don't know how she is going to react to all of this once she comes around. She cannot be left alone. Stan, you and I will go back to her, and I'll introduce you as someone who is here to help. I will tell her I must be questioned separately and will be back with her in a little while. You can ask her whatever you need to ask. When you are done, we can regroup and decide how to proceed but I'm telling you right now, she saw and heard *way* too much."

"Stan, just do it," Rhodes commanded. "Now tell me what happened." She was clearly frustrated.

Stan put in an earpiece so he could listen in on the team's conversation. Then they walked back through the door and over to Anne, still seated on the couch and hunched over with her head in her hands. Dolan set the purse down on the couch next to her.

"Anne, this is Stan. He's one of the authorities I told you about."

She looked up at them, her normally perfect, radiant hair was a mess with random strands pasted to her cheek as her tears had dried.

"He is going to ask you questions about what happened. I am going to be questioned also, but it must be done separately, OK? I need to leave you alone with him for a while. And don't worry about him, he's a nice guy, we know each other. I'll be back when I'm finished."

She watched him as he spoke, looked at Bolden, then back to Dolan. "OK, fine. But someone needs to answer my questions as well. Who is going to do that?"

She seemed to be in a better frame of mind now. "Stan can do that, and I'll be here afterwards to answer any others you might have. Everything is going to be fine." *Nothing is fine right now*, he thought.

"OK," she conceded.

Dolan returned and proceeded to explain everything that happened, every detail. He sent them the photo of Varayev and the email address Yuri had given him. They listened attentively as he recounted what happened in the hotel room. When he was done, Rhodes and Welker both sat there, absorbing it all and thinking. While Rhodes seemed to be weighing the positives and negatives before she responded, Welker just looked upset. No doubt, he was thinking he had failed. He failed to notice their target, Varayev. He failed to follow up on the Russian Yuri after noticing him in the university square. If he had, he may have recognized him tonight. Finally, he failed the mission. They did not capture the assassin. He was dead and could not be interrogated. They would get nothing from him that might help locate Lefebvre or the cell in Germany, or to prevent any future attacks. He wasn't used to failure. He'd probably enjoyed nothing but success over the course of his long career—he was that good. It was why he was chosen to be their point man in the field for this op.

Rhodes finally spoke. "Michael, you shouldn't have walked Anne to the hotel, and especially not up to her room when you knew we would lose visual contact. It wasn't part of the plan and it put you both at risk." With the teaching moment out of the way, she switched gears. "That said, who knows what would have happened if you hadn't, and if the intel Yuri gives us helps locate Lefebvre or the cell in Germany, we will be happy with the result. We can't change how it all went down but based on what we know now, I believe you handled it well. Or as well as anyone could have given the circumstances. Once Stan is done debriefing her, we'll ask her to sign an NDA.

"Michael, I expect you to shape Anne's thinking on this. She should never, ever consider breaking the terms of the agreement. I expect you to say nothing about your role with the Agency or this mission, of course. Howard, please weigh in if you disagree. She's heard too much for you to make up a story. Tell her the truth—that you work for the U.S. government on a contractual basis, whenever they have need of your services and expertise. It's an extension of the agreement you had with your job in Paris two years ago. In this case, you are in Berlin for your sabbatical and there happened to be an international security issue you were asked to help with that caught the attention of an adversary. That adversary is now removed from the picture, and everything is fine. End of story."

"Sounds good to me," said Welker. "Be ready to deflect a shit ton of additional questions after you feed that to her, though."

Rhodes continued. "Bringing her to the duplex was probably the right decision. She saw and heard everything; you needed to manage her and contain the damage. And there is serious damage here. But I do see a few positives to take away from this. One, the threat to your life is eliminated, Michael. I don't see that there is any immediate risk now to you moving forward. Two, we found out that Russia knows about SCALPEL. They may not know the scope of our mission, but at minimum they know we're after Lefebvre and the AMA. And they know a few of us are involved. In and of itself, this does not constitute a total compromise. It is probable the Russians have kept this information to themselves and wouldn't use it against us unless we demonstrated in some way that our objectives conflicted somehow with theirs. For now it appears we are aligned in that regard and it's something we can use. We'll have to do more analysis and it makes our way forward more complex—these are new, serious considerations to be factored in.

"Third, we may now have a potential ally in the larger mission. I am not saying we should trust this Yuri, and certainly not the GRU or the Russians in general. But if we have something they want, or they think we can get it for them, that's an advantage. And if everything is true, they took a big first step tonight with the transparency they demonstrated in what was revealed to Michael. Now, I'm just shooting from the hip with all this. After I talk to Dittrich he may call off the operation. I don't know. I'm going to suggest strongly against it, however, as we first need to see what the GRU is going to give us tomorrow. It might be useful; it might be nothing. If useful, it could make the untimely death of our target irrelevant. And I'll see what we can dig up on Yuri. Find out who he really is. Was Varayev wearing gloves?"

"No," replied Dolan. You might be able to get his prints off the gun; you will certainly find mine. But I didn't touch the silencer. That's your best bet."

"OK. Stan, take it to the embassy tomorrow so they can get started on it. Take Alpha Bright back too. If we're lucky we'll get more than just prints from the gun. As for our cover, we must assume they know who we all are. Take precautions accordingly. The facts at hand point to just Michael and Mike Collier being compromised. They already knew Mike was the Berlin Station Chief, apparently. That's not a revelation in and of itself. It's their business to know. Heck, we know who their Berlin Station Chief is too. To that point, his involvement has been tangential at best. I don't see it as a serious problem. Michael, you are clearly uncovered now, but you'd more or less need to be if you were going to collaborate with the GRU in the first place. He wants to deal only with you, so that's what we will do. Some kind of quid pro quo might end up proving advantageous in this situation. If what they provide helps lead us to Lefebvre or his son, we'll make sure the CLEARCUT team is prepped and ready to execute the endgame mission. Then we'll give Yuri the coordinates, afterwards. This is the way I will spin it to Dittrich.

"In the meantime, gene sequencing has been completed for the Marburg virus that was released in Amman. It is a novel strain. There was no vaccination or treatment in the first place, but this one is hardier than previous strains. It remains viable much longer outside the host. Scientists believe it may have been developed specifically to survive longer in water. The cases in LA, Syria and Egypt, those people all died. And new cases are popping up elsewhere. Not a lot, but enough to make everyone incredibly nervous. So far, it's still contained but we absolutely must prevent any future attacks and do everything we can to eradicate the virus. Any questions?"

"No," Dolan replied.

"None here," said Welker. "But we're not finished with Anne—we need to go back to her room and sweep it carefully. To make sure they removed the body and did a good job with the cleanup. If tonight's events in that room were to lead German authorities back to Moscow, oh well. But we don't want anything leading back to her, or to Michael."

"Do what you need to do," said Rhodes. "I need to collate and prep all of this for Dittrich. I'll get back to you as soon as I have directions from him. In the meantime, keep me apprised of anything new."

"Will do," said Welker.

They cut the power to the monitors and Dolan helped Welker put the Alpha Bright and Intelink laptops in the safe with Varayev's weapon. Then he used the custom tweezer tool to remove his earpiece, setting it in its case to recharge.

"Stan should be about done with her by now," said Dolan. "Listen, she needs to stay here tonight. I doubt she would go back to that room anyway. I wouldn't want her to. She is supposed to check out in the morning and head back to Paris, but she can just leave from here. When are you going to go sweep it?"

"Get the keycard from her, I'll take care of it tonight and bring back anything she left in the room," he replied.

"OK. Thanks Howard. By the way, how'd your BPM presentation go today?"

Welker looked surprised. "Oh, that went well actually. I was almost hoping it wouldn't. I don't need the money and to be honest, it's a distraction right now. But I don't have to follow up for a few weeks and I passed most of the work off to my team. Hey, listen." He grabbed Dolan's shoulder, stopping him. "I was pretty pissed at you. You went off script, again. To be honest, I was going to rip you a new one when I got back but now that I know what really happened, all I can say is, good job. I'm impressed with how you handled that situation. I failed you out there and you still managed to come out of it in good shape."

Dolan smiled. "I have a good teacher."

Welker held on to his shoulder and looked at him squarely. "Seriously. Keep it up and you may just make a living out of this."

"Thanks Howard," Dolan replied, nodded politely and went back to Anne. Stan explained briefly what they'd talked about and left to type up and print the NDA next door. Dolan took the room key back to Welker, then returned and sat down next to her.

"How are you feeling?"

The tears were gone, and her face had regained its color. She was like that, acutely in touch with her emotions but never willing to let them consume her. She looked at him tenderly with a broken smile. "I knew you were involved in something like this. I knew you were lying to me about it, but now I understand why. It's OK. But I have to say, in my whole life, that was the worst date I have ever had."

Dolan wrapped his arms around her immediately and held her tight, caught somewhere between relief and amazement at her strength and resilience. "Thank you, Anne," he whispered into her hair. "You can stay here tonight. You won't have to go back to the Ritz. I'm having a friend check you out of your room. They will bring your things here this evening. Make sure the room is clean, that everything is taken care of. I'll take you to the train station in the morning."

She held him for a moment, let go. "I want to make sure you're alright. Help me." Anne took off his jacket and unbuttoned his shirt.

She slipped it off him and pulled his tee-shirt up over his head, revealing the bulletproof vest underneath.

"Lean forward," she said, and he did. Anne inspected the vest where he'd been shot. She prodded the wide but relatively shallow hole. The bullet went maybe a third of the way in, morphing into a fat silver nugget as it penetrated. She helped him get the vest off and caressed his back, carefully tracing the dark blue and red concentric circles radiating outward from the point of impact with her index finger. She stopped, placing her hand on his shoulder. Dolan leaned back and winced in pain. She then took his right forearm in both hands, once again inspecting both sides. "And this? You can tell me the truth about this now."

He looked at her sheepishly. "Yes, you were right Anne, it was a bullet. It went straight through and hit me here," he pointed to the smaller scar on his right pectoral.

"Oh Michael, that's twice you were nearly killed!"

"I wasn't though, my arm saved my life. By the time it went through there was not much velocity left. It didn't even crack a rib." He began to put his shirt back on.

"Whatever it is, this is a seriously dangerous thing you're involved in. For me as well, I think you can agree. What if someone finds out about what happened in my hotel room Michael? What if they come to me, the police I mean?"

"They won't Anne. If you remember, the man who died, he was a hired killer. From Chechnya. He worked alone. No one will ever report him missing and no one will ever care. He was a great prize for the Russian who shot him. And the Russian needed very much to make sure there was no evidence left behind. As far as the world will know, it never happened. It was a non-event."

"A... non-event? These curiously worded falsehoods you have in English... Mon Dieu Michael, we almost died," she replied. "And not knowing if something like this might happen again, it is frightening, like nothing I've ever felt before. And I'm not yet in a mental state where I can fully and correctly process all of this. It's going to take some time."

With a twisted, sinking feeling Dolan realized he hadn't had time yet to process all of it fully himself. Though they'd come out of it alive, miraculously, in hindsight it had been a terrible idea to involve Anne.

"Anne, as long as you don't ever say anything about it, you'll be fine. In the very unlikely event anyone ever asks you about what happened there, say nothing at all, then contact me. OK?"

"OK."

They sat next to each other in silence for a few moments. Finally, she looked at him. "You need to figure some things out, get through whatever it is you are doing here and put yourself in a safe place. When all of that is done, then you owe me a date, *mon canard*. A very nice one. Actually no, I think you owe me much more than that. I'll get back to you on it."

He tossed the vest into the corner of the room and looked at her. Again, Dolan marveled at the understanding on display, and her composure given the circumstances. She really was one in a million. *One in a billion.* It was unbelievable to think he'd ever be as happy to owe anyone anything as he was just then, in that moment. As he thought about it the moment passed, suddenly replaced by a gruesome image of Claire's bloodied, cadaverous form in the basement of Lefebvre's hideout. The extreme juxtaposition of emotions that ensued caused him to shudder and he immediately pushed it away, still not knowing what it meant or why he continued to be haunted by it.

Perhaps these events were just the beginning, that his dream was a symbolic foreshadowing of what was yet to come. It wasn't Anne in the dream, but it was beginning to seem like it may as well have been.

CHAPTER TWENTY-SIX

Sharif looked around the old warehouse. It was in extreme disrepair. There was trash everywhere, and graffiti covered every wall, the floor, even the high windows that weren't already broken. There was no electricity. *Probably no running water*, he thought with a frown. A forty-foot wide, fetid-smelling puddle of water in the middle of the expansive, empty building indicated a leak in the roof. He hoped it would not rain while they were there.

A semi-truck with its trailer was parked at the far end of the warehouse, in the corner. Its auxiliary power unit whined, providing power to keep the contents refrigerated. Several petrol cans sat on the floor near the side of the truck. Roller conveyors had been set up between the middle and back of the trailer and three tables, the first and third of which held machines they would use to automate and accelerate their work. There were two large, aluminum cases resting on the middle table. Several large, brown boxes were stacked to the right side of the third table. With the five of them laboring nonstop, they would be able to process their cargo in relatively short order. According to Hakeem, it all had to be done within a twelve-hour window to ensure virulence would be maintained through transport, right up to the moment of delivery. They would need to work rapidly and efficiently to be able to do it.

He set his heavy backpack on the floor and looked at Taweel, handing him a pair of latex gloves. "Here, wear these. We cannot leave fingerprints anywhere. This is our home for the next few days. I know, it looks terrible but it's everything we need. When we are done, we will go back, but we may not be returning to the compound. My father will tell us our destination after our mission is complete. It's as simple as that."

Taweel nodded as he set his pack on the floor as well. He scanned the place as he put his gloves on. "Yes sir, this is all we need. We were lucky to find this warehouse. Where is Abdul? I want to meet him."

"Abdul is working right now. We will get to meet him sometime tonight. And when he gets here, don't freak out. He's not exactly what you would expect." Sharif began walking to the semi. "In the meantime, he left us some food, clothes and blankets. We can have a bite to eat, and then clean up a little in here. We should at least get all the trash away from the area where we will be working. We'll be sleeping in the truck."

As Sharif climbed up inside the cab and began going through their supplies, he felt oddly safe, and happy. To be sure, there was nothing about spending several days and nights in this dump that pleased him. In fact, this was quite a step down from the level of comfort he enjoyed in Algeria. But he made it back to Europe, and whatever Taweel and his father thought, he had no intention of returning. He would complete the mission, and then he would remain here, in hiding. Taweel and Abdul would be punished severely for allowing him to stay. But Sharif didn't care. He would cover all the bases—fulfil his destiny as Allah's right hand in the holy war against his people's enemy, and then he would literally become a new person. Start a new life. The fake ID and papers he used to get here would give him a start. He'd need a completely new identity at some point of course, but he had fifty thousand euros in cash, and he was smart. He would figure it out. He had to.

◆

"I agree, Lauren. We should press on for now." Dittrich sounded almost apathetic over the phone. He probably hadn't gotten any sleep. None of them had. And this was just one more in a long list of significant operational problems. Rhodes held her breath, hoping he had a plan.

He continued. "There is too much at stake. But as for the future of SCALPEL, it doesn't look good. It doesn't matter if the GRU or SVR keeps this to themselves or not, they are our number one adversary. At some point they will use the information they have against us. They've been following and collecting on our field officers and will continue to do so. They're collecting on our methods.

"Now, I received a briefing from the Russia desk, just before this call, and we know who Yuri is. We also have some information on Varayev—I'm sending it over to you. But Yuri...believe it or not that is his real name, his last name is Kuznetsov. He was in Spetsnatz for years and worked in the Kubinka-2 Special Purpose Center, then at some point moved over to the main intelligence directorate, the GRU. The Russia desk thinks the SVR won't get involved because their bioweapons programs fall mainly under military jurisdiction. They think the AMA captured one of their scientists who may have worked on weaponization of the Marburg Virus. We're coming up with a list of possible names. We also think that by telling us that they know who we are, and in turn by being transparent about Yuri's identity, they are demonstrating a legitimate willingness to work together. It is also highly likely that Yuri is on the way out, nearing retirement. This is his last hurrah. Outing himself is of little consequence."

Rhodes' head was spinning. How could Dittrich be so matter of fact about it? She was going to lose her job because she couldn't keep her people covered. Because they'd been compromised for God knows how many years, and she didn't even know it. There was nothing worse than that in this business. SCALPEL was done. *Lauren* was done.

But she still had a job to do. "Understood. That all aligns with what Thomas and I put together. Speaking of Thomas, he reconfigured Sentient to include all our Chechnya intel, everything we have on Varayev, and a few other related fields. He'll continue to update it as we get more, from what you send us and from whatever we get from the GRU. And the Berlin team is helping us analyze imagery. They have extra time to dedicate to that in the near term now that the primary mission is essentially over."

"I wouldn't say it's over," countered Dittrich. "It's just being recharacterized. The focus is now on the Offenbach area. I'd move Welker and Bolden down there now. Let Dolan continue with his work at the university for now but come up with a plan to move him down in the next week or so. And for God's sake, give me something useful from that multibillion-dollar AI piece of shit so I don't feel like we're wasting all our bandwidth on it. No pun intended."

She stifled a groan. He knew that she knew the secondary mission had always been Offenbach, and that she drew it up that way personally. "Yes sir. Offenbach is part of the plan of course. We are getting data back from Sentient, but until we can limit the scope of what we are looking for, it will continue to give us a broad range of outputs with low levels of confidence. To date, all we've done is widen the scope. But I expect that to change now. We have a lot of new data now that will help. On that note, we are trying to narrow down where and when the next attack might happen. The 'when' hasn't changed much; probability is still high another attack will occur sometime in the next six months. However, when we first began with Sentient it was focused almost exclusively on North Africa and the Middle East. As we feed it more information that has shifted towards West Europe. Israel remains in the top spot, but now Germany and Italy are numbers two and three of probable target countries. We are shifting our analysis efforts accordingly. One of our key mitigation initiatives is to notify all European community water supply authorities to shift from monochloramine, if they are currently using it for disinfection in their public supplies, to chlorine and to err on the higher side of concentration. Barring unforeseen circumstances, all of Europe should be on chlorine or some antiviral equivalent within days. Israel has already done it. Accomplishing the same in North Africa and the rest of the Middle East will take longer, but it's in motion."

"OK, good," said Dittrich. "The CLEARCUT team here is making sure the WHO, the CDC, and all other major U.S. and international health organizations receive all relevant information needed to prepare for an immediate and coordinated multinational response in the event of another attack. And the Agency is opening channels with select foreign government counterparts in parallel. In the meantime, we sent a cable out to all U.S. embassies, consulates, and DOD installations in North Africa, the Middle East, and Europe to be prepared for a possible biological attack. The governments of Algeria, Jordan, Israel and others are working closely with us to locate anyone associated with the AMA. Algeria is still being a pain in the ass but they're on board now.

"Listen, I know it is difficult to hear you might have to disband SCALPEL and find a new job in the Agency when we are done with this operation, but stay focused. The task at hand is to find Lefebvre, determine the AMA's plans and to stop them. Let's do it right. Play along with the GRU, but don't assume anything they say is the truth. We need to intercept the virus, capture and rendition or kill Lefebvre and erase the AMA from the face of the Earth."

CHAPTER TWENTY-SEVEN

It was a quiet ride to Berlin Hauptbahnhof, the capital city's main station. Anne seemed largely recovered. They held hands, saying nothing as the taxi moved through the rainy morning traffic. Welker retrieved her things and swept the room the night before. The Russians did a good job, he reported. He was hard pressed even to find where the bullet hole in the ceiling had been. Toothpaste…

Dolan walked with her to the train platform. He promised to visit her as soon as he could, and for at least a few days once his work at Freie Universität was complete. They agreed to abstain from communicating for a while, at least until things settled down. It was better to let the trail go cold in case local law enforcement got wind of any weird goings-on at the Ritz and began asking questions. Besides, Dolan needed to focus. It would be far too easy to overthink about her. To need her.

Then they waited. Anne was emotionally spent, and he was just thankful, relieved she'd forgiven him. When the time came, they held and kissed each other deeply, her lips lingering on his as the final boarding call was made. Anne then skipped playfully to the train and paused on the bottom step, giving him one last, longing look before turning up inside the passenger car. *Straight out of a movie*, he thought. *True love is a bizarre and powerful thing.* Even after lying dormant and untended for two years, after everything that happened yesterday, theirs had persisted. It overcame. Rather than impacting their relationship in a negative way, it was as if their fateful ordeal the night before had fed it. Made it stronger. The fear, the adrenalized shock of a shared near-death experience needed somewhere to go, some outlet, and it transmogrified into and strengthened their love. It was a testament to what his good friend and mentor Père Aubertin, *God rest his soul*, had taught him—that love trumps everything.

The platform emptied as he watched Anne's train disappear from the station. He turned to leave and accidentally bumped into someone, causing the man to drop his briefcase. The contents fell out around their feet.

"Entschuldigung," Dolan apologized. He bent down to help him gather his things, among which he noticed a thick white envelope with the name *Michael D.* scrawled across the front. He glanced at the man out of the corner of his eye. The Russian didn't look back or say anything as Dolan took the envelope and placed it in his jacket pocket.

"Vielen Dank," said the man curtly before walking away with his case and melting into the crowd.

The intel on Varayev.

Dolan took the U-Bahn to Dahlem-Dorf Station and went straight to the duplex. Bolden wasn't there, probably at the embassy. He sent the team a secure group text about the envelope. It was unsealed. He took out the sheaf of papers and unfolded them, then looked inside the envelope and held it up to the light on the ceiling, then did the same for each individual sheet. No evidence of a hidden bug or microchip. The report was in Russian. He was curious about what was it said but would have to leave it for the Russia desk to interpret and analyze. After placing it in the safe, he headed back up the street to the University. He was running late but it didn't matter; Möller expected him to be there, but not at a specific time each day.

The work Dolan needed to do today was time sensitive—he had to come up with a credible reason to move to Offenbach, temporarily. It was already Thursday and it needed to be coordinated for next week. There was one major university there, but it was a school for art and design. As close as Offenbach was to Frankfurt, however, he didn't have to look far for a good candidate. The Frankfurt University of Applied Sciences had a robust research and development department, but more promising was the Institute of Medical Virology at University Hospital Frankfurt. One of Europe's leading virologists worked there and was well published. After six phone calls and three emails he'd set up the introductory meetings he needed. It was enough to justify a detour of at least a couple weeks.

Dolan met with Möller to inform him of his trip and assured him he'd still make it for dinner that Saturday. He planned to leave on Sunday. They decided to use the opportunity to review his progress. It was too early in the game to show him very much, but Möller was convinced he was on the right track. There was an abundance of data that came out of the 2020 Coronavirus pandemic, and a year later scientists and statisticians were still trying to refine their conclusions. Much progress had been made, despite the fact China fudged their case and death numbers. They sowed disinformation from the start. The virus proved to be less fatal, but far more contagious than originally thought.

In May of 2020 Germany's federal intelligence service, the Bundesnachrichtendienst, or BND, leaked a report to the German press claiming China had urged the director of the World Health Organization to 'delay a global warning' about the COVID-19 pandemic and further, to hold back information about human-to-human transmission of the virus and that for whatever reasons, the WHO director complied. The BND estimated this resulted in a delay of over a month in the global effort to better understand, contain, and react to the spread. Added to that, the long incubation period of COVID-19 and large numbers of asymptomatic carriers resulted in many countries taking a less than optimal approach at mitigating the spread and impact of the disease. The vaccine had only become available in mass quantities very recently, and its effectiveness had yet to be fully studied. Then, there were the countries whose governments concluded that the virus shouldn't be contained at all. The elderly and infirm, and those with comorbidities were sheltered in place, away from the rest of the population, but beyond that the virus was essentially allowed to run its course. Children still went to school, businesses remained open. It appeared that the young, the healthy, and even healthy, older segments of the population were highly unlikely to die, or even to become overly sick from COVID-19. It was a gamble that paid off. Sweden was one of those countries, and their population reached herd immunity by the end of July 2020. Their case numbers and deaths due to the disease approached zero while much of the rest of the world continued large-scale efforts to stem the advance of higher case numbers.

Marburg Virus was altogether different. The death rate was remarkably high, and there were no asymptomatic carriers. If you got it, you were in for a rough ride and would most likely die. The symptoms manifested quickly. Added to that, it was a more virulent, more viable and novel form of Marburg, perhaps even genetically modified. It was scary as hell. Though it was easier to contain than something like COVID, it was the alarming death rate that catalyzed a serious global effort to stop it in its tracks. There was a growing stream of critical data on the Marburg outbreak flowing in. Just as COVID-19 had been a year earlier, it was the number one hot topic for anyone and everyone in the medical business, worldwide. Dolan had already set up channels to obtain all that information as it became available. He would be using it and a select few modeling scenarios from both outbreaks, two vastly different diseases, to do his research.

His second and equally important research topic was past and present international cooperation in the areas of pandemic prevention, containment, treatment and vaccine development. He would focus on all those that have had a measure of success, and those that looked promising. There were many in the latter category that formed in response to COVID-19. Then he would begin to think outside the box. For instance, how might NATO or the African Union play useful roles? The United Nations was the parent organization of the WHO, but that didn't mean they had nothing else to bring to the table. What about France's Doctors without Borders? And the Coalition for Epidemic Preparedness Innovations, the CEPI? What intrigued him most was the possibility of forming a network of these and other large, health-focused nongovernmental organizations, led by a small board of directors consisting of members of participating (and paying) countries. Given the WHO's fumbling response to COVID, they would have to take a backseat in the decision making but would still have a major role given their influence and resources. The World Bank had a long, successful track record providing financial and technical assistance to countries across the globe to improve health—they could coordinate funding.

For it to work, a majority of first-world countries would need to sign on, agree to invest as they were able, and to comply with board decisions, even if they had no direct representation. A small board was key. There shouldn't be too many cooks in the kitchen, and they must be empowered to make targeted, apolitical decisions quickly and for the benefit of the global majority. It was the basic framework for a seemingly good idea, at least on paper. But he needed a lot more data and expert help with the analysis of it before he could entertain any of it seriously.

When he was done for the day, he returned and Bolden was back from the embassy, receiving a briefing from Freeman on the Varayev intelligence. He looked up as Dolan entered the back room, waving him in.

Freeman was live on the screen. "Hi Michael. Nice work last night. I'm glad everyone is OK. How's your back?"

"Thanks Thomas, it got a little hairy, but it worked out," Dolan replied. "My back hurts, but nothing is broken. I'll be fine. So what did the GRU give us?"

Freeman nodded. "Well, it appears to be a summary of everything Russia has on Varayev that was typed up specifically for us. Or at least everything they have on him that they want us to know. His given name, birthplace, a lot of biographical data. A long list of confirmed, and even longer list of suspected crimes. Places and dates he has been spotted or suspected to have been. Associations. Even a partial medical history, his blood type. But the most useful thing I think is a list of his known and suspected aliases. It's something I can use to try to pinpoint electronic communications between him and the AMA. Cell calls, texts, emails, chat rooms. If I can do that, I might be lucky enough to get a fix on the cell in south Germany. Once we have that, it could then help lead us to Lefebvre's location, or the location of the virus and bioweapons, the future attack locations and dates, all of it."

Bolden was nodding. "Yep. It might not seem like this information is that useful, but it really could be. Sometimes it's the most obscure, seemingly irrelevant detail that proves most valuable to us."

Dolan agreed. A simple street address on a list of investment properties provided by the French Internal Revenue Service proved to be the key piece of information that led to his takedown of François Martin and the cell in Berlin. With it he was able to disrupt the AMA's plans to attack Paris and U.S. Embassy Berlin. And the address would have meant nothing to him had he not first noticed it scrawled somewhere else, on a sticky note hidden in Sharif's Paris apartment.

"OK, thanks. This could be helpful," replied Dolan. "I've made plans to travel to Offenbach on Sunday." He looked at Bolden. "When are you and Howard headed down, and where are you staying?"

"Howard left this morning. I've got some paperwork to close out at the embassy today, then I'll head down. We are staying at our safehouse in Frankfurt. If needed, we have access to our consulate there. Do you have a hotel yet?"

"Yes, I have reservations at a Marriott on the edge of town. It's out of the way, between Frankfurt and Offenbach actually. I have a meeting set up with a doctor at the Institute of Medical Virology, at the Frankfurt University Hospital."

"You know Michael," Freeman responded, "before this is over, some of the information you are gathering might actually prove useful to this mission."

"I doubt it," Dolan chuckled. "To be clear, choosing the topic of my research had little to do with the mission itself, except insofar as the Marburg outbreak has put a spotlight on it and nudged me in a certain direction. I decided on this general topic some time ago. So yes, there's a correlation but really, it's coincidence."

"You know," said Bolden, "you might want to swing by the embassy at some point, now that Varayev is out of the equation, and meet with the Economic Section. I can set it up for you if you like. They focus mostly on commercial and U.S. trade policy in Germany, but they have strong ties with a variety of NGOs, think tanks and other important businesses and institutions. They might be able to grease the rails for you and your research."

"That's a great idea, Stan. I appreciate it."

Freeman segued impatiently back to the mission. "OK guys, during the transition to Offenbach I need a little more of your bandwidth on helping to analyze the images Sentient is kicking out. I just sent a new batch with my comments. Stan, you and Howard can go through them over the weekend at the safehouse. Michael, if you don't mind, now that you're no longer being hunted, could you take a look and get back to me before you leave on Sunday?"

He had accomplished a lot in his first week, and since he already met with Möller yesterday, he could justify working from the duplex on Friday. "Sure Thomas, I'll have it done tomorrow."

"Great, thanks. I won't downplay the volume of it though, it's a lot of images. Between the four of us I hope we'll find something. Regardless, Lauren and I agree that things are beginning to come together. The question is, will it happen fast enough—will we get what we need in time. That's it from me. Anything else from Berlin?"

"No, I think that's it, thanks Thomas," replied Stan.

"Thanks Thomas," Dolan echoed.

They turned off the VTC and Dolan returned to his side of the duplex. He was going to order out tonight. Pizza in Germany wasn't particularly good by American standards, but there was one place he found in Dahlem that wasn't bad, and they delivered. Afterwards, he planned to settle in and get a head start on the Sentient imagery. He was never trained on how to analyze reconnaissance imagery, but he had been a consumer of quite a bit of it over the years. Preparing for combat flights in Afghanistan, in his Joint Staff work, and elsewhere. He understood the process. And when he put his mind to it, he never forgot what he saw. This gave him an incredible advantage; he possessed the ability to correlate small details with other information gleaned from an entirely different place and time. Hours or days, or even months before. And it didn't have to be imagery, it could be a single word on a document, or the sound of someone's voice in an audio file, anything. Anything at all.

CHAPTER TWENTY-EIGHT

"What am I looking at?" asked Dittrich. He twitched his nose as if his mustache were bothering him. Rhodes asked him to come to SCALPEL headquarters in Clarendon for the briefing, and he was not happy about having to make the trip from Langley. The irritation he exuded made her and Freeman uncomfortable as they sat on either side of him at the conference room table in The Pit.

Freeman knew Dittrich's demeanor would change because he had good news. With a red laser pointer, he circled an area on the large screen. "It's a compound in Syria, about twenty kilometers east of Daraa, near the Jordanian border. There isn't much else in the area. Three structures and a high block wall surrounding the property. This one is the main house; this other one is a storage building. This third one, we're not sure but we think there is a basement or underground room below it. The wall around the site was built only five years ago, much newer than the structures. And these…" Freeman put the red dot between two nondescript blobs next to the third building, "weren't there until recently. They appear to be piles of dirt. We think it was excavated out from below the third building."

"This site was kicked out by Sentient?" Dittrich asked.

"Yes. With a nineteen percent level of confidence that it is Lefebvre's hideout. We understand that conflicts with the general assumption Lefebvre is still in Algeria, but nineteen percent is much higher than anything else we've looked at so far. As you'll see on this slide," he clicked forward, "there has been recent activity on the property. Here you see three figures unloading a truck and bringing everything into the third building. And though we never were able to apprehend Saleh Attar and Fadi Hafif after they left Issam Yassefe in Amman, we were able to trace their route partway into Syria. They were heading in a direction that would have brought them here. We can't positively identify them as any of the three in this image, but conversely, there is nothing here that would rule out the possibility."

As Freeman spoke Dittrich's facial expression transitioned from one of annoyance to curiosity. "Yeah, the Syrian kid, Issam Yassefe is dead now, but we were able to get quite a bit from him before he croaked. What you are you telling me then, is that we might have been looking for Lefebvre in the wrong place, the wrong country this whole time? Every other bit of intelligence supports the theory he is still in Algeria."

"What I'm saying," responded Freeman, "is that it's a good possibility. We dug into the records of this property. It was owned for years by the family of a sheik who passed away fifteen years ago. His wife died three years later, and they had no children. The extended family sold the property to a Syrian real estate investment firm that pretty much exists only on paper. It remained unoccupied until the excavation activity began five years ago."

Dittrich's frown had returned. "It's pretty thin Thomas. The communications we intercepted about the contract hit on Dolan went between Germany and Algeria, not Syria. How do you explain that? Do you have anything else?"

Freeman had a flair for the dramatic whenever he was asked to give a briefing, and everyone was used to it by now. "Yes, there's more. As for the communications, they use a VPN at both ends and each time they send one out it bounces between several servers around the globe. Whoever set up their security did a magnificent job—it's difficult to conclude definitively that Algeria was the origin or final destination of the messages. Based on the information we have though, the probability of that is high. But it is also possible one of the servers they bounce off is in Algeria, and that's just where the trail dead-ended each time. Which is a good segue..." He advanced to the next slide displaying what looked like a purchase order in Arabic.

"As you know, Lefebvre is now the defacto leader of the AMA and is incredibly careful about communications and operational security. He stovepipes and compartments everything. No one person outside Lefebvre knows everything that is going on within the AMA. This is how he's been able to remain financially and operationally viable even as we and other nations have frozen his assets and shut down his businesses. We might be able to eliminate a portion of his organization, but there is little if anything that ties one piece of it to the next.

"They made one mistake with this property, though. A fiber optic line was installed four years ago, terminating at the building in question. It was incredibly expensive to do so because of how remote the property is. The payment was made from the same Swiss account François Martin used to purchase Hemoxin gas from Rolf Haussmann. It's the one piece of information that Haussmann gave us, thus far, that has proved to be valuable."

Dittrich's eyes went wide. "Holy shit."

"Yeah, holy shit," Rhodes cut in. "Sir, this is very good, actionable intelligence. For now, we only have the still imagery. I want to dedicate continuous satellite surveillance to the property as soon as possible. I recommend you loop in the DEVGRU team immediately and prepare them for the possibility they could be headed to Syria. The blueprint guys there at Langley and the setup team at Harvey Point should build a mockup of the property immediately. We are running out of time. Once we have eyes overhead, we can analyze any activity on the ground and improve the plan.

"Additionally, I did some brainstorming on this, I'm thinking outside the box here, but we could set up out of Mashabim Air Base in Israel, just West of Dimona. DEVGRU can insert from there, it's probably an hour max by helicopter from the north, through the Golan Heights. The flight would be quicker if we overfly Jordan but I'm not sure we want to involve them in this. And..." Rhodes paused, almost like a child preparing to ask for something her parents would not likely agree to, "we could move a couple of our MQ-9 Reapers there from Djibouti. European Command already has a joint Air Defense presence at Mashabim, it's been there since 2017. We can use the Reapers for additional reconnaissance and as part of a potential strike package. We'd need to coordinate quickly with EUCOM and the Israeli Defense Force."

This caught Dittrich by surprise. She was coloring outside the lines. "Wow, Lauren you've been doing your homework. That all sounds plausible, and I'll investigate it but there are many more moving pieces here than you may be aware of. You should be focused on completing the Germany assignment. Root out the cell in Germany, wherever it is, and get what you can out of it to help us intercept the virus and prevent further attacks." Dittrich stroked his moustache, thinking. "Good news is, I don't think Israel would give us any pushback. We'd have to work with Mossad on it, let me see what I can do. As for the satellite, I'll have it tasked by tonight and send you details on the feed, which we'll be monitoring from Langley as well. I'll go through all of this with the larger team in the next CLEARCUT standup meeting, tomorrow morning at six. You can join from here. Great work team, keep doing good things!"

Dittrich patted them both on the back as he got up to leave. He had come in with a scowl and was leaving with a smile. That was good. Rhodes hoped that if they could pull this off, and do so in spectacular fashion, she might just be able to save SCALPEL. They could regroup, form up under a new name with a modified but similar objective, just different enough to throw off the Russians. She would need to bring in new blood. Heck, she was operating undermanned already. She still needed to fill the position vacated when Stone was killed. They were such a small unit; it shouldn't be terribly difficult. Dolan and Welker were part-timers. She was confident neither she nor Freeman were compromised. Welker had been seen by the GRU, but that didn't mean they knew who he was. Dolan and Collier were really the only ones, and as Berlin Chief of Station Collier was more of an administrative resource than a field officer for SCALPEL. Though Rhodes knew he had great potential and would be an asset to the team, she realized she may have to cut Dolan out. It made her feel guilty, as if she were thinking of doing something immoral. But she had to consider the greater good. It was justifiable and would be easy. *To excise him.* Again.

CHAPTER TWENTY-NINE

One of the six burner phones in the bag of food and supplies began ringing, waking Sharif from his nap. He grabbed the bag, fumbling through them before finding the right one. He answered, "hello?"

"It's me. I'll be there in fifteen minutes."

Sharif pressed end, removed the battery and sim card, then placed everything back in the bag. He opened the passenger side door and got out. Taweel was sitting on the floor, near the edge of the big puddle.

"Taweel!" He yelled, bag in hand as he closed the door. "Abdul is almost here. We have work to do, get ready."

He jumped to his feet, excited to finally be doing something. As Sharif walked over, he became serious. "Sharif, when does the attack happen, how will it happen? Will we be safe? Will we be able to get away?"

Sharif looked at Taweel. Such a smart kid; a genius with networks and computers but when it came to the world, he knew pretty much nothing. He was intelligent but naïve, and that was a dangerous combination. Sharif would have to watch him closely. "It's a good plan, Taweel. Yes, we will be safe. In fact, we will prepare for the attack right here in this old warehouse. Once we are done with our work, Abdul will make the delivery, after which we can return to my father. It's a great plan, in fact. And it is simple, so there is little risk. This is what went wrong with our plan two years ago in Paris and Berlin—it was too complicated. Too many loose ends. Too many variables. You saw how well our attack in Amman worked. Because it was simple. The greatest risk to us in all of it is the virus itself. If we wear our protective gear, that risk is eliminated as well. Let's wait until Abdul is here so we can go through the whole plan together in detail."

"Sure Sharif," he replied.

A short time later they heard a vehicle approach outside. Sharif went to the huge sliding door on the front of the warehouse, undid the latch and began pulling it aside. A small BMW sedan with three men inside drove in slowly, coming to a stop a short distance behind the semi-trailer. Sharif and Taweel walked over to greet them.

"As-salaam 'alaykum! You must be Abdul. Welcome," Sharif said to the driver as he got out and closed the car door.

"Wa 'alaykum salaam," replied the young man. Abdul had somewhat curly, dark brown hair and striking blue eyes. He was of north German descent; his family was from Hamburg. Tall and strong, he was an imposing man.

Taweel remained silent and was clearly nervous. The other two men appeared to be of Middle Eastern descent, but this man named Abdul, he couldn't appear any more European if he tried. They were all wearing surgical gloves.

"Taweel, this is Abdul, Razan, and Milosh. Razan is from here and has been with the AMA for many years. He's Syrian. Milosh is originally from Kosovo. In 2012 he left Pristina to train and fight with ISIS in Syria and returned home three years later. He escaped to Germany after his government tried to put him in prison for his beliefs. Now he's with us. Abdul is originally from France and came to us four years ago. He converted to Islam and has proven himself during that time. We couldn't possibly have executed this plan without him." Sharif walked to Abdul and embraced him. "Welcome, my brothers." Razan and Milosh stood silently.

"Thank you and welcome to Germany. My English is not particularly good, I apologize," said Abdul humbly in a thick French accent. "In case you were wondering, Abdul is not my given name; it is a name I chose for myself. I am happy to meet you and work with you in the name of Allah. I will show you how we are going to do this, OK?"

Taweel was unconvinced. He knew there was much about the world he had yet to learn, but he was smart and had listened closely to his Imam's teachings over the years. He knew the Quran back to front. He hadn't simply read it, he *understood* it. Yes, there were many Americans and Europeans who have converted to Islam and some who had joined the AMA, but they were tolerated by the true Muslim fighters. Occasionally, one or two proved valuable as faces for their propaganda machine. But most of the time, they were simply put up with and were most certainly never centrally involved in operations. They were never assigned a critical or primary role.

These western converts were almost always mentally broken somehow. Something bad happened to them that they could not reconcile. It destroyed them to the extent that their own religion, the ideology or theology they were taught and grew up with was exposed as fallacious—an apocryphal framework of beliefs, shallow and useless. So they looked elsewhere, believing the only way to fix themselves, to make sense of their fractured lives was to completely and radically change *everything*. Taweel didn't consider them true believers; they were pretenders who were seeking something revelatory that would never come to them because their purposes for converting to Islam were tainted and selfish at the core. Sharif was right—Abdul was not what he expected. He worried that Sharif, who didn't understand Islam the way he did, would be blind to the dangers of trusting him. He would have to keep an eye on this one.

"Come over here, let me explain." Abdul smiled and motioned for them to follow as he walked to the three large tables. The whine of the truck's auxiliary power unit sounded louder than it should inside the large, cavernous building. As he approached the tables, he turned to face the group and pointed to the semi, speaking loudly to be heard over the noise of the APU.

"The truck is half full, from the middle to the front end of the trailer. We will offload from the middle," he pointed to the roller conveyors leading to the truck's set of side doors, "and move the cases along the conveyor to these tables, where we will open the bottles, put the virus inside, and then cap them again. As each case is finished, we will stack them on the floor until a pallet inside the truck is uncovered. We will then carry the empty pallet to the back of the truck and use the second conveyor to move the completed cases to the end of the trailer and rebuild the pallet. We will do this nonstop until we are done."

Sharif was nodding in approval. So far, everything his father had told him about the plan was proving to be true and going like clockwork. And Abdul appeared to be a good recruit; he knew what he was doing, and his English was not bad at all.

Abdul continued, taking position in front of the first table, on top of which was a strange-looking machine. "Razan speaks only German, and Milosh speaks Albanian with a little German, but they already know what's going on. I've gone through this with them multiple times. Their job will be to move the cases from the truck to these tables, and then from here back to the trailer and to rebuild the pallets. Taweel, you will uncap all the bottles using this machine. It's quite easy. You turn it on here," he pointed to a big green button, "position the case underneath, then use this lever to lower this top part onto the bottle caps. As soon as you have it aligned correctly you add pressure to the lever, and it will unscrew and remove all the caps at once. The caps are ejected into the big bin behind the table. Then you slide the case to the middle table."

He looked at Sharif now. "This is the most important part, when we put the virus in the bottles." He tapped on one of the cases. "You have the virus?"

Sharif nodded. "Yes, it's in my backpack."

"Good. We will attach the bottle containing the virus to a machine in this case that delivers one tiny, measured drop of the virus solution into each bottle. Once we have it set up you will see how it works but again, it is quite simple. You slide the case underneath, lower the multichannel system so each of the pipettes goes into a bottle, and then you press the button. Then you raise the pipettes and carefully slide the case to me. The machine on the third table is the same as on the first, except instead of uncapping the bottles it screws new caps on them. From the time that we open the virus bottle until the time we all leave this building we will need to wear masks, gloves and plastic suits. I have these in the trunk of my car. When we are finished there is a big metal drum outside where we will burn them, along with the pipettes and tubing from the middle table. Since it is not airborne, and if nothing is spilled, we will be fine. Afterwards, we will clean up and get ready to leave. I also have five AK-47s and three handguns with ammunition, should we need them."

Taweel had so many questions. He was becoming more uncomfortable by the minute. "Abdul, what are you going to do after all this? How will you cover your tracks? People at your work will notice the truck is missing, and what about this equipment? Everyone will know it was you who made the delivery. Eventually they will find this place. You will be the prime suspect."

Abdul looked at Sharif questioningly, then back to Taweel. Sharif didn't tell him. "I am well trusted by my company; I have been a good worker there. The truck would only appear as missing a few hours or so after my scheduled delivery is completed. No one is looking for it right now. I will take it back as soon as we are done. And these machines, they are old inventory. No one cares and no one will miss them. It will be days before the outbreak can be traced back to me. What will I do afterwards, Taweel? I will be going back with you and Sharif. There is nothing left for me here. There hasn't been, for a very long time. My destiny lies with the AMA."

Now Taweel was surprised. While on one hand it implied Abdul might in fact be fully committed to their cause, on the other it was a complication he hadn't foreseen. It was added risk. It meant the plan wasn't as good as Sharif made it out to be. The authorities would not be looking for him or Sharif, no one knew they were here. But there would be an immediate and global search for Abdul. Getting away was going to be much more difficult than he had expected.

Sharif saw the tension and decided to ease it by changing the subject. "Abdul, tell us about the scope of our attack. How many people will die? How many bottles of water?"

Abdul turned back to Sharif. "There are twelve pallets of water. Each pallet holds one hundred and twenty cases, each case has twenty-four bottles. That's thirty-four thousand, five hundred and sixty bottles. To answer to your question Sharif, this will be a glorious, terrible apocalypse beyond anything the world has ever known."

CHAPTER THIRTY

Dolan rubbed his temples. After a one-hour jog that morning he'd showered, eaten breakfast and retrieved the Intelink laptop from the safe. Then he set to work reviewing the imagery and analysis Freeman sent. He was seven hours into it and his mind was wandering. To his research. To Anne. To his troubling dream—the 'epicenter tripping' and 'emotional disinhibition' of his dorsal prefrontal cortex. Each time he quickly walled it off, conscious of the fact it was a practice that if left unchecked, could again lead him insidiously down a long, dark path. One that would be difficult to escape. There had to be a balance somewhere, but he had yet to find it.

Freeman had grouped the reconnaissance photos based on their calculated intelligence value: low, medium, and high. Each photo was accompanied by varying amounts of relevant data and in some cases, an analysis that Freeman had already made. He'd already gone through all the high value imagery. These included the shots of the compound in Syria, and he agreed with Freeman—there was something significant going on there. Its proximity to the attack in Amman, and the paper trail linking the property to Lefebvre made it easy to conclude this could be an AMA hideout and possibly their base of operations. The virus could very well have been prepared and weaponized there. These conclusions made it difficult for Dolan to fully concentrate on the much larger collection of photos that were of low value, the vast majority of which had little data and no analysis.

The minimum data present for each photo included its assigned intelligence value, coordinates, date and time the photo was taken, and which satellite took the photo. It also included the why. Why the Sentient AI assigned a specific value to the image. In most cases it was because the property or building was associated with Lefebvre, his extended family, or to his businesses and shell corporations. The intelligence value was listed as a number representing a level of confidence that it was Lefebvre's hideout. In most of these low value photos the level of confidence number correlated directly to the strength of that association. Intuitively, it was an important data point to acknowledge. Not because the correlation was correct; rather, because it struck him as a potential flaw in the algorithm Sentient was using, as Lefebvre would surely choose a hideout that was as disassociated from his past as possible. If he had written that algorithm, Dolan would have reversed the formula at a certain point so that it would begin to assign an increasing importance to imagery as the association weakened. With this in mind, he adopted a new method for reviewing each of them, spending more time on the images with the very lowest values.

It was beginning to grow dark in Dahlem as he finished, and he was dispirited that he found absolutely nothing worthwhile to communicate back to Freeman and Rhodes. As a special operations pilot he'd always felt bad for the intelligence officers and analysts—this was exactly the kind of work he'd always imagined they were stuck with doing day in and day out. Endlessly combing through mountains of information to find that one thing that might be useful to the mission.

It was akin to how he felt about the game of golf. It was an endeavor that required the player to put adrenaline on pause and forget about the final score, forget about par—the only thing that mattered was this one stroke. Until the next one. A lot of time and focused effort was required to reach the goal. With the smallest of errors, by overlooking the tiniest detail you could immediately find yourself in an exceedingly difficult place, off-track and further from the goal than when you started. To make matters worse, when it came to intelligence analysis you didn't even know up front where the stupid little hole was—you were lucky if you ever found it. He chuckled at that but couldn't shake the feeling of uselessness, so he decided to go back through the lower value images he reviewed prior to the point where he made the change in his approach. It was perhaps fifty images and wouldn't take too much additional time.

Halfway through, something caught his eye. It was an overhead image of a compound, not unlike the one in Syria. The property was in southern Algeria and owned by a Canadian natural gas corporation, purchased years ago from one of Lefebvre's companies after prospecting efforts had proven unsuccessful in the area. It had all the appearances of being deserted; apparently, the Toronto-based company had no immediate plans for the property. Something looked unnatural about the photo though, a red dot on the roof of one of the buildings. He zoomed in and held his breath. There was a person on the roof. He couldn't tell much about the person, but he recognized something. Something he'd seen before, in Paris a little over two years ago. The red dot wasn't just red, it was red and white. A red and white cap, and it had a certain pattern to it. It looked similar to the Francopharma baseball cap Sharif wore on occasion. It was one of those promotional items the company would just give away. He offered one to Dolan at one point but he declined, explaining that he couldn't possibly wear it, as it didn't have a Red Sox logo on it. The probability that anyone in Africa would wear a baseball cap was already slim. That it was a red and white cap being worn on a remote, abandoned compound previously owned by Lefebvre was nearly zero. It was Sharif, it had to be.

◆

It was six a.m. on Saturday and the team was meeting via encrypted VTC feed, including Collier and Dittrich. Welker and Bolden joined from the safehouse in Frankfurt. Dolan's theory about Sharif's cap was probably enough to generate a group discussion, but there was more. There had been another breakthrough with Sentient.

"Go ahead Thomas," said Rhodes.

"Thanks Lauren. As you may have heard, Michael found something in an image from one of the Black Sky satellites." He shared his screen to display the zoomed-in photo. "This was taken ten days ago. It is a compound in southern Algeria owned by Northleaf Gas, a Canadian firm. The property includes over forty thousand hectares of surrounding land. They purchased it from one of Lefebvre's subsidiaries four years ago and have done nothing with it since. They have plans to renovate the buildings two years from now and using newer technology, attempt to succeed where Lefebvre failed in finding oil or gas. In any event, you see the red dot there, it is clear this is a person standing on the roof. It is the only indication the place is not abandoned. Sentient assigned a very low intelligence value to the image in part because the property is now owned by a Western country. However, Lefebvre could have kept a presence there if he were aware that Northleaf was going to leave it vacant for a period.

"In and of itself, this is not enough to interest us. However the person on the roof is wearing a very distinctive hat, a red and white baseball cap." Freeman zoomed in on the red dot. "The resolution of the photo isn't good enough to make any kind of ID, the angle doesn't get his face anyway. But we were able to conclude with a high degree of confidence that the person is an adult male. I was in touch with Northleaf earlier today and they confirmed they currently have no one on site and haven't since the purchase. The cap is similar in color and appearance to that of a promotional Francopharma cap that Michael knew Sharif Lefebvre to wear. Francopharma is the French pharmaceutical company Sharif worked for in Paris."

"Team, this could be something and it could be nothing," interjected Dittrich. "It's almost discouraging to think the compound in Syria might be the wrong target, however there are several possible scenarios to consider. I highly doubt it, but the Lefebvres might be separated—Sharif could be in Algeria, and his father in Syria. Or they could both in Algeria, or both in Syria. Or they're in neither place, and this is just some random Algerian who just happens to be wearing a red baseball cap checking the place out. The bottom line is, we need the NRO to put eyes on this compound as well and hopefully we'll get some sort of confirmation, and soon. We need more than visible spectrum.

"Now, I'm not trying to put a damper on this news but ongoing activity at the compound in Syria has been confirmed, and we got a positive ID on Saleh Attar—he is there and there are others we have yet to identify. This greatly increases our confidence that Lefebvre could be at the Syria compound. The Seal Team is enroute to Mashabim Air Base in Israel as we speak, and we moved two Agency Reapers there from Djibouti yesterday. We will have a strike package ready to go by tomorrow. In Lauren's estimation, it is better to hit them now and find out whether Lefebvre and his son are there than to wait for confirmation from surveillance. That could take months. Even if they are not there, we have a good reason for going in now—we must obtain every bit of intelligence we can gather about where and when the next attack may take place. Attar's presence verifies it is an AMA hideout. Now listen, if Lefebvre isn't there the raid could tip him off and he could go even deeper into hiding. This could make things more difficult for us but according to Freeman's analysis, the potential benefit outweighs the risk involved."

Rhodes noted Dittrich mentioned her name as he laid out the Mashabim Air Base strike plan for Syria, the plan she came up with. It was a good sign, and she took heart in the fact he had concluded hers was the best way to proceed.

Freeman waited for Dittrich to finish, then took over. "That's the plan for now. Execute the strike on the compound in Syria and establish surveillance on the property in Algeria. The second development concerns the location of the AMA cell in South Germany. The intel on Varayev given to us by the GRU yielded some positive results. I ran his known and suspected aliases, along with other data through Sentient and came up with an IP address and location. Whoever was communicating with Varayev did so at an internet café in Offenbach. I sent you all an email with the details and needless to say, this is big. It gives us a date, a time, and a place that will hopefully lead us to one of the members of the cell."

"It also means we need all hands on deck in Offenbach," said Rhodes. "Michael, can you head down today, instead of tomorrow? And I know you would have told us but just checking, have you had any further contact with Yuri?"

"Sure. I have train tickets for tomorrow; I can try to change them. If not, I'll just rent a car. I'm invited to dinner at professor

Möller's place tonight, I'll have to cancel. And no, nothing from Yuri. I suspect there won't be, unless the GRU suspects we've located Lefebvre, or are hot on his trail and haven't told them yet."

"Good, thanks. Our game plan for Yuri remains the same—we wait until the last minute before telling him. Russia has a strong military and GRU presence in Syria. If we get confirmation Lefebvre is there, we don't want the Russians engaging before we do."

"Stan, I have some valuable demographic and chatter data from the BND for the Frankfurt area," Collier interjected. "Offenbach has a high concentration of newer-generation Muslim immigrants. While they are generally well-behaved, there are some definite pockets of concern. It will help."

"Thanks Mike. Asking you for that was on my to-do list."

Welker had been silent until now and was impatient to move the meeting along. "Guys, we are going to have to get whatever we can from that café. If they have interior video surveillance, we need access to the recordings. We need streetcam footage from outside if it exists. Would it help to bring the Alpha Bright laptop down? Michael would need to swing by the embassy and sign it out. Thomas, if we can identify the exact computer that was used to communicate with Varayev, would you be able to get anything useful off it?"

"I might. If you can determine which one was used, I can remote in but one of you would need to be there and logged into it at the time. After that it depends on whether they did anything else on the computer before or after sending the message to Varayev. If they did, like access their personal email or bank account, anything like that, then we have him. If not, and if there is no video of the guy it may yield very little. These café computers are typically set up to automatically delete all personal data and search history once a user logs off, but not to shred the data. In other words, the information is deleted but remains on the hard drive until it is overwritten. And even when overwritten, it is still possible to extract the original data, but that requires some serious forensics. We will see. I'm already looking into whether security and traffic camera video exists. As for Alpha Bright, we could definitely use it once we identify and locate one or more of the cell members, to track their movements. I'm surprised you didn't just bring it with you."

Collier replied. "I told Stan to bring it back to the embassy, that's on me. We only have one and it gets used a lot here. If you consider it a priority, I can release it again, but remember the protocols. If you keep it at the safehouse, someone must always remain with it, even when it's locked up. If you need to you can check it in temporarily at the consulate."

"Well, that settles it then," said Dittrich. "Michael, you will swing by the embassy and pick it up on your way out of Berlin and drop it off with Stan and Howard. The three of you will work with Thomas to get whatever you can from the internet café and hopefully identify the cell member who was there. At this point, we have no evidence the cell is active, other than the communications with Varayev. In other words, it may be difficult to identify other members and could take some time. If they are communicating or associating with each other, it's an indication they may be planning something. Let's get to it."

"Roger that," replied Dolan.

"Thank you, sir," said Rhodes. Freeman got up from his chair, muttered something about getting a bite to eat and left the room. Rhodes kept staring as her team began dropping off the monitor, wondering whether SCALPEL would be disbanded just as summarily once Operation CLEARCUT was concluded. There would be meetings; the Director would probably be involved and would make the final decision. The last time she was in this position SCALPEL had become a 'political liability.' While that situation was serious enough, being compromised was something altogether different and nearly impossible to repair. She couldn't let it get to her though; the work they were doing now could very well break everything open. SCALPEL might just save the day and in doing so, save itself. Her unit may look quite different on the other side, but it would be there. *I will make sure of it.* She pulled her eyes from the screen, noting the yellowing *Arm Pit* sign on the wall above. With defiant determination she stood up, strode over and took it down, wadding it into a tight ball and throwing it fifteen feet away into the wastebasket by the door. *Swish.*

CHAPTER THIRTY-ONE

Dolan packed a bag, checked the safe and equipment in the adjoining apartment and called the professor to cancel dinner. Möller was disappointed and suggested a compromise, to come by his place for coffee before he left the city. Dolan began to decline that as well—he was already delayed in having to swing by the embassy—but then he gave in. It was an awkward situation. From Möller's perspective, there was no good reason for Dolan to leave town on Saturday instead of Sunday, for a meeting that wouldn't happen until Monday.

The additional stop in his itinerary forced his hand; there was no good way to get to Möller's house using public transportation unless he took a taxi. He decided to rent a car in nearby Zehlendorf instead of taking the train to Frankfurt. It would save time and frankly, the thought of carrying Alpha Bright around in public made him uncomfortable. He would have a coffee with Möller, swing by the embassy to sign out the laptop, and drive directly to the safehouse in Frankfurt. He would make a slight detour along the way, though. Möller's house was in Potsdam. It would be easy to make one additional stop, a brief reconnoiter of the property François Martin used to plan and prepare for the gas attacks on the Paris Métro and U.S. Embassy Berlin. So much happened there. Happened to *him* there.

Little had changed along the rural road. He knew where to slow as he approached the property, tapping into the memory of his fateful drive along this road two years ago. Given his condition and that it was raining that night, Dolan was surprised he remembered anything at all. The long gravel driveway would be on the right, just past the next curve. He rounded the bend and there it was, the entryway now marked on either side by a round red reflector atop a silver metal stake. He drove a few meters beyond and pulled over, parking just off the pavement. Dolan left the engine running—this wouldn't take long. He had no agenda. As he walked up the drive the September morning chill made him wish he hadn't left his jacket in the car.

As he walked up the driveway the house came into view from under the awning of red and browning leaves above. At first glance he speculated the property had been abandoned; the yard appeared unmowed. The home was in good repair, however, perhaps even recently repainted. Though the grass was uncut the property was well-tended. As the sun overhead moved from behind a cloud the area became awash in warm, bright light and it was then he noticed the wildflowers. The new owners intentionally left the yard to thrive naturally. It was a sight out of place, out of time; arguably impossible for this late in the year, yet there it was. Considering the death and destruction associated with the place, one might call the look of it funereal. But it wasn't, it was the opposite—it was a celebration of life.

Movement in the tall grass to the right made him stop and think briefly of finding cover, but he remained still. *I have no reason to hide.* As he searched for the source a small blonde-haired girl suddenly appeared, as if by some perfectly orchestrated magic trick. She must have heard him approaching and popped up, looking straight at him.

She was perhaps four years old, clutching a multicolored bouquet in her right hand. If he had a camera with him, he would have taken a photo. The emotional juxtaposition of this exquisite moment with the memory of a place stigmatized by bloody violence and pain nearly brought him to tears. He smiled instinctively and she smiled back, her golden hair and bright blue eyes catching the sunlight.

For three or four seconds they stood there silently, smiling at each other. Then Dolan turned resolutely and walked back under the canopy of turning leaves towards the rental car, certain that whatever reason he may have had for stopping there, it no longer mattered. It had been borne of events long past and his new memory of this place would eclipse any from before.

◆

"I didn't say much about it on Thursday, but I was busy, and it was a sudden request. I've had some time to think on it now, and I'm surprised you are heading to Frankfurt after being here only a week. Therefore I wanted to make sure we spoke today. My belief is it would be beneficial for you to remain here at Freie Universität for a few more weeks at least, to build and strengthen the foundation for, and the direction of your research. You need to seek out and consider a wide range of subtopics, then prioritize and groom them. Only when that is done should you engage directly and deeply with the relevant experts, officials, and organizations. If you put the cart before the horse, well, you run the risk of latching onto a theory prematurely. You'll fall in love with that theory and spend the rest of your time here searching for the data that supports it. When you finish, the evidence you've gathered will no doubt end up reinforcing the conclusions and recommendations of your dissertation, but detrimentally, it will be in the absence of considerations for other, potentially more salient theories. You'll pigeonhole yourself. And remember that my name is associated with this project as well…" He sipped his coffee.

Dolan was caught off guard. It hadn't occurred to him that Möller would press him to visit this morning just to dissuade him from travelling. What he was saying made sense but leaving for Offenbach was unavoidable. He would have to convince him.

They sat in ornate black, wrought iron chairs drinking espresso on Möller's patio. Birds chirped in the trees surrounding his modest backyard as the temperature warmed. Dolan selected a butter cookie from the assortment between them on the matching table and took a bite, chewing thoughtfully.

"Would it allay your fears at all to say that I've considered this, and that a temporary change in venue will not affect my approach at all? The opportunity to meet with this renowned virologist at Frankfurt University Hospital might not come around a second time. Doctor Schröder is terribly busy, and between research projects. Though the timing may seem inopportune for you and me, that I contacted her and was able to gain an audience when I did was quite fortunate."

The old fighter pilot took a cookie and smiled. "I would not say I have any fear, only that even with the best of intentions, as humans we can get sidetracked at times and end up in a place we never intended. You may be familiar with the common German saying, Ordnung muss sein. There must be order. While we Germans tend to laugh when we hear it as it has become so cliché, it is nonetheless true. Our approach must be ordered from the start, and through and through if we are to do this the right way."

It was Dolan's turn to chuckle. "Yes, I am familiar with it. I like to think I live my life, more or less, according to that cliché. I do understand what you are saying, though, and if it makes sense, I think this will reconcile things. I will conduct and conclude my research opportunity with Doctor Schröder. I will document everything, put it aside and return to the university. We will then pick up where we left off. I will consider my engagement with her a valuable opportunity to collect raw data and results, nothing more. I won't let her influence the direction of my research, no matter how convincing she is. If what she shares with me turns out to support what we both agree is the best theory, then we will use it. If not, it may provide perspective for an alternate theory that can still be included in my dissertation as such."

There was a pause as Möller considered Dolan's statements. "You know, it is funny you use the word 'reconcile.' Reconciliation is an interesting thing. All that is required is accord. If you and I agree, then we have reconciliation. It does not guarantee that the agreement is sound. In fact, as the parties involved are less and less logical or intelligent, or more and more emotional, the act of reconciliation becomes less and less meaningful. The Catholic Church would say that reconciliation, or the sacrament of penance, is an accord with God where forgiveness is predicated on trust that one will be diligent in doing the right thing moving forward. That one will accept the will of God. On the face of it, this concept is illogical because men are flawed, and God is not—it's a bad deal for God. I would argue however that God's goal with reconciliation is quantity, not quality. If man is mostly good, it's a win. But neither you nor I are God, there is nothing to be forgiven here and I do not consider either of us to be unintelligent, illogical, or overly emotional. My point is that my goal for you is quality—not quantity. And your work cannot be 'mostly good.' That said, you can do as you please if it's not contrary to the goals we've established so far. To maintain some state of order in your approach our accord requires just two things—my trust and your diligence. I challenge you to do as we have laid it out. When you return, we will as you say, pick up where we left off."

Though it was strange to hear a fellow former military pilot speak this way, Möller was no ordinary pilot. It was why he was chosen to work with Parliament. He was intelligent, eloquent and diplomatic, but possessed the capacity as well to be forceful and compelling when the situation dictated. His was a laborious, philosophically laden concession, but also a warning. There was reason and purpose in what he said— Möller's time was valuable, and the research topic was globally relevant. He was invested in this and was ensuring Dolan was as well. Möller was also complimenting him in a way; he wouldn't have said all that, and in that context, if he did not believe Dolan possessed the capacity to create something that was useful for the world. Something that would have great impact, with the potential to save lives.

The road through the world of academia was littered with worthless research projects and hollow theses and dissertations, refuse created for no purpose other than to check a box, complete a degree, or to garner unwarranted attention and fame. Möller expected more from him than this, much more. And Dolan expected no less himself. The challenge for Dolan to deliver at that level went far beyond anything Möller could have suspected, however. The stress of it all was just beginning to creep in. He would stave it off for now. It was a satisfying irony that this stress was driven by other, higher priority tasks that, God willing, would also have great impact and save many, many lives.

CHAPTER THIRTY-TWO

By the time he reached the safehouse it was dark. Dolan signed Alpha Bright over to Bolden who handed it to the 'housekeeper.' Gertrude was a longtime CIA employee whose job it was to live there, manage the house, and maintain the appearance of an uninteresting and reclusive retiree. He and Bolden joined Welker in the electromagnetic and soundproofed basement for a briefing with Rhodes and Freeman. The strike at the compound in Syria was planned and prepped. DEVGRU was standing by and both MQ-9 Reapers were armed and ready to take off at a moment's notice, capable of providing real-time electro-optical and infrared video feeds. The Reapers could also be used to take out the buildings, vehicles, or personnel if necessary. There was tension in the air; all were hopeful that Lefebvre was onsite and would be captured. If Sharif were with him, even better. But Dolan's gut told him otherwise.

The screen on the wall flashed and Rhodes appeared, in The Pit with Freeman at her side. "Hello Team Berlin. Hey Michael, glad you could join us. We expected you earlier."

He kept them waiting. "I know, sorry. I had to make a detour to see Möller. He was concerned about me taking this trip. It was necessary to convince him otherwise."

"Fine. Let's get to it then. Seal Team Six will hit the Syria compound within days, perhaps as early as tomorrow. Goal one is to capture Lefebvre, his son Sharif, and if the Russian is there, to collect him as well. For anyone else at the site, the protocol is to capture if there is no resistance, kill if there is. Goal two is to collect all evidence and intelligence on the AMA's attack plans, location or locations of the virus, and anything else that has strategic or other value. If there is a lab…if this is the location where they weaponized the virus, or if the virus is there, they will photograph everything, obtain a sample if they can and burn the place down. DEVGRU has MOPP gear if they need it.

"Michael, Dittrich instructed me emphatically that we *do not notify* the GRU of this operation, and I agree. We don't know if Lefebvre is there and we do not want to compromise the strike in any way. If we had confirmation of his presence, we might take a different approach, but we don't so this is the way forward. If it turns out he is there, or if the Russian is there, we will let them know afterwards and proceed accordingly. Depending on who he is, we may even decide to keep him."

"Understood," Dolan nodded. He was immediately conflicted about her last statement. "Will we be able to watch the feed when it goes down?" Dolan had a bad feeling from the moment he walked into the safehouse, and it was getting worse by the moment. He wondered if he should compartmentalize it. There was no logical reason for it, other than all the unknowns. *People fear what they don't understand.* He understood that it was better to meet fear head-on. To learn about it, mitigate it and defeat it. Or, to constructively exploit it, if possible. But

Dolan was inextricably tied to too many of those unknowns. The most disconcerting of which, he was the only member of the team here whose cover had been verifiably compromised by the GRU. A misstep in their approach with Yuri could affect him directly.

"We'll have it here, but you will not. The audience is being approved at a very high level and it's a short list of names. Listen, we need to make this meeting short so Thomas and I can join Langley and the CLEARCUT team for another briefing. Thomas?"

Freeman scooted his chair forward and smiled. "Hi guys. I verified that the internet café in Offenbach has security cameras inside. They use a cloud service for recording storage that I was able to access, and the quality of the footage is quite good. Based on the timestamps on the messages sent to Varayev I was able to determine with a high degree of certainty there are only three computers that could have been used for the communication. We might have to check all three to find the right one. Bottom line, there were seven computers being used at the time in question. Two users were young women who appeared German, probably high school students. With two others the footage gave me a clear view of their computer screens and I was able to rule those out. The other three were being used by men, all looked to be in their late twenties or early thirties. Two who could be middle eastern and a third who looked European. I've emailed you the details and the plan, which we can execute tomorrow when they open at nine. We have two options. Tomorrow we can have the three of you go in individually, preferably one right after the other, each of you accessing one of the computers. Once we have the right one, I will scan it remotely. The second option is to have just one of you, preferably Stan or Howard, go in three separate times until we find the right one. There is more risk with the first option."

Welker was frowning. "Thomas, why the hell can't you just hack the café and be done with it? This seems like small potatoes to me."

Freeman reacted sheepishly. "Believe me, I tried. There are twenty-five computers, all of them on a virtual private network and they are using the very latest security and firewall technology. This is Germany, after all; they take protection of personal data and private information very seriously, much more so than here in the U.S. Added to that, even if I had the IP address for the exact computer that was used, I wouldn't be able tell you where it was physically in the room— the IP only tells me that it's somewhere in the vicinity. This is the reason we needed the video footage. If I could get by their network security, I would have to hack each of them sequentially until I found the right one, and I would still need someone to upload the forensic tools with a USB key. I can't install those from here. We must do it this way. It's all in the plan I emailed to you."

Rhodes smiled knowingly, having heard this sort of explanation from him more than once before, and Welker gave in with a grunt.

"Lastly," Freeman continued, "we now have a dedicated satellite over the compound in Southern Algeria. We've been monitoring for several hours with no physical activity; however, there is very faint, continuous electromagnetic emanation observed in one of the buildings. It is impossible at this point to tell what might be causing it. I did some checking and there is no active electricity service connected to the property. If the compound were in fact abandoned for all these years, an emission like this would be an unlikely occurrence. We'll continue to monitor and apprise you of any developments."

Thomas prefers Stan or Howard over me because I am burned. Dolan wondered how long they'd let him continue as part of the team. It could be that just as he'd gotten started with SCALPEL as an equal team player, he was now on the way out. 'The Michael Dolan Experiment, Phase Two' would be over soon. They seemed already to be discounting him, which could explain in part why they were focused almost entirely on Syria and very little on Algeria. It had been his input, his recommendation that they do the opposite.

"Are we working at all with the Algerian government on this?" asked Dolan. "I know there has been some ongoing coordination with them to locate Lefebvre and root out the AMA in general, but specific to the compound?"

The slightest hint of a frown appeared on Rhodes's face as Freeman slowly slid his chair back to its original position. "We are proceeding carefully," she said. "Algiers Station believes that if we involve them too early, they will want to take control and it would complicate things. Added to that, there is not much to go on at this point, certainly not enough to draw up a strike plan. If you want my opinion, and this is just between us, we should have had a second SPECOPS team prepped and ready to go all along. Not specifically for Algeria; a second team would be able to strike in parallel or consecutively wherever they are needed. The one team we do have is busy, as we know. Even if things go smoothly, we wouldn't be able to get the planning done and reposition them for a strike in Algeria or anywhere else for days, and we absolutely cannot go into Algeria without doing it bilaterally—if we did it would destroy any semblance of mutual trust we have gained thus far. If things do not go smoothly in Syria, if there are U.S. casualties, a strike in Algeria could be a week away or more. I pitched the second strike team idea to Dittrich, but it didn't go any further. The dominant theory among the analysts and CLEARCUT team leadership is that the Syria compound is ground zero, the site in Algeria is likely nothing, and to have a second team involved right now would splinter our resources and divert our focus unnecessarily."

His bad feeling—Dolan decided it was a fear generated from helplessness. It was foreign to him, something he couldn't remember having felt this strongly before. There were very few times in his life when he hadn't been the one in control. And those few times—he had compartmentalized that fear and it had worked. But those were simpler situations. This one was overly complex and multifaceted. A matrix of difficult and interconnected issues, some of which were unquantifiable. It was a challenge to process fully.

Unfortunately, he was still the new guy, and he was already damaged goods. Whatever he thought, whatever he said would be heard but not necessarily listened to. *I am being marginalized.* He wasn't a hundred percent sure the person wearing the red cap on the roof was Sharif, but who else could it be? It was not the only factor to consider, either. The property was formerly owned by a company within Lefebvre's conglomeration of corporations and subsidiaries. That Lefebvre no longer owned it, and that it was known to be purposefully vacant for the time being was precisely what made it a perfect candidate for Lefebvre's hideout. *And there is an electromagnetic signature emanating from one of the buildings.*

He hoped they were right, that his fear was unfounded—that Lefebvre and Sharif would be located and captured in Syria, that the compound in Algeria was in fact abandoned. That while it was likely Hakeem would not break easily, Sharif would probably give in right away and reveal their entire plan. The AMA could then be rooted out and would very quickly cease to exist. Any future attacks would be snuffed, and any remaining incidence of the virus would be located and destroyed. A fairytale ending. But this was no fairytale. As it stood, to be hopeful in this situation seemed almost irresponsible. It was hope itself, and not his fear, that was unfounded.

CHAPTER THIRTY-THREE

After reviewing the plan, the team decided on option one. Freeman seemed indifferent about the choice, and Rhodes agreed with Welker that the risk involved was probably lower than Freeman originally estimated. Though the GRU was aware of Dolan they appeared to be, for the moment, working with SCALPEL. Option two would take longer and delay their operation unnecessarily.

Bolden would enter the café first, a few minutes after they opened. Then Welker would go in, followed by Dolan. There was enough time planned in-between to verify if the workstation was the correct one. If things went their way, Dolan wouldn't even need to take part. They spent some time that morning with the housekeeper altering their appearances; a wig for Welker, glasses for Bolden, a fake mustache for Dolan. He'd never grown a mustache before, not even on his combat deployments. As he looked himself over in the mirror it looked strange to him. Strange, but natural. A little older, but normal. *That's the point of course.* It was one of Gertrude's many talents and she had an entire back room set up and stocked for just this purpose. Each of them took turns receiving a thorough course of cosmetic treatment; makeup to change skin tone, to add a freckle here and a scar there. She chose clothing for them that had been carefully altered to slightly manipulate perception of their body types. All in all, it was just enough to prevent anyone from recognizing them. If the GRU were truly intent on surveilling them, it wouldn't necessarily work but being recognized today wasn't the only reason for taking the extra precaution—it would likely prevent them from being identified later by someone else who just happened to be there that morning. Added to that, everything they did or said today would be recorded inside the café, recordings that could be reviewed later.

Dolan waited at a bookstore across the street while Welker sat in his beautiful, black Mercedes G63 SUV. He shook his head again, wondering how Welker could justify renting a 150,000-euro vehicle on a government expense account. Welker had a litany of reasons, some of which made sense, others, not so much. They all had earpieces and identical USB keys with the essential forensic tools. Freeman was looped in to tell them what to do. No one was armed, though there were weapons hidden in the Mercedes should they need them. Dolan was secretly hoping both Stan and Howard would strike out, that they'd have to use him. *Selfish, I know.* But it was his nature to be the one to act, to be the one who made a difference. If there was one thing about being a spy that Dolan didn't particularly like, it was all the dead time in-between the adrenaline. It was akin to grading reports back at BU. There was so much preparation, analysis, and culling through the chaff before he got to that one gem of a paper.

He broke from his train of thought and realized he was standing there in the quaint bookstore pretending to be interested in a tome on *Motherhood and Maternity*. He hadn't bothered to translate the German title as he wasn't truly reading it and was thinking of other things. He'd picked up a random book. Dolan needed to be more careful. Little things like that would be caught by a trained adversary.

He placed it back on its shelf and moved to a different section. He chose a book about German military warplanes and found an empty chair.

He listened as Bolden went in, made a decent excuse about which computer he preferred when the attendant assigned him one randomly, and went to work. Bolden and Welker would check the two that had been used in the security footage by the middle eastern looking men. If those didn't pan out, Dolan would check the one that had been used by the European. If none of the three gave them what they came for, it was back to the drawing board. It would mean that Freeman's analysis had been wrong.

It didn't take long for Freeman to determine Bolden's was the wrong computer. After he checked out, Welker went in and also asked for a specific workstation. He did so in such a casual and natural way though, the attendant probably thought nothing of it, which was remarkable considering two consecutive patrons on a slow Sunday morning just made strange, similar requests. Both his and Bolden's German were impeccable, and they'd been in the game for years. It didn't bother them at all. Dolan's continued to improve, though he was still nowhere close to being comfortable with the language in casual conversation. He wouldn't be able to act as naturally as Bolden and Welker had making a third consecutive, unnatural request. It would be Dolan's face that stood out in the attendant's mind. If anyone were to be remembered, it would be him. *Good thing for the mustache…*

He flipped through the pages of his Flugzeugbuch, pausing at each photo to appreciate the beauty and historical relevance of each airframe. No one would ever catch him pretending to be interested in aviation. Even as he enjoyed the book however, he continued to focus his attention on what Freeman was telling Welker, and it was looking as if Dolan would need to go in after all. Neither of the first two was the computer the terrorist had used.

Freeman told him to get ready to enter the café. Dolan stood up to put the book back where he found it but then stopped, deciding instead to buy it. It was a good book. He paid the young lady at the counter who placed it inside a brown paper bag. He walked across the street and went inside, ignoring Welker and Bolden in the SUV, parked just down the way. They would drive around a bit while he was inside.

"Guten Tag," he said to the attendant. As he began to speak, he saw a woman in the corner of his eye taking a seat at the workstation he needed. The plan just changed. He couldn't walk out now; he'd have to wait and come up with a reason to switch computers once she left. The man assigned him a station by himself across the room. He walked over, logged in and began surfing the web.

"There is a woman at the workstation we need. I am at the wrong one. Stand by," whispered Dolan.

"Of course," replied Welker sarcastically. "Three fucking people in the place and one of them chooses our computer. Dolan, you can…"

"Silence please," Freeman cut in. It was strange hearing him interrupt a seasoned field officer; he was usually the quiet and reserved one. That is, until the op required his IT expertise. Then he was in charge.

"There are a couple of ways to do this," Freeman continued. "We can wait until she leaves, and you can figure out a way to switch computers. Or one of you can go back in later."

Welker began to speak again, this time Dolan cut him off.

"Guys, relax. I will wait. Let's not change the plan. Stand by." Dolan was on a Bundesliga website, doing his best to appear interested in German soccer.

About forty-five minutes later the lady got up from her chair. The café was beginning to fill up now; Dolan had a small window of opportunity. As she walked over to check out, he reached behind his computer and disconnected the ethernet cable. Using his pinky finger, he reached inside the port, feeling for the wire contacts. With his fingernail he bent the outermost wire across the others and reinserted the cable. Then he refreshed the screen. When the "no internet connection" message popped up he rose from his chair and notified the man behind the desk. He asked if he could take the one the lady had just left. It seemed to be working fine for her, after all.

With an exaggerated look of concern, the attendant walked with Dolan back to his computer and fiddled with it for about a minute, then rebooted it, trying to get it back online. When that didn't work, he gave up and told Dolan to go ahead and take the other workstation. There was a patron on either side of him, and though there were small partitions in between each workstation, whatever he said could be heard. If they really wanted to, they'd be able to lean back in their chair a bit and see his screen. He sat down and muttered, as if to himself, "boy this place is packed." He wanted Freeman to know they needed to be careful.

"Understood," said Freeman. You won't have to say anything. Clear your throat to say yes and exhale, like you are sighing, to say no."

Dolan cleared his throat subtly to let him know he understood.

"Alright, all you have to do is insert the USB drive. A program will launch automatically in the background that will bypass security and about ten seconds later I should see your computer. For now, just surf the web or something to look busy.

Dolan fished the key from his pocket and inserted it, then navigated back to his Bundesliga site.

"OK, I'm in," Freeman announced.

Several minutes passed and Dolan began to worry they'd reached a dead end. Freeman kept his microphone live. The team could hear his rapid keystrokes and Freeman muttering under his breath as he worked his nerdy magic. He swore a few times and each time Dolan's worry was heightened.

"JACKPOT!" Dolan jumped a little in his seat at Freeman's exclamation. Neither of his internet café neighbors seemed to notice.

"Are we good?" Welker asked.

"Oh yeah, we're good," replied Freeman. "Michael, you can remove the key and leave. We have everything we need."

Dolan deleted his search history, closed the browser and logged out. He pulled the USB drive and put it back in his pocket. After checking out he left the café and walked down the street two blocks, Flugzeugbuch in hand, then down a side street where Bolden and Welker were waiting for him. After he got in Stan started the SUV and drove off. There was little to discuss on the ride back to the safehouse; Freeman would brief them on the details of what he'd found via secure VTC.

The face of the enemy was becoming clearer, and changing—it wasn't just Sharif and his father anymore. This made him feel different about the whole operation, that it was marginally less personal for him. On one hand, that was unfortunate. It signified that Dolan's hatred, the driving force that fueled his need for revenge was less important. His hate of Sharif for murdering Claire. For Hakeem's attempt to assassinate him and nearly killing Anne in the process. Sharif's betrayal of their friendship in becoming a terrorist; the betrayal of his country, of humanity itself. Incomprehensibly, these things were somehow less evil.

On the other hand, hate was an imprecise motivator. Powerful emotions often lead to unpredictable and disadvantageous outcomes, particularly when the subject of one's hatred is inaccessible. Dolan knew this. There would be no opportunity for a total reprisal without the ability to confront Sharif directly, and he was on a different continent. At this point, the prospect was highly unlikely. Even if they managed to capture and rendition him back to the States, it wouldn't be the same. It would be tightly controlled; he wouldn't have the option to exact his revenge on his terms.

He had already decided not to continue boxing his hate away, not completely. Instead, he would access it and use it carefully. He would study it, learn from it and let certain, relevant pieces of it escape when the moments were right. Dolan planned to exploit it without allowing it to subjugate him. He would direct his hatred and control it, use it within the scope and context of his mission to exact as much of a perfect revenge as he was able. To do anything less would be his own, unforgivable betrayal.

CHAPTER THIRTY-FOUR

"You did a good job," Welker acknowledged to Dolan. They were waiting in the living room at the safehouse while Bolden prepped for their debrief in the basement.

"Thanks," said Dolan. "It wasn't much, to be honest. Not compared to what went down at the Ritz. Or in Potsdam, for that matter."

"True. But again, you demonstrated the ability to think on your feet without raising suspicion. At the Ritz, and in Potsdam you were reacting instinctually. There was an element of luck of course at the Ritz with Yuri interceding but that's immaterial. The point is, during these relatively mundane, smaller ops you have time to think; you don't necessarily feel threatened. We feel safe because, well, because there is no imminent danger. That's when we get relaxed. When we are too relaxed, we lose sight of the big picture and can make bad decisions, or less effective ones. You kept your cool and waited. You figured it out. Not necessarily an easy thing given you were the third of us to go in. Anyway, as I said before you seem to have a knack for this work. I'm glad you're on the team."

Dolan took the compliment silently.

"Michael, on another note, are you worried at all about this situation with the GRU? About how that might affect your future with SCALPEL?"

Dolan perked at that. "Is it that obvious? Yes, I'm concerned. I feel like there won't be a good opportunity to discuss it until this mission is over, and when all is said and done, I'm burned. It's not like all this was for nothing. I'm honored to be part of what we are doing, and I want to make sure Sharif and Hakeem get what's coming to them. But when and if that happens and we are done, I don't know. I guess I'll go back to Boston and pick up my life where I left off."

"Good. You're prepared for the possibility that this was a one-and-done. Or I guess in your situation you could say, two-and-done. But there was also a chance it might not pan out that way. I don't want to get your hopes up, but your demonstrated effectiveness as a field officer has not been lost on me or Lauren, even Dittrich. What I'm trying to say is, there are ways to come back from it. Collier was compromised during the drone attack operation in Algeria, though his was not so cut and dry as yours. Look at him now—he's a station chief."

Dolan chuckled. "Yeah, he might not be the best example. We both know his compromise was the main reason for the gas attack on the embassy in Berlin. They were trying to kill him, specifically."

"Not quite. They could have taken him out a lot easier than the way they went about it. Collier wasn't the reason for the attack; the AMA wanted to take out as many high-ranking U.S. officials and their family members as possible. Collier was more like the cherry on top."

He was right, thought Dolan. "OK, I'll give you that. But it's my perception that Collier was one of Dittrich's favorites. I'm not sure I have that going for me."

"No, perhaps not. Suffice to say that I'll put in a good word." He shifted in his armchair, visibly intent on changing the topic. "Anyway, what about this dream you told me about, where you end up shooting Claire at the end. Has that dream reoccurred?"

Dolan nodded uncomfortably. Sometimes he forgot Welker was a psychologist and that one of his directives was to make sure Dolan didn't wig out or go rogue. "No, it hasn't reoccurred. I had it just the one time. And yes, I've thought about it since we last discussed it but it's not something that is bothering me to any great degree. I was worried that it would. There was another dream I had, years ago that would reoccur. The content of it was disturbing, in much the same way as this one, and I would think about it a lot. The last time I had it was in Berlin, back in 2019. Whatever was causing its reoccurrence was reconciled with the end of that mission. With how everything went down. I found some peace after that."

Welker regarded him with a hint of compassion and then smiled, pursing his lips. As if he saw something in Dolan that he saw in his younger self. "I find it surprising you open up to me about this stuff, to be honest. But it's a good thing. Evidence of a healthy mind. I think you're going to be just fine, Michael Dolan."

Dolan knew he wasn't patronizing him—it was genuine. He cared. What a strange, cool dude. He admired him. Welker was simple on the outside and complex on the inside. An essential trait of a good spy, he mused. Bolden then entered the room, beckoning them to the basement.

With Freeman by her side, Rhodes was waiting for them on the large screen on the wall. Dolan and Welker took their seats as Bolden enabled the audio.

"Good afternoon team. We have much to go over, so please save your questions for the end. I'll let Thomas get to what he found at the internet café in a moment, but first, the strike in Syria is about to go down. We have the green light and should have boots on the ground within the hour. Both Reapers are in a low altitude holding pattern just outside Syrian airspace. They will go in if necessary, but for now we don't want to tip anyone off that something is going down. If we do need them, they'll fly in under the radar, which is spotty at best. It will be enough of a challenge getting two helicopters in and out without being noticed. We are more worried about the Russians than Syrian intervention. As you may know, Russia has considerable military presence in the country. They have forces at Tiyas Airbase near Damascus, but we are more concerned about Shayrat Airbase, just north of our ingress route near the border, as most of their aircraft are based there. Normally we'd give Russia a heads-up before taking any military action in the area, but this isn't something we want them to know about. It could get ugly if they notice us going in.

"If all goes according to plan we will know soon if Lefebvre and his son are there. I will debrief you on the outcome of the strike as soon as I can break away from the CLEARCUT team, but don't expect anything for at least a couple hours. You should all sit tight at the safehouse in the meantime.

"As for the compound in Algeria, the National Reconnaissance Office informed us late yesterday there were other demands being levied against the use of our satellite, and that we would lose it in the next few days unless we obtain some hard evidence the AMA is there. Well, it didn't end up taking that long. We had already lost the feed by the time they gave us the warning. Up until the point it was retasked, the faint EM signature continued to be the only activity. A farmer was herding goats at one point on the southern part of the property, but he never approached the compound. Neither we nor anyone else on the CLEARCUT team has received anything additional to reinforce the idea it's a valid AMA target. What I want to do is see what happens in Syria. We can then reevaluate our approach for Algeria if necessary. At the very least, if the raid is not successful, we'll have additional leverage to try and get the satellite back. If that doesn't work, we can ask the Algerian government to go check it out for us. OK, Thomas go ahead."

Freeman slid his chair slowly forward once again, an unnecessary and somewhat irritating maneuver. He was the subservient type; Dolan wondered how long he would last in the field. *Probably about ten minutes.* "What about the Black Sky satellites? I thought we were paying for those?"

"We still have them," said Freeman. "But they are in traditional orbits and have no ability to loiter over a target. The revisit rate is pretty good, so we'll continue to get updates, but they'll be periodic. They are not the kind of satellites we can use to direct a mission or maintain video surveillance. Alright, switching gears—great work at the café. We thought we'd find our terrorist with one of the first two computers, but it just goes to show you that appearances can be deceiving, and anyone can be the bad guy. So, there was nothing useful at all on the hard drive—there was no additional activity before or after sending the message that would help us ascertain his identity. The video we have of the guy is decent but not good enough for face recognition technology. And if he had no prior record, which he doesn't, it wouldn't have helped us anyway."

He had Welker, Bolden and Dolan in suspense, wondering how it was good news that there was nothing on the hard drive and that the video was useless. Rhodes was doing her best to mask her frustration but failing, wanting him to get on with it so she could jump to her other, more important meeting.

He went on. "However, once I was in the network, I was able to access the computer at the checkout counter. Our terrorist logged off workstation thirteen and exactly one minute and forty-two seconds later, a credit card was used to pay for that session at workstation thirteen. The card belongs to a French man named Abdul Collignon. He was born Albert Collignon and changed his first name a year or so after moving to Germany." Freeman hunkered over an offscreen keyboard for a moment to project a picture of the man on the right side of their screen.

"He is unmarried, has an apartment in Offenbach and works as a truck driver. His home and work addresses, phone number, all of it is in my report. He's originally from a small town near Lyon, the son of a French soldier who was killed in 2011 in a friendly fire incident near Mazar-e Sharif in Afghanistan, almost immediately after he deployed there. Roman Catholic family. The tragic circumstances of his father's death made headlines and could very well be the genesis of his radicalization. His mother died of cancer four years later. He moved to Germany in 2016 and has no social media accounts as far as I can tell. I haven't had enough time to investigate things like email or clubs and affiliations, and I haven't analyzed his financial accounts yet but all the details you need to get started are included in what I sent. I'll pass on whatever else I find."

"Nice work Thomas!" Welker said enthusiastically, turning his attention to Dolan. "This is a big deal, and it's a rare thing. Tracking these douchebags down normally takes a lot longer than this. When it does happen quickly, it's usually because they're amateurs. They screw something up, leave something behind. Yes, using a personal credit card might qualify as amateurish, particularly in a country that still uses cash for almost everything. If he were German and not French, it is likely he'd have paid with euros, and we'd have gotten nothing from this. So, everything I've seen to this point leads me to believe these guys are the real deal and this breakthrough is the result of Thomas' exceptional forensics work."

Dolan acknowledged Welker's mentoring with a nod as Freeman blushed lightly, said 'thanks' and mumbled something about it being 'a team effort.'

"Listen, that's all we have time for. Sorry for cutting it short but I really do need to run," said Rhodes. "I want to add, and I don't know if you've been watching the news over there but just as the world's financial markets were beginning to make a comeback, it was announced about an hour ago that there have been two new outbreaks of Marburg. This has sent them tumbling again. One in Egypt and another in California. In both cases a person was infected in Amman and got on a plane to fly home. Both individuals were identified, quarantined and subsequently died, but not before they'd infected several other people. Even though Marburg is less contagious and easier to contain, to this point the Amman attack has been more destabilizing, financially and geopolitically, than the entire COVID-19 epidemic. This is not the Coronavirus. It is very, very scary and people are afraid. Another successful attack could very well plunge the entire world into complete chaos. I am not being dramatic here—this is real. There is no option except to succeed in stopping them. Dittrich is working with the Director and others at the highest levels to provide us the operational latitude we need to ensure success. Even if it's not palatable, legally speaking.

"The next step is to review the data on Collignon and to put a surveillance plan together. Don't waste too much time on it, though— I'd like to see you tracking his movement, activities and communications by the end of the day. As for the Syria strike, I'm pretty sure Thomas and I won't have time for another VTC, but I will send you all an email summarizing what went down. Take care, and good luck."

The monitor went blank abruptly. They had seen the news and it was sobering. Dolan's education and experience gave him special insight into how these attacks could in fact lead to the terrible place Rhodes just described. He wasn't sure the globalized nature of the new world was resilient enough to recover quickly from a second attack. It could take years, or longer.

Bolden pulled up his classified email and opened Freeman's report on Collignon, displaying it on the widescreen monitor for the group. They reviewed the information together. Dolan remained quiet as Welker and Bolden discussed how best to surveil him. A little over an hour later they had a plan. Welker would remain in the field with Bolden in the safehouse monitoring Alpha Bright and Dolan getting 'over-the-shoulder training' at his side.

Dolan wondered if the team had been discussing how to handle him behind his back. How to best mitigate the potential effects of his blown cover. He wasn't angry—he knew it was necessary. But he was frustrated. Very. He'd been unofficially demoted to a status somewhere south of sidekick. But there was nothing he could do at this point except to help the team in whatever capacity he was able.

It continued to concern him that the strike in Syria may not pan out the way they hoped. That neither Hakeem nor Sharif would be there. That any intel they found might be of little value. If they did capture anyone during the raid, the AMA's operational and communications security was so good they probably wouldn't know enough to be useful. The strike would alert Hakeem and Sharif, wherever they really were, and give them the time they needed to go deeper into hiding. To accelerate the timeline of their attacks.

There was still one card Dolan could play. It would mean doing something contrary to guidelines they'd been given. Doing it would be justified, however, if he turned out to be right. *Lauren said it herself, operational latitude would be needed to ensure success.* There was risk involved, but even if he were wrong the fallout would land primarily on him. It wouldn't hurt the team, not in the foreseeable future anyway. If he were right, it would have an immediate, positive impact on the mission. And at the same time, in a marginally satisfying, vicarious manner, he might be afforded some slice of revenge.

CHAPTER THIRTY-FIVE

Dolan made himself comfortable in an overstuffed armchair with a good view of the monitor. Bolden configured Alpha Bright with a split screen. On the left was a map of Offenbach, Welker's position marked by a green dot. The camera feed was on the right. For now it was configured to track Welker; they would add Collignon as soon as they located him. The feed was jittery, rapidly swapping from camera to camera and at times going blank attempting to catch up to Welker as he drove his rental SUV through town towards Collignon's apartment.

Gertrude opened the door and stopped at the top of the stairs with a tray of snacks and carafe of coffee. "Am I interrupting?" she asked them.

"Not at all, thanks. I was just thinking about coffee," Bolden replied.

She poured two cups and placed the tray on the large wooden table in the middle of the room, then left back up the stairs. Dolan got up, took one of the mugs and returned to his chair. He was comfortable with feeling nervous right now. He could always turn it off if he wanted but found it to be useful at times. Peak performance occurs once a certain level of stress has been reached. Dolan understood this well and tried to keep himself in that place whenever the situation dictated. Allowing a certain amount of adrenaline into his system helped. He had to be careful though, adrenaline has other effects that can be counterproductive—it routes more control to the midbrain and consequently, less to the cognitive areas. With too much adrenaline a person can enter fight or flight mode and their ability to reason goes out the window. Dolan was limiting it to a tiny trickle, just enough to keep him on his toes.

He was nervous because they would soon be learning the outcome of the DEVGRU raid in Syria. He would know then whether the decision he made earlier was the right one. He was nervous because at some point he was going to have to tell Rhodes what he did and wasn't sure how she'd react. Welker might just smile and shake his head; Bolden would probably sit there looking shocked. Dittrich was either going to fly off the handle in an expletive-laden tirade, or he was going to promote him. But he was more concerned with what Rhodes would think. Probably that he'd gone rogue again, and that whatever the outcome was it didn't matter, because she would see it as a breach of trust. One more reason to let him go. But none of that mattered now. It was done and he'd face whatever consequences there might be.

"Welker is there at the apartment building," Bolden announced without looking back. "According to the plan he'll observe the windows for a while, see if there's any activity inside. If not, he'll make the call. He'll go in if Collignon doesn't pick up. See what he can find."

There was no activity in the windows. After thirty minutes Welker called the landline in the apartment. There was no answer. They suspected he might not be there; truck drivers made regular deliveries over the weekend. He was probably working. Welker picked the lock and went in. Dolan and Bolden sat there for the next two hours while Welker went through each room, photographing and describing everything he found through his earpiece. He installed three motion activated cameras and a cellular relay that would autorecord to an Intelink cloud server. They could also link live feeds from all three directly to Alpha Bright. Unfortunately, there was no cell phone, no computer or tablet; nothing they could pass off to Freeman to crack and analyze. That was always the hope of course. For the most part, the apartment was clean. No obvious smoking guns. The absence of electronics reinforced their assessment that the AMA was well-trained, careful and thorough.

Welker relayed the pictures back and they set to work printing and hanging them on the wall alongside hardcopies of the rest of the information they'd accumulated on the cell to this point. There wasn't a lot to go on yet, but it was beginning to take shape. The entire southside basement wall was treated with whiteboard paint. They used dry erase markers to make notations and draw lines and arrows between documents and photos, identifying relationships and firming up timelines. As Welker drove to Collignon's work address, they went through everything he photographed searching for clues.

Welker headed to the trucking company headquarters. It was nearing the end of the day, but their front office was still open. In the meantime, Dolan had found something. Whether or not it was useful remained to be seen. A document found among a stack of pay statements and other work-related papers in a filing cabinet at Collignon's apartment. It was a list of properties owned by the trucking firm. There were thirteen—one in Berlin, another in Hamburg. Two in Munich. Five in smaller cities across Germany and four in and around Frankfurt, including the company headquarters in Offenbach. In and of itself, that information wasn't revelatory. What could be, however, was the contact information. That column had no phone numbers, names, or email addresses for two of the properties. Instead, the word

'GESCHLOSSEN' was printed in that field. Closed. One of them was in Wuppertal, on the west side of the country. The other was just south of Frankfurt. That location was circled.

When Welker arrived, he went straight in and asked to speak with Collignon. He introduced himself as a lawyer for an insurance company and explained that Collignon's mother had died with a life insurance policy no one knew about. They'd done their best to try and locate him over the years to transfer the funds but just recently found out he'd left France. They only had his work address. The notification had to be done in person.

It was risky. The plan required Welker to confront him directly. As a psychologist and experienced interrogator however, he was comfortable with the approach. And it was the most efficient way to get as much information as possible in a short period of time. He would lure Collignon to a nearly empty bistro nearby. What happened after would depend entirely on Collignon. As a member of a terrorist cell, especially if it were active or about to activate, he would be highly suspicious of anything out of the ordinary. If he reacted normally, if he wasn't nervous, it might be an indication they have the wrong guy. It was possible Collignon had been paid or convinced to send a message to Varayev that he didn't understand. That he wasn't part of the cell at all. In that case, Welker would shift the discussion to get him to reveal who put him up to it. Getting from Point A to Point B in that conversation was quite a stretch—Dolan was interested to see how Welker might pull that off. It would need to be a delicate and surgical line of questioning. If Welker believed they had the right guy however, he'd set up another meeting at a location they could control and perhaps even detain him at that point for interrogation. If he tried to bolt at any time, Welker would either incapacitate and detain him or signal Bolden and Dolan for backup. They couldn't let him escape if he knew or suspected someone was on to him.

Their plan came to an abrupt halt right there in the front office, however. The shift manager told Welker that Collignon made a delivery the night before and was supposed to make three more today but never showed up for work. He called Collignon several times and left messages. It turned out he had a work cell phone—Welker wrote it down, thanked the manager and left. Bolden then sent Freeman an emergency request to locate the cell phone and send them the metadata they needed to set up tracking on Alpha Bright. If Freeman were successful and Collignon had it with him, it would be a huge break. If it was a newer model cellphone it might be possible to track even when turned off.

Dolan was already beginning to tire of being a spectator. "Howard, rather than coming back here, why don't you go check out the closed location south of Frankfurt. It's probably thirty minutes from where you are. At the least, we can scratch it off our list as a possible base of operations for the cell."

"Makes sense to me. I'll let you guys do all the boring shit. I'm no good at that analysis stuff anyway. Just tell me who to shoot."

Dolan and Bolden laughed in unison. Welker was good at almost everything. It was why he was always given the benefit of the doubt and a near-blanket license to do whatever he wanted. He always got results.

Just then the laptop made a ping noise. Freeman had located Collignon's phone and sent them the information they needed. Bolden read the email quickly and typed the necessary codes into the system. They stared expectantly at the monitor. Thirty uncomfortable seconds went by. Then, a red dot appeared uneventfully on the map. The right side of the screen remained blank.

"Will that map show us the address? Or can you zoom all the way in?" asked Dolan.

"You can do both, actually," Bolden replied. He scrolled the mouse wheel and the map of greater Frankfurt converged on immediate area around the red dot, showing street names and points of interest. It was a rural area south of the city.

"Stan, Howard...can you hear me, Howard?" asked Dolan.

"Loud and clear," he responded. "Go ahead."

"It's the same address as the vacant trucking property. He didn't show up for work today. Something is going down, or it's about to. We should be there to give you backup."

There was a moment of silence. "I don't know..." Bolden replied hesitantly. "Someone should stay here to monitor Alpha Bright. Howard can do some recon first, then we can make a decision."

"Do you think we might be too far away? A lot can happen in the half hour it'll take us to get there. Right now all we have is Collignon's location, there are no cameras Alpha Bright can even tap into. There might not be any within kilometers of the site. We can ask Gertrude to monitor the map." *We need to go.*

"But if he begins moving..." Bolden stuttered.

Welker interrupted. "Just figure it out, people. I'm good with whatever you come up with. I'll be there in about ten to fifteen minutes."

Dolan stood up and walked to Bolden who was staring at the screen, indecisive. "Stan, I am going. Are you coming with me, or are you staying here?"

Bolden swiveled in his chair to face him, surprised at his moxie, and conflicted. Dolan found it odd at first; Bolden was a seasoned field agent. This sort of decision shouldn't flummox him. Unless of course he'd been told to keep the cuffs on Dolan. At least one of them should go, but Bolden also felt it was important for someone to monitor Alpha Bright. If Welker was in downtown Frankfurt with cameras everywhere the system would run almost independently. Without those resources, however, it required constant management. Dolan wasn't yet fully up to speed on how to do that. Until now, he was the one they'd been tracking with it. There had been no good reason or opportunity to teach him.

"Go," Bolden said, finally. "I will monitor from here and coordinate. If we need additional backup, I can call it in from the consulate, or from the BND if things really go sideways."

Bolden was right. There were things that could be done from here that were more difficult to do in the field. It made sense for him to remain here.

"OK. I'll need comms," Dolan responded.

Bolden opened a drawer and gave him the earpiece, which he quickly inserted and sound checked. "I'll need a sidearm."

"Howard has four in his SUV..."

"Just give me a weapon and three clips. We don't know what the situation will be by the time I get there. I need to be ready the moment I arrive."

Bolden didn't wait for him to finish He opened another drawer and handed him a holstered pistol with three full clips. Dolan put on his jacket and placed the clips in his pockets. He removed the handgun from its holster and checked the breech. Then he put it back, strapped the holster to the inside of his left ankle, and pulled his pantleg down to cover the gun.

Bolden offered him a flashlight with one hand and put his other on Dolan's shoulder. "Here. It's getting dark. Good luck. Stay with Howard and follow his lead. Oh, and take these." He opened a second drawer and handed him a small silver case. "There are three inside. One syringe will knock someone out for twenty-four hours. We'd rather have them alive, of course."

"Thanks Stan." Dolan put his jacket on and pocketed the flashlight and case. Then he strode quickly across the room and up the steps, past a surprised Gertrude in the hallway and out the front door.

CHAPTER THIRTY-SIX

Ivan Vasnetsov shifted his position carefully. His right leg was asleep. Almost immediately a prickling sensation coursed from hip to ankle. He pinched his thigh, barely registering any feeling. It was the hundredth time today. Lying prostrate with little room to move for the past seventy-two hours had become unbearable. He was afraid to leave his hiding place. His freedom was at stake. He had heard nothing but silence for days and he couldn't remain here forever.

After Sharif gave him the key to his electrocution collar, he hid it in a drawer and began plotting his escape. He knew it wouldn't be easy, even with guards that had become complacent. They knew if Ivan ever tried to escape, he wouldn't make it very far before the collar subdued him. There had been long periods of time recently when there was no guard at all. But the lab was next door to the operations room, and people were always coming and going from there. If anyone were still in the building, he would have heard them. If he was in fact alone and was able to make it down the hall, up the stairs and out of the building, there was the additional problem of not knowing where he was. Which direction to go. How to get help.

With Sharif's promise to give him the key, Ivan decided he would escape as soon as he had it, in the middle of the night. Then he did what Sharif requested. Ivan accelerated synthesis and production and delivered the final batch of Marburg. It was his best work yet, by far the most viable, the most virulent and in record time. Hakeem even came in to congratulate him, laughing and smiling. That made Ivan angry. He had two reasons to smile—his next attack would go forward on time and as planned, and he would finally be able to kill Ivan. Hakeem was pure evil; of this, Ivan had no doubt. In contrast, when Sharif thanked him, it had been genuine. He even gave him a hug and wished him well when he gave Ivan the key. Though it was likely Sharif presumed Ivan's escape attempt would fail and that he would die during the attempt anyway, he felt Sharif was rooting for him to make it out alive. There was still good in him.

He'd noticed something was going on shortly after he delivered the last batch. Whenever he left the lab to use the restroom, Hakeem's team seemed to be busier, and on edge. They were packing things up and stacking boxes at the end of the hall near the stairwell. One morning he heard his guard outside the door speaking with someone about 'moving out soon.' They were abandoning the compound. This is when he decided to change his original plan.

He had already set aside enough food and water for several days. He hid his stores in the ceiling by removing a panel in the corner of the room, right above where the ladder was routinely kept, leaning against the wall next to his soiled mattress. The lab ceiling was suspended, and the panels wouldn't support him, so he removed several boards from the sides of the megabat cages. He fed them up inside through the corner panel and laid them inside across the metal lattice structure, creating a floor in the dark, two-foot space. Someone might notice the missing boards, but no one besides him or Sharif had gone into the bat room in months. And Sharif had already left with the final container of Marburg virus. There was no longer any reason for Hakeem to keep him alive.

That evening he waited until he suspected the guard had left his post. Ivan went to the door and opened it slowly, looking down the hall in both directions. No one there. He closed the door and went to the drawer where he'd hidden the key and removed the collar. Then he went back to the door, again looked in both directions before walking about fifteen feet down the hall towards the staircase and placed the opened collar on the floor near the wall. Then he went back to the lab, climbed up the ladder into the ceiling and replaced the corner panel.

He was unable to sleep that night, expecting at any moment the collar would be noticed and commotion would ensue. But nothing happened until the next morning. Eventually he heard someone come into the lab and look around, somewhat frantically and muttering beneath their breath. He heard them open the door to the bat room and close it about two seconds later. Then they left. About ten minutes later Hakeem came in with at least two of the guards. He heard Hakeem ask them several questions; neither guard had any answers. It was clear by then Ivan's ruse had worked. They were convinced Ivan already escaped the building.

The next two days were interminably long. It was an excruciating exercise in sensory deprivation interrupted only by the discomfort of laying on hard planks. Hakeem's men came through the door one last time early on the second day. It sounded as if they were packing up things from the lab. A short time later the lights in the lab were extinguished and a long, deafening silence ensued. The only things he heard in the hours that followed were the sound of his own breathing and the minimal noise he made when eating or urinating into a plastic jug. After three days in the ceiling he'd had enough. It was time to go down, reconnoiter the basement to see if anyone was still there.

He almost fell going down. It was as if he forgot how to use his limbs. Ivan paused at the top of the ladder, his head still up inside the ceiling. He listened carefully but heard nothing. It was absolutely pitch black in the lab. After a moment his legs began to feel somewhat normal, and he finished his descent. He made his way by feel to the opposite corner of the lab and found the drawer where he kept a flashlight and turned it on. Ivan then tiptoed to the door and pressed his ear against it. Hearing nothing, he opened it slowly, again tiptoeing as he moved into the hall, pointing the beam one way and then the other. It was the first and only time that the lights in the hall had been turned off.

Increasingly hopeful he was now alone, he stopped tiptoeing and walked toward the stairwell, pausing at the open door of the operations room to look inside. The furniture was still there, as were the widescreens on the wall, but the computers and other equipment were gone. A surge of joy swept through him as he scurried towards the stairs and up to the first-floor door. Holding his breath as he opened it, Ivan saw no one and immediately ran down the hallway to the building's entrance, bursting through it and into the night air. Ivan would have to go back and get his supplies for the journey, wherever that took him, but for now he was simply overcome by his apparent freedom. He went perhaps ten meters before looking up. The sight of a quarter moon and a billion stars punctuating the jet-black backdrop of space caused him to drop to his knees in awe. Something he thought he'd never see again in his lifetime, the night sky. So vast, so beautiful.

In that moment he reaffirmed his vow to do things differently this time, to be a good man and to help others with whatever time he had left on this Earth. He thanked God over and over for his good fortune and for the opportunity to change his life. But a noise broke him from his prayer, something off in the distance. Someone yelling. He stood up and listened and there it was again, someone yelling at him from a ridgeline a hundred meters or so in front of him. He couldn't see who it was, but it was *what* they were yelling that made him feel suddenly and completely overcome with happiness and gratitude. Someone was asking him what his name was—*in Russian*. He wouldn't have to find his way through the wilderness with no passport, no money, and no help. He was being rescued by his countrymen!

"I am here! Yes, it is me, Doctor Ivan Vasnetsov! I was kidnapped and held prisoner, but I have now escaped!"

Ivan began running toward his saviors, crying now to the point it was difficult for him to see. Suddenly, he was knocked forward ten feet by a concussive blast that ruptured both his eardrums. He hit the ground hard, his face scraping the ground. He laid there for a second, until he was sure he was not badly injured, then turned his head back to see what had happened. A great column of smoke and dust hung above and rolled outward from where his prison had stood. The entire building was gone, pieces of it strewn here and there, but much of it had fallen straight down into where the basement had been. *Where he had been.* Did his rescuers blow up the building? Why would they do that? He would have heard them inside. No, he realized Hakeem must have wired the building with explosives before leaving.

Ignoring the pain from his ears and face, he got up slowly and again began running to the ridgeline with his arms held high in the air, unable to hear himself yelling his own name. Within fifty meters Ivan could make out the silhouettes of three men, one standing and two crouched down, waiting for him. *To save him!* Just then he was blinded by a bright light, shone directly on him. He stopped, not quite knowing if he should continue toward them. A second later he was again knocked to the ground, this time backwards as a sniper round penetrated his torso. It tumbled as it moved through him, the incredible energy of the bullet transferring to and liquefying the organs and tissues within his chest cavity. The round took out three vertebrae as it left his body, leaving a five-inch hole in his back. He crumpled to the ground in a heap, facing the now dispersing plume of smoke. As his last moment in life passed, he noticed something rise from the rubble and take flight. Eerily majestic, the huge bat spread its wings wide and flapped powerfully, circling up and above the wreckage of the compound. Then it dipped one wing, accelerated and flew off into the night.

CHAPTER THRITY-SEVEN

"Hi Lauren. Thanks for getting back with me so quickly. We may have a situation here and I wanted to keep you in the loop. We may need assistance." Bolden was in the safehouse basement, pacing as he talked.

"OK, fill me in quickly. Then I have an update for you. Go ahead," she answered.

"We have Collignon's location. He's at a vacant property owned by his trucking company, just south of Frankfurt. Added to the fact it could indicate cell activity, he didn't show up for work today. We suspect something is going down and we're looking into it. We could use Thomas' help."

"Well, I'm glad one of us has good news. I'm still at Langley but I'll give Thomas a call and have him connect with you. You're at the safehouse?"

"Yes. Well, I am anyway. Howard was in the field when we located Collignon, so he redirected immediately to the property. He should be there any minute. There was no time to plan anything, right now we're just reacting. Michael and I decided he should head out to provide backup for Howard, so he's enroute as well, probably twenty minutes behind. It was the only call. I stayed here to monitor Alpha Bright."

Lauren sighed disapprovingly. "Stan, I don't like it. I know you're thinking on your feet right now but Michael's too new, and he's burned. Every time he comes and goes from the safehouse we risk compromising it and everyone who uses it. Do you even need AB for this?"

"It's not just about Alpha Bright," he responded. "It's much easier to run coordination from here for resources and additional backup if needed. Out there all I have is a cell phone and Dolan hasn't been trained to do this yet. So yes, I think I needed to stay here. What have you got for us?"

"OK. Stay on top of it and keep me apprised. On my end, the strike in Syria is complete. Unfortunately, Lefebvre wasn't there. Neither was Sharif. There was evidence they may have stored the virus there, probably in the lead up to the attack in Amman. No casualties. The DEVGRU team went in just after dark. There were four targets inside one of the buildings. Minimal resistance: they were caught completely by surprise. Three shot and killed and we have the fourth in custody. Stan, the compound was definitely going to be a headquarters of some type. There was a lot of IT equipment, monitors, routers in the basement. It looks like they were in the process of setting it all up. In hindsight though, I think we may have gone in too early. I have a suspicion Lefebvre was enroute. That things were getting too hot wherever he was hiding. In any case, the other very interesting thing that happened was our helos were intercepted by three Russian Mi-28 attack helicopters ten minutes after crossing the border. 'Intercepted' might be the wrong word. They never got close. We were about to cancel the operation, but they kept their distance and eventually flew off. If we were spotted on radar or from the ground, they couldn't have had enough time to scramble and converge on us that fast. They would have had to have been in the air already, or at least in the immediate area. It was as if they knew about the mission ahead of time and wanted to verify what we were doing, but not to interfere. I've never heard of anything like this before. They made no attempt at radio communication and did nothing overtly antagonistic. They did not reengage after that."

"Holy cow, that is strange. Is there any chance information about the op was leaked to them, from Mossad maybe? I can't see how that would have benefited Israel. At this point though, a win is a win and I'll take it. Even if Lefebvre wasn't there, it's still a win. Hopefully, we will get good information from our captive. What about intel gathered from the building?"

"They just landed at Mashabim. They have all the computer hard drives, every piece of paper. A couple cell phones. Our relationship with Mossad is excellent, I don't think they would have done something like this behind our back but it's possible. We'll see. But there's another important update, and it's significant."

"What is it?" Bolden asked.

"One of our Black Sky satellites passed over Algeria about forty minutes ago. Thomas called me as soon as he heard. Stan, one of the buildings at the compound we were monitoring, it's no longer there. It's been destroyed. We have several still images."

There was a moment of silence as Bolden processed what she'd said. "Was it the building with the faint EM signature?"

"Yes," Rhodes replied. "We're looking at all the images now but at first glance, there is nothing to suggest it was any kind of attack, that there was any fighting, nothing of the sort. It's hard to tell if you ask me; it was already dark when the photos were taken but the ambient light was good. According to our analysts here it does not look like an aerial bomb or missile attack. It doesn't look like the result of a ground attack either. The debris dispersion pattern does not support either scenario."

Another moment of silence. "Huh, so it was blown up from the inside then? The AMA covering their tracks maybe? The Canadians are going to be pissed..."

Rhodes sidestepped the weak attempt at humor. "Maybe. We don't know what it means yet, but I have a feeling it's not a coincidence. Thomas is getting in touch with Northleaf Gas to see if it was scheduled for demolition. Even if it were, it wouldn't have been done at night, but we must rule it out. If the answer is no, I'll consider asking Algiers Station send someone down to investigate, or at least to get the Algerian government to do it. We would need to know what happened there, if for no other reason than to rule it out for good as an AMA hideout. If we are lucky, it was, and Lefebvre and Sharif were inside when it was destroyed."

"We are never that lucky," Bolden countered.

"I know."

♦

Dolan listened carefully as Bolden relayed Rhodes' new information. Welker was on-site now, having parked down the road from the property. He found cover with a good vantage of the front of what looked like an abandoned warehouse. There were two vehicles parked in front next to a rusted fifty-gallon drum. There was a bad smell in the air, like rubber burning. Alpha Bright put Collignon inside, very likely with one or more additional suspected cell members. Dolan was five minutes away.

The strike went down pretty much the way he thought it would, though the MI-28s were an added wrinkle. Apparently, Russia felt it was better the U.S. knew that *they* knew what DEVGRU was up to. It was a very Russian thing to do. As for the destroyed building in Algeria, he did not expect that. He wasn't surprised it had been destroyed; he was surprised it appeared to have been destroyed from within. It didn't add up. It made him worry that Hakeem and Sharif had been able to escape yet again.

He saw Welker's car on the side of the road ahead and pulled up behind it. He parked, crossed the street and set a good pace towards Welker's position. As he walked, he prepared mentally, getting into his zone. His heart rate was already right where he wanted it. Dolan narrowed his focus, concentrating on what might lay ahead. It could be quick and easy, they might take Collignon and whoever was there by surprise. They could give up immediately and that would be it. They could run. Or there could be a firefight. The latter two were more likely but he was banking on a fight. Ideologically radicalized terrorists tended to bare their teeth when cornered. Dolan considered the possible outcomes and played them out in his head. It would be better had Bolden come along, especially if there were more than two or three inside the building. Even more so if they were armed and on edge, which was likely.

Bolden keyed his mic just as Dolan arrived at Welker's hiding spot. "Guys, I'm looping Thomas in. Right now, all I have on Alpha Bright is your positions and Collignon's. The accuracy seems tight, it looks like he is near the back of the warehouse, away from the front entrance."

"Copy, Stan. Thanks. Michael! welcome to the party," said Welker as Dolan moved up next to him. He was crouching behind a bushy overgrowth in a grove of trees, seventy or eighty meters diagonally from the warehouse, night vision goggles trained on the front entrance. "No activity so far. There is a light on inside, but it is faint and goes in and out. Probably a flashlight."

"Understood," Dolan replied. He crouched down beside Welker and checked the breech again on his Sig Sauer P229. He surveyed the area around them. It was an industrial block that had seen better times. The dim light added to the desolate atmosphere. He noticed while driving along the road the buildings in the vicinity were rundown and most were abandoned. He calculated this property had gone unused for many years. The overgrowth along the periphery was dense. It would provide them with good cover for now.

"Team, this is Thomas. I have information and blueprints for the building. It's been vacant for twelve years. It is a standard warehouse setup. No electricity. There is a large open area through the front door and a small office immediately to the right of the entrance. There is a row of small rooms along the back, offices and restrooms most likely, and a door in the middle of the building on the south side. That door is on the right from your position. There is another door on the south end of the east side. That's the back side, opposite you. Sending both of you images of the layout."

"Got it," Welker replied. He kept his NVGs trained on the warehouse while Dolan pulled up the image on his cell. He showed it to Welker. "Thomas, are you ready to copy? I have details for both vehicles. Michael, reduce the brightness on your phone." There was a hint of irritation in his voice.

Dolan complied immediately. "Sorry."

"Ready to copy," said Freeman.

Welker relayed the make, model, color, and plate number of both cars to Freeman.

"Got it," Freeman acknowledged.

Welker looked to Dolan. "Notice anything else from the blueprints?"

"No. It's a simple floor plan and there is no second level. If they are in any of the smaller rooms, we'll be able to get on top of them quickly but if not, we'll be exposed as soon as we go in, unless we go in from the back. All the windows are too high to see through from outside. But each door appears to have a small window."

Just then, a notification appeared on Dolan's phone, a text from Anne. *Perfect timing.* Dolan decided to ignore it but just as quickly, he changed his mind. It would only take a second to read. He tapped the messaging app.

"Hey you… I know we agreed to not communicate until you are done with whatever you are doing, but I'm worried about you. Can you just let me know if you're OK?"

He thought about answering, then dismissed the idea. *Stay focused.* He hadn't thought about Anne much in the last couple days. That doesn't seem right…

Welker looked at him. "We may not need to go in. It might be better if we don't. We can get them when they exit the building. If they don't come out together it could complicate things, though. To be honest we should have another body here. One spotter and two for the execution." *Interesting choice of words,* Dolan thought.

Welker stood up and moved behind a tree, checked the breech of his own P229, then tucked it back in his pants. "I want you to stay here and let me know if you see anything. I'm going to have a look inside."

"Sure," Dolan said as he took the NVGs, looping the strap over his head. Do you want my flashlight?"

"Don't need it. Anyway, it will highlight my position if I turn it on. And it's better if we allow our eyes to adjust to the low light."

Dolan felt sheepish. His inexperience was showing. These were things he already knew and had practiced time and time again flying night combat missions. *Pull yourself together.*

Bolden's voice came through. "Guys, depending on what we find, there are several options in play. We have assets here in Frankfurt I can call in to help if necessary. Let's not do anything impulsive."

"Don't get your panties in a bunch, Bolden," replied Welker sarcastically, already fifty meters away to the southeast and moving towards the building. Dolan watched as he went to each vehicle and planted a GPS tracker in the rear wheel well of each.

"I'm seeing both cars on my screen now," Bolden informed them.

Everyone remained quiet as Welker paced silently to the south side of the warehouse. From his position, Dolan could no longer see him and considered moving to keep him in view.

"I'm at the south door, there is a window in it," Welker was whispering now, but his voice was clear. "There are three targets standing inside," Welker reported. Looks like they are having a heated discussion. I recognize Collignon, and there are two others. Both average height, black hair, slim build. One is a little smaller than the other. I don't recognize him. The other guy has his back to me. They have what looks like a small battery powered lantern, on the floor between them. There are three tables with some sort of equipment set up in front of the rooms across the back. A few boxes on the floor. Nothing else."

"Can you take a few photos with your phone and send them to me?" asked Freeman.

"Sure, I'll send you a few, hold on. Not sure how good these are going to look though. It's dark in there."

Dolan kept the NVGs trained on the front of the building, moving back to the right every few seconds to spot and track Welker's retreat from the south side. But he wasn't coming into view. Then, two pops. Gunshots. And another.

"Howard, status?" Dolan asked urgently. Nothing.

"Howard, can you hear me?" he asked, more urgently. Still nothing.

"What's going on?" Rhodes asked in a strained voice.

"I'm changing position, team," replied Dolan. "Shots fired. I can't see Howard and he's not responding."

"Michael, what's going on?" Rhodes's voice was now panicked.

"Stand by." Dolan abandoned his position and ran through the trees, across the warehouse driveway and back into the overgrowth on the opposite side. He found new cover behind a row of evergreens that would give him a clear view of the warehouse. He parted the low tangle of branches. He trained his NVGs on the south side and his blood ran cold. Welker was laying on his back near the door, surrounded by three men standing above him. One of them was yelling, another appeared to be hurt, but not badly.

"Welker is down. Repeat, Welker is down. Three targets are on him, they are dragging him inside the building. I am going in. I think he is still alive."

"NO, stand down Michael. DO NOT engage, repeat, STAND DOWN. You will wait for backup; do you hear me?" Rhodes couldn't believe the op had gone south so quickly. "Stay where you are and monitor until backup gets there. Stan, get your guys there NOW."

"I'm already on it," came his reply.

Dolan had already left his new position and was moving around the property within the treeline, his mind made up. They would finish Welker off, or he could bleed out. Either way, he didn't have much time. "Negative Lauren, I'm going in. By the time backup arrives, Howard will be dead and these three will be long gone. I don't have a choice. I'll keep you updated."

Rhodes knew in her gut that he was right, but she couldn't risk losing two of her team. She may have already lost Welker and she knew what that felt like, when Tony Stone was killed in Marseille. When Sharif shot him. She did not want to have to go through that again. She couldn't. It was too much. Rhodes was unnerved now, finding it difficult to maintain her composure, to think straight. "Listen, you will wait for backup Michael. That's an order!"

But Dolan had already turned his earpiece off. There was no point in keeping it on. It was a distraction, and he couldn't afford to be distracted right now. He sent Bolden a quick text that he would be comms out for now. His phone was on and set to silent; they would have his position and could message him.

CHAPTER THIRTY-EIGHT

By the time Dolan reached an optimal position to advance on the warehouse, Collignon and the others had moved Welker inside. There was a dark splotch on the concrete where Welker had lain. Dolan picked his approach and moved quietly from cover to cover, briefly pausing each time to listen and to verify no one was watching him; never exposing himself for more than a second or two. He held his P229 with both hands, at the ready position. He reached the rear of the building and stood against the wall immediately adjacent to the back door. After turning off the flash on his phone camera he bent down and moved in front of the door, holding it just high enough to snap a photo through the window. A quick review of the grainy shot revealed little. A short hallway, one door on either side. The end of the hallway was open to the main warehouse area. Welker and the terrorists were not visible, a faint glow emanated across the floor from the right.

Dolan tried the door, but it was locked. *Shit*, he thought. *I'll have to pick the lock.* He should have practiced it more. He took a small case from his jacket pocket and selected two lock pick tools. He could hear yelling inside now—they were interrogating him. That was good,

Welker was still alive. And they were distracted, at least for now. He needed to get inside fast. *FUCK!* It wasn't working.

It had been an unnaturally cold day; it was even colder now. His fingers were going numb as he fumbled with the tools in the dark. Just as he was about to give up and try another way in, he felt the tumblers move just right. He twisted the lock and the deadbolt retracted. Dolan turned the knob and opened the door carefully, just enough to slip inside. He remained close to the right wall and walked heel to toe, gliding silently past the two rooms as he listened for any activity inside. There was no strip of light below either door. The only noise came from one of Welker's captors, yelling in German. His words echoed preternaturally off the walls of the expansive, shadowy interior.

A French accent, probably Collignon. But Dolan noticed the man's German wasn't good, bad in fact. Collignon had lived and worked in Germany long enough to speak better than that. And the voice seemed oddly familiar. Dolan continued to the end of the hall and peered carefully around the corner. To the right he saw them, a trail of blood led from the side door to three men silhouetted by a small lantern on the floor next to an unmoving Welker. Two of them held what looked like AK-47s; the smaller of the two had his with the barrel to the floor, leaning on the stock and clearly in pain. The third, the one yelling, held a handgun and was waving it around, then pointing it at Welker's head, then waving it around again as he continued to yell. Dolan squinted in the dim light, and it was becoming clear to him. He couldn't see the face but the voice, those mannerisms. He knew who this was.

Something dark and sinister began to build rapidly within Dolan; an ungovernable rage he'd kept at bay for more than two years now. Ever since that fateful phone call in Potsdam as he sat physically and spiritually broken, nearly dead in Anne's Peugeot. When Sharif confessed to him that he murdered Claire. It was a revelation that had changed everything. He decided then in that moment to seek a terrible and just revenge, to find closure the only way that made sense. To make things right. That meant killing Sharif. However, Dolan was robbed of that opportunity when he escaped to Algeria. And he was right here, right now, incredibly. Fortuitously.

Dolan slipped back into the hallway and placed the NVGs and flashlight on the floor near the wall. He pushed his rage down, keeping it small and contained. In this moment he needed composure, total control. Then he went back, peeked around the corner again and waited for the right moment. Sharif began waving the handgun once more. Dolan immediately walked out from the cover of the hallway, his P229 trained on Sharif's midsection. He would begin shooting while striding methodically forward. Careful trigger squeezes, perfectly aimed while noting any movements by Collignon or the third terrorist in his peripheral vision.

Just as he let loose the first round the injured man leaning on his rifle shifted left and accidentally took the bullet square in the back. This made Dolan pause, though he continued to move toward the group. The shot man went down hard as Sharif looked up, now exposed. He looked confused, straining to see who it was and in an instant his demeanor became distraught. *Did he recognize me?* At the same time, Collignon brought his AK-47 to bear. Sharif kicked the lantern hard, and it skittered across the floor, going dark as Dolan shot twice more at Sharif, missing.

The interior of the warehouse then erupted in the cacophony of a hail of bullets as Collignon let loose on full auto, spraying back and forth in Dolan's general direction. Dolan immediately dove to the right and rolled into a kneeling ready position. Each individual report from

Collignon in the now pitch-black warehouse was accompanied by a muzzle flash, creating a surreal strobe effect. Their movements were caught in a rapid succession of still images, confusing Dolan's aim. As he pulled the trigger to take Collignon down he saw Sharif running toward the front door. It was a sight straight out of a hallucinogenic dream as he splashed through the huge puddle in the middle of the warehouse, each flash capturing a different pattern of the midair water spray cast up by his footfalls.

Two trigger pulls later Collignon fell dead right next to Welker, one bullet having penetrated his liver and the other, his heart. Dolan ran back to the hallway and felt around on the floor for his gear. He turned on the flashlight and pointed the beam first at Collignon, then at the other terrorist. No movement. He walked over and checked their pulses, confirming both were dead. He kicked their weapons away and went to Welker. His eyes were open, and he looked worried. He had reason to be, having been shot in the neck and shoulder. It was his neck injury that looked to be the worst of the two. Dolan tore Welker's shirt sleeve off, tied it around his neck and applied pressure to the hole in his shoulder with his thumb. Outside, tires screeched as Sharif pulled away.

"What the fuck are you doing, go get him, damn it!" Welker said, coughing. "You can't let him escape. He's the lynchpin to everything."

"Don't worry, we can track him. No one wants Sharif more than I do. Are you able to keep pressure on this?" Dolan grabbed Welker's right hand and moved it to the wound on his left shoulder.

"Yes. Get going or you'll lose him. Take the Mercedes, all our extra gear and weapons are in the back."

Dolan reached into Welker's pocket for the keys and using the phone app, turned his earpiece back on.

"Team, this is Dolan. I'm inside, I have Welker. He is hurt and needs immediate medical assistance. Shot in the neck and shoulder. He's lost a lot of blood but is conscious. Collignon and one other terrorist are dead. The third is Sharif Lefebvre and he's escaping now. I am going after him. If we could a get a satellite feed to track him, it would be extremely helpful."

"Copy all," said Bolden. "Your backup is ten minutes out. They are Agency officers from Berlin Station assigned to Frankfurt. They have medical equipment in the van and one of them is a medic. I have Sharif's vehicle location; he's headed south on the adjacent road."

"Great work Michael," Rhodes cut in. "Thomas will work the satellite. Stan, can someone from the backup team peel off and join Michael?" She felt foolish congratulating him when she should have been remonstrating him for disobeying orders. But if Welker pulled through, it would mean he made the right decision. And if he can catch Sharif…

"Negative, there are three of them, but they only have the one vehicle. Michael would have to wait," Bolden replied.

Welker tugged on Dolan's pantleg. "Tell them my earpiece isn't working. It stopped when I was hit in the neck."

The conversation had to be cut short. He needed to leave now. "Everyone, Howard's earpiece is kaput. Stan, I'm going to call you on his phone and leave the line open. Listen, I am not waiting, he already has a head start. If one of the guys from the backup team wants to tag along, he will have to catch up, the keys to my car will be with Howard. It's the grey BMW parked on the east side of the adjacent road, just north of the warehouse. I'm taking Howard's SUV." He fished Welker's phone out his pocket and dialed Bolden, setting the flashlight, the keys to his car and the NVGs with the phone on the floor. Then he ran over to the tables and quickly surveyed the equipment, taking photos with his phone.

Dolan suspected he knew what it was all for. "Stan, call the trucking company on another line and find out what it was that Collignon delivered Saturday night, and to where. They have some sort of bottling assembly line set up here. It could be they were in the latter stages of preparation for an attack, or they may have finished their work and the attack is already in motion. It looks like it may be the latter. And make sure the backup team doesn't touch anything. If what they were bottling was Marburg, the virus could be all over this place. I'm sending you some photos of the setup."

"Shit, OK, understood. Thanks Michael," Bolden replied.

Dolan persisted. "I want to make sure that you do Stan—to be clear, I think Collignon's final delivery on Saturday night *was the actual attack*. Which would mean we are twenty-four hours too late."

Rhodes cut in again. "It's clear Michael. We'll investigate it right away. Go get Sharif."

As Dolan ran to the front door, he heard Welker's strained voice. "And get my weapon back from that motherfucker!"

Without breaking stride, Dolan yelled, "I will Howard. Hang in there."

CHAPTER THIRTY-NINE

"He's still on autobahn five. Going fast and about fourteen kilometers in front of you, Michael." Luckily, Freeman was able to task a satellite quickly and was sending him live updates. Bolden had the sat feed connected into Alpha Bright. It would be nearly impossible to lose him.

"How'd he get so far ahead of me?" queried Dolan. "He had maybe a five-minute lead."

"Like I said, he's driving fast, 180 kilometers per hour at times," Thomas replied. "You won't catch him until you speed up, or if he slows down or stops somewhere."

"OK. Well he must stop at some point. Hopefully he was low on fuel when he started. Let me know if I begin to close on him, or if I get any farther behind."

"Copy that," said Freeman.

As Dolan drove, he could sense it, the rage. He tapped into it mentally, but just a taste. He had decided before to access and use it deliberately, to control it. To him it felt like a great building being gutted by fire. The windows and doors were shuttered and from the outside, nothing appeared out of place. But on the inside, it burned hotter than the sun. Eventually, containment would be broken. Sharif, Dolan's revenge, they were *so* close. It was difficult for him to maintain restraint. But he continued to hold it in and would do so until he confronted him. Thirty minutes from now? Thirty hours? When the time came, he would show Sharif the front door of that building and invite him in. Sharif would comply, in part because he'd be compelled by their interwoven, complicated bond. But also because Dolan wouldn't offer him any other choice. He would open the door, and as if from the very depths of hell, the impossibly powerful, richly oxygenated backdraft of all his pain, his years of anguish, would rush in and explode in an all-consuming conflagration. Sharif would be no more. Dolan would finally be at peace.

Team, our backup just arrived and at first glance, it looks like Howard will pull through. Our medic will take him to Krankenhaus Nordwest in Dolan's rental. They called ahead and he'll go right into surgery. The other two are cleaning up all evidence we were there and will leave the rest. When they are done, we'll send an anonymous tip to local law enforcement, and make sure they understand a biological agent is involved. They can take it from there."

"Thank God, nice work Stan," said Rhodes.

Dolan's grip on the steering wheel loosened marginally as he let out a sigh.

Bolden continued. "Yes, but we have no time to dwell on it. I just got off the phone with the BND. The trucking company wouldn't tell me anything about Collignon's load over the phone, they sounded suspicious when I asked. So, I called in a favor. They're a big company and deliver everything from raw materials to foodstuffs across Germany and all over the EU. Much of their freight is bottled drinks though—juices, sodas, water, etcetera. A lot of it is water. Collignon transported over fourteen hundred cases of bottled water to the

Frankfurt am Main Airport on Saturday night. I did a little more digging and it looks like it's a weekly shipment that services thirty-eight of the ninety airlines that operate out of there, including almost all the U.S. carriers. Water from that delivery is also sold at many of the stores and concession stands in the terminals."

"Oh my God... No, no no..." Rhodes lamented.

Her words echoed in Dolan's head as a chill went down his spine. The attack was far more sinister and potentially devastating than any of them could have imagined. Frankfurt was the busiest airport in Germany, the fourth busiest in Europe and averaged 200,000 travelers per day, flying from there to every corner of the globe. It was much busier than normal in late September with Oktoberfest in full swing, which was bigger and better attended than in years past to make up for its cancellation in 2020 amid the COVID-19 pandemic. And most flyers will drink a bottle of water, either in the terminal or on the plane. The Marburg Virus will be spread to the entire world in a single day, and it could already be happening.

"Yes, I know," said Bolden. "I hope those pallets haven't been broken down yet and we can just contain it all, but we must make some calls right now and we'll need all hands on deck. Lauren?"

"Agreed," Rhodes replied. "Stan, call airport security immediately, then the BND. I'll contact Mike Collier in Berlin, there are specific protocols he will need to run through, a lot of other calls he needs to make. I'll loop in Dittrich as well. Thomas, Stan, and I will have to pivot to this immediately and it will require our full attention. Michael, I know this is far from ideal, but the best course of action for you right now is to suspend your pursuit of Sharif. I will have to retask the satellite we are using to track him up to the airport and we won't have time to get another, not for a while. We'll continue to have his GPS position and can reengage once we have control of those pallets but in the meantime, we wouldn't be able to support you. Turn around and go back to the safehouse, do what you can to help when you get there. Stan, you can pass all the details about Sharif to the BND when you call them. Make sure they have the GPS signal. They would love to get their hands on him after what happened in Potsdam and the Berlin incident two years ago. We'll lose control of Sharif, but we can work out a deal to participate in the interrogation once they have him. The most important thing is that he's apprehended. At his current speed he'll be in France or even Switzerland soon, my bet is he's headed for France. I'll notify the DGSI as well, they can preposition at the border."

Dolan thought about how he would answer. Even as she had begun to speak, he knew what she was going to say. He'd already built so much cognitive and emotional momentum toward settling things with Sharif that it was hard to accept. But he had to proceed carefully. If they were going to succeed as a team, he couldn't appear to have his own agenda.

"I understand Lauren. I'll turn around and head back."

"Thanks Michael." Rhodes sounded relieved. No doubt she was worried Dolan might try to go after Sharif on his own. "Stan, let me know the second you find out what's become of those pallets, and what airport security is doing about it. Let them know it could be a biological agent. I'm not sure they have the right hazmat gear. If it's already been distributed, they will have to recall the flights that have left, send all taxiing aircraft back to their gates. The airport will have to be evacuated, and each person screened before they leave to see if they drank any water from either of the terminals, or if they were served water on their plane. If the answer is yes, they'll have to be quarantined. Heck, anyone who's been near someone else who drank water will have to be quarantined. Aircraft that don't have enough fuel to return will have to be quarantined and dealt with at their destinations. For flights from Frankfurt that have already landed elsewhere and deplaned in the last day, the passengers and crews will have to be tracked down. But as you said, Stan, hopefully the pallets are still intact. I must go. I'll be in touch soon." She and Freeman dropped abruptly, leaving Dolan and Bolden alone on the call.

"Stan...Listen, I am not going back to the safehouse. Not without Sharif."

"What? You just said..."

Dolan cut him off. "I told Lauren what she wanted to hear so she wouldn't worry. Listen, I am going to be a fifth wheel if I go back there. Sharif is the only one who can give us any details about the plan—if it's Marburg in the bottles, who else might be involved, whether there are more attacks planned. He is the only one who might know where his father is. If I break off my pursuit now, he may never be caught. He's highly intelligent and resourceful. I am going to catch him, and I need your help to do it. I know you are now slammed with this emergency but all I ask is that you let me know if he turns off the autobahn, or if he stops anywhere. Keep the corner of your eye on Alpha Bright. And delay telling the BND about him. That's all I need. Do that for me and I'll get him."

Dolan could hear the wheels turning in Bolden's head.

"For the record, I am against it. We can't operate this way, Michael. We were given a directive and we need to follow it. But something tells me I'm not going to sway you on this, and I agree that we could benefit greatly right now from the information he has. I'll do what I can, but I can't keep it from the BND. You'll have to catch him before they do. And if you do catch him, for God's sake don't lead the BND back here to the safehouse. Keep your eyes open. As for Alpha Bright, once we lose the satellite feed, and without me constantly managing the system, it is largely useless. It was designed to track people in cities, not vehicles on the open road. All I really have at this point is the GPS signal. If he leaves the car, you'll be on your own. I'll cover for you as long as I can, but only to the point it begins to jeopardize our team or any other aspect of the mission."

"Understood. Thanks Stan, appreciate it. I'm turning off my earpiece. And I won't be answering my phone, so text me with any updates."

"Will do. Good luck, Michael."

"You too Stan." Dolan tapped the power button on his earpiece app and the line went dead. He propped the phone up on the center console so he would notice Bolden's texts right away. Then he pushed the accelerator, weaving the powerful black Mercedes SUV around and between cars on the autobahn as if they were standing still. He almost didn't notice them as his mind went back to the burning building. To revenge, to the rage. *Just a taste.*

CHAPTER FORTY

"Lauren, hello. Tell me you have positive news from Frankfurt." Dittrich looked haggard on Rhodes' secure VTC screen. He hadn't slept in two days, and it made him appear a decade older. Rhodes wondered if she looked just as bad, having been up even longer.

"Sir, well it's not all good, that's for sure. But first, Welker is still in surgery and he's stable. Looks like he's going to be fine."

"Excellent. I wouldn't have expected anything else. Howard's a resilient old bastard. He's gotten through a lot worse. We had some fun together back in the day. What's going on at the airport?"

Rhodes took a swig from her bottle of water, eyeballed it for a second due to the irony, then continued. "Collignon's delivery was found in a warehouse on the south side. According to the paperwork in receiving there were twelve pallets, each containing one hundred and twenty cases. All twelve pallets were there, but one had already been broken into. Twenty cases were missing, delivered to seven shops in both terminals. You probably saw on the news already; the airport is in complete lockdown and it's crazy. Once we told the BND they rolled on it hard. There may be more responders there right now than flight passengers. The really, good news is that we were able to get to it before any of the cases were delivered to an airline. There will be casualties, for sure, but it will be limited and controlled." She then went on to fill him in on all the relevant details.

"In the grand scheme of things, a big win," Dittrich quipped. "Listen, you may have come to the same conclusion as me, I don't know, but this wasn't an attack on Germany, or on the world as it would seem to most. Not at all. The AMA did their homework and spent years preparing. To be honest, I've never seen such sophistication. They were working on these virus attacks well before Paris and Berlin. Think about it, all the research involved. The patience. Not just in the processing and weaponization of the virus, but in deciding exactly how, where, and when to attack in Amman. They injected the virus into a pipe that led directly to the U.S. Embassy, and immediately after they'd switched from using chlorine to monochloramine in the public water system to ensure maximum effectiveness of the virus. And in the case of Frankfurt, in choosing which trucking company to infiltrate. They purposefully placed Collignon with this company because they have a contract with all but four of the U.S. and U.S. affiliated airlines. These were, unequivocally, attacks on the United States of America. And now that we've foiled their plans in Frankfurt, it's time for us to strike back, and hard. Where we seem unable to make any headway, though, is in locating Lefebvre and his core group. Any news from the BND on the son, Sharif? He's the next best prize, to be sure. It's unfortunate as hell you had to break off pursuit when you did; you were so close to nailing him. Did you consider just letting Dolan go after him?"

Rhodes shifted uncomfortably in her chair. "Sir I did not. Once we learned of the location and nature of the attack, there was no time to do anything but react to what was going on at the airport. If I had let him continue, Dolan would have been left blind without the satellite, and without resources or backup. I think it was the right call to turn it over to the BND. They have the GPS signal from Sharif's car. They may already have him in custody at this point, I don't know. The bottom line is, I couldn't put him in that position, as new as he is. Yes, he is extraordinarily adept at this line of work, but he can also be impulsive and then there is what happened in Paris and Berlin, when he went off the reservation. He still needs consistent monitoring and mentoring, and he will for a while before he's ready to operate solo in the field."

"And yet..." Dittrich looked away from the monitor for a second, as if to structure his next thought carefully, "...it was he who saved Howard. Howard would have died."

"Yes, he might have..." agreed Rhodes.

"And he took out Collignon, and the third terrorist."

"Yes."

"And though it didn't go down the way we would have liked, he prevented both the Paris subway attack and the attack on our embassy in Berlin. Lauren, the way I see it, Dolan has been almost singlehandedly responsible for most of the success SCALPEL has had since 2019."

"Sir, these are all team efforts and..."

"I said *almost*," countered Dittrich, pointing his finger at her through the monitor.

Rhodes realized these were things Dittrich had been thinking about for a while. *He is ambushing me*, she thought. She would not be able to convince him to see things her way. Her efforts to save SCALPEL hadn't had the effect she'd hoped for. And she was unable to reconcile the value Dolan's abilities brought to the team with his unpredictable nature. There was one fact though, that he couldn't refute or fix.

"He's burned."

Dittrich let out a sigh. "Yes, he's burned. It's unfortunate and it happens. OK, let's switch gears. What's your assessment—was this it, the AMA's main and final attack? Do you think there are more in the pipeline? Our analysts seem to think the AMA is going underground for now."

"I would agree with them," said Rhodes. "AMA internet and dark web chatter was building after the Amman attack and in the days leading up to Frankfurt. It peaked when news networks began reporting on events at the airport. Thomas has been monitoring and in the last hour we've seen it subside to almost nothing."

"Right. Well, Saleh Attar and Fadi Hafif, who gave the virus to the boy Issam in Jordan and taught him how to deploy it, they were both at the compound in Syria. Attar was killed and as you know we have Hafif. He's holding out but we believe he doesn't know very much. It's part of the reason the AMA has been so difficult to root out, they compartment their communications and planning to an extreme degree. The forensics are ongoing, but it looks like all the IT equipment was new and hadn't even been used yet. We're working on the two cell phones, they are encrypted. Not much in the way of hardcopy intelligence. We do have enough though to believe things were getting hot wherever Lefebvre was laying low and that he intended to move there. He may have been enroute. If only we had watched and waited."

Yes, if only we had watched and waited, thought Rhodes. It was she who had pushed the strike, and the plan was largely hers. He was assigning the blame to her, and it was not so subtle.

Dittrich went on. "Which brings us to Russia. We think they knew about our strike ahead of time, and that for whatever reason, they were OK with it. But in true Russian fashion, they couldn't just let it happen, they had to let us know that they knew. And we understood their primary interest in Lefebvre was that he was holding one of their scientists, a scientist who was most likely responsible for weaponizing the virus. They would not want us to capture him. If they suspected we were targeting Lefebvre in that strike, I find it curious they didn't contact us ahead of time, to suggest a joint operation or to negotiate a transfer of the scientist if we were able to capture him. Or contact us after the fact, at the very least, to see if we had him. Something that, at least until now, hasn't happened. It was as if they knew he wasn't there."

"I agree, something was going on and it might have been Mossad, though I can think of no reason why they would do it."

"I don't think it was Mossad. So now we come to the big question, where is Lefebvre? Dolan seemed to think he was at the property in southern Algeria. All due to a baseball cap if I remember correctly. Sharif's baseball cap. But Sharif is not there, he is in the wind, somewhere in southern Germany right now. Nonetheless, a building on that property was destroyed not too long ago and I can't help but wonder if that was Lefebvre covering his tracks, before getting out of dodge. It is unlikely, but could he also have known ahead of time about the strike in Syria, and worried that the Algeria compound was next? Could he have been tipped off by the Russians? There is enough precedent for something like that to be a credible working theory."

Rhodes was becoming more uncomfortable by the minute. Dittrich had an affinity for micromanaging her operations, but he'd never showed *this* level of interest before. Not to the point where he was already aware of much of what she was prepared to brief him on. "I don't know, sir. I think it's premature to call that a working theory. The level of activity at that compound, up until the point it was destroyed, suggested that it was most likely *not* where Lefebvre was hiding out. In fact, when Thomas ran it through the Sentient AI system, the probability came back incredibly low, less than half a percent confidence, I believe."

"Hmmm," said Dittrich, stroking his beard. "Is Thomas there with you?"

"Uh, he's in his office. You want to pull him in?" asked Rhodes.

"Yes. I want to run an experiment. It shouldn't take long."

Rhodes got up and walked out of The Pit, down the hall and fetched Freeman.

"What is it?" he asked.

"Just come with me. Dittrich has a question for you, I think it's about Sentient."

"Hello Thomas!" Dittrich said enthusiastically as they both sat down.

"Hi sir. How can I help you?"

"This should be easy. Lauren tells me that Sentient kicked out a very low level of confidence that the Algeria compound might have been the Lefebvre hideout. Is that right?"

"Um, yes sir. It was less than a percent. Zero point three, to be precise."

"When was that calculation made?" asked Dittrich.

"Sir, it was just one image from a Black Sky batch. There were a bunch of different time stamps. I don't remember exactly, but it was over two weeks ago. I can find out."

"No, no, that's OK. Do you have access to Sentient right now, there in The Pit?"

"Sure, I can pull it up. Why?"

"I want you to run it again, now. Have we uploaded our reporting yet from the Syria strike? And from Germany?"

Freeman and Rhodes both knew where he was going, and it was something they would have done anyway, to revisit and recalculate certain probabilities once new information came to light. But they just hadn't had time.

"Sir, to be honest, a lot of the recent reporting has not been completed yet. But everything from Berlin has been submitted and analyzed, and some of what we got in Offenbach. Of note, Sentient is already aware that Lefebvre was not in Syria, and that the building at the Algeria compound was destroyed."

Freeman slid his chair to the right, booted up the Top-Secret console and logged into Sentient, then navigated to the AMA case folder and scrolled to the satellite imagery queries. "Give me a second, I have to find it. There are hundreds of these."

After three minutes he slid his chair back, a serious expression on his face. "Sir, Sentient is now telling us there is a sixty-two percent chance that Lefebvre was in fact hiding there, at some point."

Dittrich was nodding. "Listen, I get it. Hindsight is twenty-twenty, but that's not the point. *Sixty-two percent.* In our business, and I think you'll both agree, that's an extremely rare level of confidence when there are so many variables in play. It's a great example of how, early on in these operations, seemingly insignificant details can be so, so important. We hit the wrong compound. Heck, we weren't even in the right country. Yes, there was benefit in taking out the Syria site, but it wasn't what we thought it was. As much as we like to lean on big data and algorithms these days," he tapped the topside of his head with his forefinger, "sometimes it's the little things, folks. Think about it. *A baseball cap.*"

CHAPTER FORTY-ONE

Dolan was pushing the envelope, driving two hundred kilometers per hour. It was raining now, and pitch dark. At least the traffic was beginning to thin out as he sped south. He expected Sharif would eventually jump off the 5 and head east, into France. Perhaps near Strasbourg. It had been over half an hour with no message from Bolden, and he was beginning to worry that Bolden was too busy and unable to help Dolan at all. Just as the thought crossed his mind, however, his phone screen lit up.

A text: *"Get off on L87 east. He stopped a little earlier for about a minute but then took off again. He stopped again here, just now."* The text was accompanied by a dropped pin marking the BMW's location.

He looked at his maps app and immediately slowed, almost missing the exit. Jeez Bolden, that was close, he thought. Sharif might have stopped for fuel. Or he could be trying to switch vehicles. It was likely he suspected authorities had a description of his car and had the license plate number. Whatever the reason for his stop, he wouldn't risk leaving the older, red BMW out in plain sight for too long.

He turned off the autobahn and headed onto L87. Sharif's position was a kilometer or so down the road, on the right. He used two fingers to zoom in on the pin and saw it was in fact an Esso fuel station. The area and everything east of it was rural for some distance. *Smart. He's probably going to stay off the major highways from here on.* Dolan checked his own gauge, three-quarters full—it was a big tank. He'd be good for a while still. If he was lucky Sharif would still be there when he pulled in.

As Dolan approached the station, he saw the red BMW, the only vehicle at the pumps. But Sharif wasn't in the car or anywhere nearby. His heart sank as he realized it would have taken no time at all for Sharif to steal another vehicle and be gone already. He scanned the parking lot and vehicle again, searching for clues as he backed into a parking spot away from the station's security cameras. He noticed the license plate number was different. He hadn't paid the vehicle much attention when casing the warehouse with Welker, so he couldn't be sure it was the same car but the coincidence of two older, red BMWs in the same place within a few minutes at this time of night was too far-fetched. Sharif's brief stop earlier—*he swapped out the plate before getting fuel.* He was inside, probably paying with cash.

Dolan thought about disabling the vehicle and retrieving Welker's P229, if in fact Sharif had left it in the car. Just as quickly he quickly dismissed the idea. His identity may be known to the GRU, but right now it would be much worse for the German authorities to know he was involved in this. He had to stay away from the cameras.

As Dolan sorted through his options, Sharif walked out the front door of the station. When he stopped to change the plate, he had changed his appearance as well. He was wearing a long brown wig, glasses and a heavy jacket. Dolan noticed he'd even changed his shoes. Sharif looked left and right as he walked to the car, trailing plumes of white as he exhaled in the bitter cold. As he approached the car the rain turned to snow. Big fluffy flakes landed on the hood of the Mercedes, melting immediately.

With a full tank Sharif could now outlast him on the open road. The immediate option was to end it right here, right now. Dolan could cover his face, walk up to Sharif and shoot him in the head, then drive away. It would be done. It was the easiest way, but not the best. Dolan had things he needed to say to Sharif. He must be confronted before he dies. However, as soon as he drove off, he might lose him when his fuel ran low. The other factor to consider was that the BND should be closing in on Sharif by now, and his new license plate won't throw them off. They had his GPS location. It was likely as well they had notified every Polizei station from Frankfurt to the French and Swiss borders to be on the lookout for his car. He'd be pulled over before long. Dolan had to act soon. He picked up his phone and studied the route ahead. The next town was five or so kilometers further, with nothing in-between. If Sharif was going to continue on the backroads, there would be intersections and stoplights. Plenty of opportunities to cut him off, perhaps at the next town. There were traffic cameras at these intersections, though. He needed a better option.

Sharif got in the car, visibly nervous despite a clear effort to maintain composure. He started the engine and pulled away from the pumps. As he exited onto the access road to L87 Dolan pulled out of the parking lot and trailed at a distance. He readied himself mentally for another adrenaline-fueled pursuit, but Sharif drove right at the limit, no doubt aware of the different speed rules once off the autobahn and feeling safer with a new plate and the disguise. Snow was a factor as well; the visibility and road conditions were worse now.

As Dolan followed, he determined his sense of urgency wasn't unwarranted. If he didn't act soon the opportunity would be lost. So he decided on a course of action. Dangerous, but no riskier than any other available and realistic option. One kilometer from the Esso station and with no other traffic in sight, Dolan gunned the Mercedes, his back pressed into the driver's seat as he accelerated, quickly closing the gap with the BMW. As he sped up, time seemed to slow down. Sharif did not react, maintaining his speed and probably assuming he was an aggressive German driver trying to pass him. Dolan pulled into the left lane until the front of the Mercedes was just ahead of the BMW's left rear wheel, then matched his speed and carefully but deliberately pulled the steering wheel right, impacting the left rear fender. Neither his resolve nor his confidence wavered as Dolan made minute corrections each millisecond, manipulating the vehicle's controls with extreme precision. He continued pulling right until the BMW was sideways and directly in front of the SUV. Sharif looked left momentarily to face his aggressor, shocked and confused, his glasses gone and the long hair from his wig flying wildly. Dolan deftly pulled the steering wheel back to the left until the front of the G63 scraped further up the left side of the BMW, then pulled hard to the right again. At some point Sharif had slammed his brakes, but the rapidly accumulating snow negated any effect they might have had. Dolan then began to depress his own brakes, expecting and receiving the rapid pulsations in his right foot from the anti-lock system.

As they began to slow together Sharif's car slid away from the front of the Mercedes, still going sideways, off the road and down an embankment. At the bottom, the car flipped and rolled in a thunderous discord of breaking glass and twisting metal that was surprisingly audible within the otherwise quiet interior of the luxury SUV. Dolan came to a stop just off the road as the BMW was in its last roll and balanced on its side, teetering as if it might stay in that strange position. But then it gave in and landed with one last groaning crunch on all four, now shredded tires.

Before the BMW even came to rest, Dolan put the G63 in park, grabbed the P229 and began to make his way down the embankment. He approached from the rear, wary that Sharif could still be alert and ready to use Welker's handgun on him. But as he drew closer, he saw the blood, and Sharif's head tilted forward, his face buried in the airbag. Dolan moved the P229 to his left hand and reached in through the broken driver's side window to check his pulse. It was weak, but it was there. *He's alive. Good.*

Dolan tried the door. When it wouldn't budge, he put his handgun in his jacket pocket and reached into the car, releasing Sharif's seatbelt. He pulled the wig off and tossed it aside, then grabbed his shoulders and pulled him forward enough to reach under both armpits and lock fingers behind his back. Then he pulled him in a bearhug through the window, laying him face up on the ground. He could feel the warmth of Sharif's blood on his cheek, on his hands.

Going down on one knee next to him, Dolan forcefully slapped Sharif's face twice while reaching deep inside his subconscious to access that pulsing, obsidian box he'd kept carefully tucked away for so long. He allowed it to open then, not for a taste this time but to conjure everything from within, to fuel and empower a total and final revenge. For Claire's murder and the resultant psychological stigmata Dolan had carried ever since. The deaths of thousands of innocents in Jordan and elsewhere, for Stone's murder. For everything. He felt it build inside him as Sharif's eyes opened and fluttered, confused and afraid. Dolan reached into his jacket and held the P229 against Sharif's blood-spattered forehead, putting pressure on the trigger. The great building was engulfed with fire now as Dolan opened the door. He could sense the rush of air, beginning to pull Sharif inside.

"Do you have anything to say before you die, Sharif?" Dolan was hoping he would curse him, hate him with his last words. But he did not. He remained lost and scared, unable to move and unwilling to walk through the door. Dolan yelled at him at the top of his lungs, screaming for him to say something, but Sharif simply lay there, trembling. Dolan added pressure to the trigger, grinding the barrel into his brow. Sharif then wet himself, a dark stain spread across the front of his jeans. Disgusted and upset, Dolan stood up, looking down on him and unsure of what to do. Then Sharif finally spoke.

"I just wanted to be happy. It's all I've ever wanted Michael. I'm sorry about Claire, I told you that before. It was an accident. I wish it never happened. I never wanted to be any part of this. I thought Islam was the answer, but my father…I just never had a choice."

Dolan's rage came back instantly. "You're sorry? What about me, Sharif? What about Anne? Anne was with me when your assassin tried to kill me. Anne almost died because of you!"

"What…no, what do you mean? Assassin?" Sharif looked confused.

It was possible Hakeem hired the hitman without ever telling Sharif. In fact, it made sense to keep it from him. Dolan felt robbed, suddenly. He needed every ounce of anger available to him right now.

"Sharif, you always had a choice! Everything you've done in your life, up to this very moment, has been a choice. You could have done the right things, but you never did!"

He pointed the gun again at Sharif's head. As he squeezed the trigger, his terrible dream came to mind. The dream that suggested if he killed Sharif, it would be as if he had killed Claire. It was the last cryptic piece of his mental puzzle, the one he'd been unable to fit anywhere. He needed to complete it, to finally make sense of everything. But it was still unclear, even now. Welker had insinuated the only reason the dream was concerning was that Dolan continued to think about it. That did make sense. He worried about it because he wanted it to mean something. He desperately needed a metaphysical divination, that bright light moment. Because it was the easy way out. To have the answers handed to him, without cost. Because that's what happened with his previous dream, his recurring nightmare. *Wasn't it?* No. The recurring dream had been one small, perplexing element of a long, arduous mental process. There were many difficult decisions he made, actions with consequences he took along the way that led to that final psychical resolution in Berlin. This was no different.

It wasn't necessarily a stirring revelation, but it was valuable insight. His dream was a symptom. By itself, it had no real meaning. It was the byproduct of unreconciled insecurities and incorrect choices he had made in the past. Things he'd never fully dealt with, and all of them related back to Sharif. This new insight didn't sway him, though. Why would it? The bloody, bullet-torn image of Claire was one that might have given him pause if he determined it were a foreshadowing, or a warning. But now it meant nothing.

He continued to squeeze, and the moment didn't begin to feel as he expected it would. There was no impending conflagration, no imminent release of pain or promise of serenity. He worried instantly that none of it would come to him. His new understanding of the dream seemed to support an unfortunate theory, that the last box would remain. It would grow bigger and more menacing than before. Then his mind went back to the tunnel in Potsdam two years ago, the first time he killed someone up close. Without the clinical, impersonal comfort of the standoff distance afforded by his C-130 gunship. So close he could see into his quarry's eyes. Into his soul. It unnerved him, at the very moment it was *supposed* to embolden him, persuade him, lead him to a satisfaction beyond anything he'd ever felt before. But this, it didn't feel right. His mind stayed at the house in Potsdam, jumping forward in time to his recent visit there. What he saw now with his mind's eye was a field of wildflowers and a beautiful, blonde-haired child smiling at him. It was a bizarre juxtaposition, there in the biting cold with the wind. In the dark with Sharif's blood on his hands and face and snow falling all around. It didn't fit, simultaneously deflating and uplifting. Yet the vision persisted and all at once Dolan realized his last dark, pulsating box, the one displaying a ghostly image of Claire being pushed by Sharif from the hotel balcony in Paris, the one he'd kept so well preserved for so long and for this very moment, was gone.

It caught him by surprise; he couldn't have expected this turn of events. But he understood immediately that the decision he was making now would dictate the course of the rest of his life, and there was only one right choice to make. Dolan hit Sharif hard on the side of the head with the P229, knocking him out. He retrieved the GPS tracker from the wheel well and after a few minutes of searching, found Welker's weapon on the passenger side floor of the BMW. He wiped down each part of the car he'd touched. Then he picked him up, slung him over his shoulder and trudged up the embankment. He laid Sharif down in the back of the Mercedes and injected him with one of the syringes Bolden gave him to ensure he wouldn't wake up on the drive back. Dolan closed the tailgate, got into the driver's seat and tapped the messages app on his phone to text a reply to Anne.

"Hey you. All is good. Talk soon. I love you."

He hit send, started the engine, turned around and headed east through the snow on L87.

CHAPTER FORTY-TWO

Dolan sat with his legs crossed, appearing casual and comfortable but inside he was genuinely stressed. There was a lot to be discussed but knowing Dittrich, he might just fire him and be done with it. On the other hand, Dittrich was known to abide a certain level of insubordination if the results were favorable. That had proven true for Collier, and true for Stone at times. But they were seasoned and proven operatives, whereas Dolan had just finished his second mission. And Dittrich didn't even know him. He thought of Stone then, how much he liked Tony's Savile Row suits. The blue one Dolan wore now was an impulse buy, and for no other reason than it looked like the one Stone was wearing when they first met. Though it cost perhaps half as much. He looked at his watch, then up at Dittrich's executive assistant, hoping for some hint of when he'd be called in. But she paid him no attention.

Collier, Bolden, and Dolan were instructed to fly back to Langley immediately for their debriefs. These would normally have been done in Berlin, but the operational significance of everything that went down in Jordan, Syria, Algeria, and Germany was orders of magnitude larger than what Langley was used to dealing with. No one was ever supposed to know they'd been involved of course, and that was true for the most part in this case, but there were numerous world leaders asking questions and demanding answers. The U.S. intelligence community was being bombarded and it was all the Agency could do to keep up.

Welker was unable to fly due his injuries, so he was debriefed remotely. They brought Sharif back with them, bandaged, drugged and packed into Welker's metal box. Given Frankfurt was shut down and would be for some time, they flew out of Ramstein Air Base on one of the Agency's white Gulfstream 5s. Sharif was by now no doubt occupying a dark cell in the basement of the Annapolis safehouse.

Dolan was instructed to meet with the Deputy Director before his debrief. It was out of the ordinary. He'd been told nothing that would indicate, one way or the other, what it was about. Rhodes had met with the team via VTC at the safehouse in Frankfurt after Dolan returned with Sharif, but she said very little to him at the time about disobeying her orders yet again. She was surprised and initially angry, but then elated by his capture of Sharif. It would have been counterproductive at the time to dress him down for it. Dolan suspected she went to Dittrich afterwards, however, to lay the groundwork for his termination. So here he was.

"You can go in now, Mr. Dolan," said Dittrich's assistant.

Dolan walked inside and closed the door behind him. He remained standing in front of Dittrich's mahogany desk. It could be a quick meeting.

"Go ahead, take a seat Michael," he said, motioning with his hand.

"Thank you, sir," Michael replied, settling into the modest leather chair.

"How was the flight?"

"Long, but I managed to sleep through about half of it, so not bad."

"Good, good. Sorry for making you wait. I was on the phone with Collier. We collected two additional members of the cell in Offenbach, a Kosovar and locally radicalized Syrian, a German citizen. Good news made possible by your apprehension of Sharif. He's already talking, though he claims not to know where his father is."

"That's great news sir," Dolan responded. "It's only a matter of time before we get them all."

"Yes, it is," Dittrich nodded. "Listen, I called you in here because you and I need to come to an understanding. I've been thinking about everything that's happened on both operations you've been involved in. There are similarities in each case, and well, you are just one of the common denominators of course but the similarities are these. One, things are not always going as planned, or occasionally, things are moving forward with no real plan at all. And two, in both operations the outcomes were successful. One of those things, the successful outcomes, that's good of course. We don't want that to change. In fact, we want to tap into that and make it happen more often. But the planning problems, we simply cannot continue to operate that way.

"Lauren came to me yesterday, in person, to lobby for your removal from SCALPEL and from the Agency. We had spoken remotely the day prior, and she was already upset then that you went after Welker when she'd instructed you to stay put and wait for backup. She found out later you ignored her again in going after Sharif, and for her that was the last straw. She says you're a loose cannon and won't follow orders.

"Now, when situations like this occur, and believe me it happens more than you think, it almost always leads to *counter*productive outcomes. In stressful or dangerous situations, not following orders can cause people to be killed or worse, it can result in significant negative impact to our national security. I know you get this. But I'm being pulled in two different directions here…" Dittrich paused, momentarily in thought. "Each time you've disobeyed orders the outcomes have *not* been counterproductive. That doesn't mean you shouldn't have followed Lauren's directives, and it *also* does not mean that the outcomes wouldn't have been better had you done so. But something I must consider is that it could be indicative of a failure of leadership."

Dolan was taken aback, though he remained stoic. He said nothing, did nothing to betray his thoughts. In his opinion, Rhodes was an honest, capable leader and a good person. The only thing that seemed to hold her back was she lacked some of the intangibles Dolan felt were prerequisites to successfully lead a unit like SCALPEL.

Dittrich went on. "Now, I'm not saying that Lauren might have intentionally done anything wrong, or that any omission of action on her part has led to any failure for the unit. Not at all. What I think is this—she's become risk averse to the point that it marginalizes the effectiveness of the mission, and as such she's hesitant to take advantage of some of the unique capabilities of her team members. Blind to them, even. She wasn't always like this, to be honest. When I first brought her in to lead SCALPEL it was quite the opposite, in fact. I believe it was when we lost Tony that she began to withdraw. She began to operate almost continually *inside* the box, the box SCALPEL was created specifically to operate *outside of.*"

The direction the conversation had taken confused Dolan momentarily. They weren't just talking about him anymore; they were now discussing Rhodes. There was a bigger picture in play. Dolan came to Langley today fully expecting a pink slip, and he was fine with that.

It would be disappointing, but he had a good life and job to go back to and he'd addressed his issues with Sharif. The operation was a success even though they had yet to locate Hakeem Lefebvre. And Lefebvre's days were numbered. There were simply too many intelligence organizations from too many countries looking for him now. He was the most wanted terrorist in the world.

"So," continued Dittrich, "I'm in a bit of a quandary. SCALPEL has been too successful lately to disband. However, our run-in with the GRU in Berlin combined with Lauren's recent penchant for being overly cautious has led the Director to call for just that. But I am nothing if not adaptive, and I have a few ideas to reconcile the problem.

"Back to the GRU. Two questions, the answers to which continue to remain elusive. First, how did the Russians know about our strike in Syria, and second, why was the building at the compound in Algeria destroyed? I think the two are connected somehow and I was wondering if you had any thoughts on it."

Dolan was prepared to address both of those topics, but not with the Deputy Director. In fact, he'd assumed he would have to raise them during his debrief, as they were both geographically and operationally separated from his responsibilities in Germany. Whoever debriefed him should have no reason to ask about them. But somehow, Dittrich knew enough to speculate his contact with Yuri was a possible linkage. And he was spot on.

"Sir, I can explain how the Russians knew about Syria, and I have unconfirmed intel about what happened in Algeria," Dolan replied. Dittrich's eyes opened wide, and he leaned forward eagerly.

Dolan went on. "While some of your operatives may tend to err on the side of caution, you may have noticed I am more aggressive. I'm not saying I like to roll the dice, not at all. I guess you could say I prefer to take well-calculated risks. But I also listen to my gut. It almost never lies and in the past when I've ignored what it's telling me, I find out later that I should have listened. In any event, I had a strong suspicion Sharif was at the compound in Algeria. Not just because of a baseball cap, but because of its color, and the pattern of it. And because of several other details that strengthened my suspicion.

"Now, Sharif wouldn't have been there without his father, in my opinion. I knew him well as you know and when I saw him last, back in Paris, he was emotionally fragile. He felt alone. He's the type who always needs some sort of support structure around him, and he wasn't getting that from his terrorist ties or from his faith. You see, he is also spiritually shallow. He always had a searching soul, if you will, and as such he never believed in anything or anyone enough to create the bonds necessary to establish and fortify his convictions and dreams. I guess I realized this when we were together at the Sorbonne, but back then he had our group of friends and I had issues of my own I was dealing with. Anyway, it didn't seem like a big deal to me at the time. Most of the support structure he had dissolved when he murdered Claire, and later he slowly lost his mother to Alzheimer's. After SCALPEL was on to him, his father was all he had left."

"His mother is dead now," Dittrich said, matter-of-factly.

"Oh, I didn't know. Well, I had my own reasons for wanting Sharif captured or killed, and I could feel the possibility of that happening fade by the moment as the CLEARCUT team focused all its attention on Syria. I had no idea Sharif had traveled to Germany by then. But I knew that I could use my connection with Yuri to our advantage, and I also knew Lauren would have shot the idea down. I felt I needed to make a unilateral decision. I contacted Yuri and told him my suspicions about Lefebvre and Sharif being at the compound in Algeria, and that their scientist would probably be there as well. I told him they would have to go in immediately, because the Syria strike would tip Lefebvre off and they might make a run for it.

"While I could have given them some other story supporting the urgency to get to Algeria, it was helpful to the larger mission, to CLEARCUT, for me to tell him the truth about our strike. You see, I asked him for two things in return. One, to prevent the Syrian government, or anyone else for that matter, from intervening in our operation there. So, the three attack helicopters, they were there to protect our mission, if necessary. I didn't tell Yuri when or where we'd be going in, or any other details, only that it was imminent. I'm surprised they demonstrated their presence the way they did, but as you are aware, the Russians don't use our playbook. The second thing I requested was for them to take out Lefebvre and Sharif if they were there at the Algeria site. At the time we had no dedicated resources or plan for Algeria. It appeared to be our only chance to get them."

Dittrich's jaw had dropped slowly as Dolan began to explain everything and remained in that position. Dolan couldn't tell if he was upset or pleased, but it was clear he was incredulous. "Is that it?" he asked.

"Not quite. After our last VTC in the Frankfurt safehouse I received one last message from Yuri. Their scientist was in fact there at the Algeria compound, apparently, and they were able to retrieve him. This would imply the virus was weaponized there, and that Hakeem was there as well. But during the rescue, that is when the building was destroyed, and it was clear to them it had been boobytrapped. It exploded just after their guy ran out the front door. Sharif was already in Offenbach at that time, obviously, and if Lefebvre had been there, he was long gone by then. For some reason they'd left the scientist behind. I guess they didn't need him anymore and left him on his own. Who knows. But Yuri was grateful—he made that clear in his message." Dolan could have said more, that Yuri mentioned he'd be honored to work with him again, when and wherever their respective country's national security goals aligned. He'd hold on to that for now, though he suspected he'd be asked to provide a transcript of the email in his debrief.

Dittrich was shaking his head in disbelief. "OK. This makes everything easier, in fact. Here's what I want to do... Wait, how's your cover in Berlin?"

At that, Dolan could no longer conceal his surprise. "Um, well, it's fine actually. I emailed Doctor Schröder in Frankfurt before I left. I was supposed to meet with her yesterday. I told her I'd reschedule when I was able. And I called Professor Möller at Free University. I told both of them I returned my rental car to the Frankfurt Airport just as the authorities were responding to the virus attack and as a precautionary measure, I was told to quarantine myself in my hotel for two weeks. So, I could just head back and pick up where I left off."

"Good. That's what I want you to do then. And this is important—don't mention anything about your subsequent contact with Yuri Kuznetsov in your debrief. Leave it all out. A little nugget for you—he's not about to retire. That wasn't accurate information. Your debriefers probably won't ask you about any of it anyway, but let's keep it between you and me." Dittrich then held out both hands in a cautionary manner. "And don't worry, this is not an ethical dilemma, or a question of integrity. It's an order from me, the justification for which is based on things I know that others don't, and things that we can use to our advantage in the future if certain events come to pass.

"So, go back to Berlin and finish your research with Atlantik Brücke. Go visit Anne and make sure she's staying quiet. Then I want you to return to Boston and defend your dissertation. Get your doctoral degree. Over the next couple of years, you are going to receive additional, specialized training. And we are going to ask you to do things now and again, certain missions will pop up that we can use you for. We will have to keep you active; I don't want your skills to go stale. After some time you'll be offered a position at American University in Washington, D.C. and I want you to take it. We have a few other assets embedded there. We also get some pretty good recruits graduating out of American." Dittrich paused there to gauge Dolan's reaction, who had settled in at that point and was unreadable.

He went on. "As I mentioned, I have some ideas. Yes, SCALPEL will be disbanded but it's more accurate to say it's being paused. I'm going to put Collier, Bolden and Freeman in a holding pattern. Collier and Bolden have their day jobs in Berlin, so it'll be largely transparent to them. I'll find something for Freeman to do in the meantime. Lauren will be reassigned to a role she can handle without having to sweat all the decisions. Welker will still be around. Once you transition to American, we will stand SCALPEL back up under a new name. Bigger and better, more capable and farther-reaching. Oh, and don't worry too much about being burned. Heading back to Boston and lying low for a while, disbanding SCALPEL—from the outside, it all appears procedurally correct and if they are looking, the GRU will assume correctly that SCALPEL is kaput, and incorrectly, that the CIA is done with you. Even if they don't, there are many ways to exploit a positive association with an adversary to our advantage. So, Michael Dolan, when the time comes, I want you to lead that team. What do you say?"

It took him a while to get to the point, and Dolan saw it coming. As Dittrich spoke, Dolan was already weighing his options. The positives and the negatives. Opportunities and possibilities. Most importantly, was it what he wanted for his life, for his future? His academic career would take a measurable hit; he'd be unable to fully dedicate himself to that end. It wasn't necessarily a bad thing, however, if at the same time he'd be doing something else that was extremely gratifying. Protecting his country. Putting an end to those who would harm us and our way of life and doing so in a way that was insanely challenging. Dolan realized it wasn't as difficult a choice as it might seem.

"I'm in."

TO BE CONTINUED IN *REVELATION*

Michael Dolan is now leading the CIA beyond-black operations team formerly known as SCALPEL, his fortunes buoyed by unparalleled success in thwarting numerous terrorist attacks. After uncovering a sinister network of organizations planning a cyberattack with global financial and geopolitical implications, he must risk putting the world at war if he is to save it.

ABOUT THE AUTHOR

JOHN CASEY is a novelist and Pushcart Prize-nominated poet from New Hampshire. *Evolution* is book two of *The Devolution Trilogy*. Book one, *Devolution*, was released in 2019 and *Revelation* rounds out the psychological spy thriller series. He is the author of *Raw Thoughts* and *Meridian: A Raw Thoughts Book* as well, both compelling and mindful fusions of poetic and photographic art. A Veteran combat and test pilot with a Master of Arts from Florida State University, Casey also served as a diplomat and international affairs strategist at U.S. embassies in Germany and Ethiopia, the Pentagon, and elsewhere. He is passionate about fitness, nature, and the human spirit and inspired by the incredible spectrum of people, places, and cultures he has experienced in life.

www.ingramcontent.com/pod-product-compliance
Lightning Source LLC
Chambersburg PA
CBHW060234100726
47907CB00003B/626